Death on the Agenda

THE HENRY TIBBETT MYSTERIES
BY PATRICIA MOYES

Night Ferry to Death
A Six-Letter Word for Death
Angel Death
Who Is Simon Warwick?
The Coconut Killings
Black Widower
The Curious Affair of the Third Dog
Season of Snows and Sins
Many Deadly Returns
Death and the Dutch Uncle
Murder Fantastical
Johnny Under Ground
Murder by 3's (including *Down Among the Dead Men,*
Dead Men Don't Ski, and *Falling Star)*
Falling Star
Murder à la Mode
Death on the Agenda
Down Among the Dead Men
Dead Men Don't Ski

Death on the Agenda

by Patricia Moyes

An Owl Book

HENRY HOLT and COMPANY
New York

Library of Congress Cataloging in Publication Data
Moyes, Patricia.
Death on the agenda.
"An Owl book."
I. Title.
PR6063.09D44   1984   823'.914   84-6750
ISBN 0-8050-0507-2 (pbk.)

First published in hardcover by
Holt, Rinehart and Winston in 1962.
First Owl Book Edition—1984

Printed in the United States of America
7 9 10 8 6

To all the people, of many nationalities, who have made life in Geneva so stimulating and delightful, this book is affectionately dedicated.

Author's Note

This story is set in Geneva, and centered on the Palais des Nations. Inevitably, therefore, it involves characters who are international officials, members of the Geneva Police, and so forth. I need hardly say that none of my friends or acquaintances at the Palais or in the gendarmerie bears the faintest resemblance to any of the people in the book, all of whom are purely imaginary. Nor, to the best of my knowledge, does the Permanent Central Opium Board hold conferences of the sort which I describe here. For readers who know Geneva, I should perhaps add that the mythical conference in the book takes place in the old conference wing, which is in process of being rebuilt.

I One

"In short, gentlemen, my country has taken—and is taking—the most active steps to prevent the illegal importation of narcotic drugs. As we see it, the problem confronting our excise authorities divides itself into two facets . . ."

Henry Tibbett pulled himself together and sat up straight. The booming voice in his earphones had a disquieteningly soporific effect. He wished he could take the wretched things off, but the speaker was the delegate from Spain, and Henry's knowledge of Spanish was not sufficient to enable him to follow every word. Consequently, it was not Señor Moranta's volatile, light-weight voice that Henry was hearing, but the robust English of a tall, fair-haired young man called John Trapp, who sat in a glass-fronted booth overlooking the conference hall, performing the small miracle of simultaneous translation.

John Trapp was, as a matter of fact, dissatisfied with himself. He had been on the permanant staff of the Palais des Nations at Geneva for five years, attending numberless conferences, translating witty speeches, dull speeches, speeches on vital international affairs, and speeches on the sewage problems of Upper Nigeria, speeches on the resettlement of refugees and atomic energy and overpopulation and disarmament. By now, all speeches sounded much alike to him. The only fun he got out of his job was the determination of the perfectionist to do it well. That word "facets" had been wrong. You can't divide a problem into facets. Still, no time to worry about that now. The slightest hesitation, and the translator is lost. He went on.

"There is the question of identification of the smugglers. That is all-important, and becomes increasingly difficult. I don't have to tell you that the master-operators never carry contraband themselves, and are constantly changing their couriers. Then there is the question of actual methods of concealment. This I do not propose to elaborate today, since the subcommittee on counter-measures—of which I have the honor to be a member—is due to start work tomorrow, and will be able to produce a report far more detailed and valuable than anything we can achieve in plenary session. Nevertheless, statistics collected over the past three years show . . ."

The subcommittee. Henry, too, had been chosen, along with five other delegates to the International Narcotics Conference, to study, compare notes and report on current methods of dope smuggling and the countermeasures being evolved by the police of various nations. He allowed his attention to wander again, as he looked around the conference hall, picking out for special study the fellow members of his committee.

The hall was upholstered in the usual Palais des Nations color scheme of brown and beige. The delegates' seats, comfortable and well-sprung, were shabbily solid in the manner of the 1920's. Great slabs of mahogany had been hewn to form the desks, with their complicated panoply of microphones and headphones. Above the Chairman's head, a Cubist-influenced mural in muddy colors showed Humanity—a massive, square-jawed superman in an open-necked shirt—clasping hands with Peace. Peace was a large lady in a flowing and faintly classical garment, who held in her free hand a chunky, bored-looking dove. Henry sighed, re-flecting on the fate of that dove since the optimistic days of the early twenties, when this great palace had been built in burning hope by people who honestly believed that they had fought a war to end war, and that the League of Nations would prove an unbreakable bastion of peaceful discussion and common sense in the face of fanaticism and self-interest.

By now the dark, sprightly little Spaniard had sat down, and the French delegate, Jacques Lenoir of the Deuxième Bureau, was on his feet. With relief, Henry removed his earphones. This he could follow in the original. He liked Lenoir, and was pleased that he, too, had been picked to serve on the subcommittee. Un-like many Frenchmen, Lenoir spoke quietly and with a sur-prising lack of gesture. He was a small, brown-haired, dapper man in his forties; everything about him was neat, from his light brown suit and pointed suede shoes to his impeccably turned phrases. He was a precise, witty speaker who set problems for his interpreters.

Lenoir came out with one of his elegantly satiric remarks, and Henry glanced across the room, caught Alfredo Spezzi's eye, and grinned. Spezzi was an old friend, a young but brilliant officer of the Italian police with whom Henry had worked on a murder case in the Dolomites. He was exceptionally good-looking—tall and blond, with clear blue eyes. Henry had been overjoyed to find him in Geneva, for several reasons. First, because a familiar face is always welcome in a strange city. Second, because Spezzi's presence here was an outward sign of his rapid promotion, his transfer from Montelunga to Rome and the hierarchy. And lastly, because success, far from spoiling the young man, had apparently relaxed him. The slight tendency to pomposity which had occasionally riled Henry in the old days had evaporated, revealing a most engaging sense of humor. Henry looked forward keenly to working with Alfredo on the subcommittee.

Several places along from Spezzi sat the fourth member of the subcommittee—Bill Parkington, a large, ginger-haired American who seemed to have been carved carelessly out of a redwood tree in his native California. He stood up to speak next. After Lenoir, the contrast was bizarre, like an earnest St. Bernard following a dancing poodle. Parkington was no speaker, but everything he said was illuminated by common sense and a blazing sincerity. Henry knew that the more sophisticated Lenoir and Moranta considered Bill to be a naïve country cousin. Henry himself had great respect for the big American, for it was clear that his battle against the dope runners was a personal, deeply felt struggle, too serious to be subjected to the trivialities of wit.

Glancing up to the interpreters' booth, Henry saw that John Trapp had removed his earphones and left the hall, leaving the English-French interpreter, Helène Brochet, to wrestle with Parkington's richly idiomatic phraseology. Helène was a tall, dark woman in her thirties, with a beautiful but almost frighteningly intense face and a lovely figure. While French was her native language, her English was so perfect, so easy and idiomatic, that Henry surmised she had spent many years on the more austere side of the channel.

Reluctantly, Henry looked away from Helène Brochet, and transferred his attention to the last member of the subcommittee. This was Konrad Zwemmer, of Western Germany. To Henry, Zwemmer had been an enigma ever since the opening of the conference. He was fair, stocky, and apparently open and friendly, yet Henry had found it impossible to fathom just what went on behind the glinting rimless glasses. He sat now, very upright, polishing his spectacles and listening to Parkington with a concentrated attention which did not seem to imply agreement. Zwemmer, Henry reflected, represented the postwar generation of Western Germany, her prosperity and her precariousness, her ambivalent sense of pride in the present and guilt for the past. Not that the guilt was ever allowed to show: it simmered beneath the surface, an inferiority complex assumed by an innocent generation, the sins of the fathers visited on the sons.

These were the men who were to form the subcommittee, of which the chairman was Henry himself. Chief Inspector Henry Tibbett of Scotland Yard, to give him his full title. A deceptively insignificant man in early middle age, with sandy hair and a mild manner, and a flair for intuitive detection which he described, with some embarrassment, as "my nose." It never occurred to Henry—who thought of himself as the most obvious and uninteresting of characters—that his fellow committee members might be studying him, too, and might find him as baffling as he found them.

Bill Parkington had by now launched out into a technical and impassioned description of the newest American electronic identification system—a wonder-working machine which, when fed with certain facts, could produce the names and photographs of a limited number of suspects within seconds. The Chairman glanced up in annoyance. This was precisely the sort of thing which should be reserved for the subcommittee. As soon as the American paused for breath, the Chairman stepped in smartly. He wished the subcommittee success with its work, and requested a report at the earliest possible moment. He then declared the day's meeting at an end.

At once the hall was filled with a rustle of papers, as the delegates collected their files and their notes, and prepared to leave. The faint but continuous tapping of the verbatim reporters, as they took each speech down word for word on their machines, was cut off suddenly. Quiet conversations began, and the delegates sauntered out of the windowless conference hall into the bright sunshine of the great marble corridor of the Palais des Nations.

Whatever architectural aesthetes may feel about the somewhat weighty design of the Palais as a whole, nobody can deny the impressive beauty of the marble corridor. As wide as a street, floored with an inlaid design of colored marble from all over the world—green, black, red, white and beige—the corridor runs the length of the central building. On one side, doors open into the various conference rooms, rest rooms and offices. The other is made almost entirely of glass, and looks out over sweeping green lawns and trees, to the sparkling blue of the lake and the majesty of the mountains beyond, topped by the ever-white peak of Mont Blanc.

Now, at half past five on a late spring evening, the distant, snowy mountains had caught the last rays of the sun as it set behind the Jura, and had turned from white to rose-pink. On the lake small white sails scudded over blue water. To the right the city of Geneva was just visible—green spires and golden stone houses and tall white blocks of modern flats. The famous *Jet d'eau* fluttered like a huge white feather over the lake—a solid column of water five hundred feet high, fanned out by the evening breeze into a gentle, falling curve. Henry stood by the window wall, gazing out and marveling, as he had done each evening since he came to the city.

He became aware of a tall figure looming up beside him.

"Coming to the party tonight?" asked Bill Parkington.

"I suppose so," said Henry, his eyes still on the view. "There seems to be one every night. Who's giving it this time? I haven't even checked. My wife keeps the engagement book at the hotel."

Bill looked surprised. "Oh, this isn't one of those," he said. "Not official, I mean. This is Paul Hampton's party."

"I'm sorry," said Henry. "I seem to have been in a daze of hospitality ever since I came to Geneva. Who is Paul Hampton?"

"American," said Bill laconically. "Rolling in dough. Lives in that huge white house you can see on the other side of the lake, the Villa Trounex. I met him at the French party. Old buddy of Lenoir's. He's invited all the subcommittee delegates out to his place this evening. Wanted to have the whole bloody conference, but Jacques and I finally got it into his head that six of us were enough to inflict on a private party. Should be quite a binge."

"It'll be a pleasure to get away from official cocktails for once," said Henry—and immediately regretted it. For him, this conference represented a miraculous break in a basically humdrum and underpaid existence, and he was determined not to become blasé.

"Yeah," said Bill. "Well, be seeing you."

At the Hotel Étoile, Emmy Tibbett was taking a long, luxurious bath, and pondering for the hundredth time in the past week how lucky she was. With finances tight, and little or no prospect of a summer holiday abroad, Henry had suddenly been assigned to attend the Narcotics Conference. The opportunity had seemed too good to miss. Emmy had drawn on her reserve of carefully hoarded housekeeping money, bought an air ticket, and come with him. She was having the time of her life.

This was in great measure due to Annette Delacroix. Annette was a pretty, blond Swiss girl whom Emmy had met some years before in London, where Annette was working temporarily as a secretary at an international conference—the type of job for which, because of her knowledge of English, she was always in demand. They had become friendly, exchanged addresses, and thought little more about it.

Emmy's first day in Geneva had been a little bleak. Henry was at the Palais, and there are limits to the amusement to be gleaned from exploring a strange city alone, hampered by an imperfect command of the language. That evening, with some misgivings, Emmy had conquered her shyness and telephoned Annette, to be met with a heartwarming surge of hospitality. Of course Annette remembered her perfectly. She and Henry must come and have a drink at her apartment at once—well, then, as soon as they could get away from the official party. And she, by the greatest good fortune, was on a week's leave from the Palais and free as air all day. She would show Emmy Geneva.

Later that evening, Henry and Emmy had gone around to Annette's gleamingly modern little flat on the top of a tall block overlooking the lake. Annette, looking stunning in a pale blue silk dress, opened the door to them and said, "Henri . . . Emmie . . . it is so good to see you. Be angels and pour yourselves drinks—I am just on the telephone. Please excuse me."

She went back to the phone, and Henry heard her say, *"C'est un peu difficile ce soir, John, j'ai des invités . . ."*

Quickly, Henry said, "Annette, don't let us interfere with . . ." but she silenced him with a smile and a gesture. To the phone, she said, *"Oui . . . oui, d'accord . . . au revoir, chéri . . ."* Then she put down the receiver and came over to them.

"But it is *drôle,* Emmie," she said. "I work now at the Palais, and my first job when I return from my vacation is with Henri's very conference, *les narcotiques et stupéfiants*. And before that I have a whole week for myself and I am dying of boredom."

After they had been there for a few minutes, there was another ring at the door, and John Trapp arrived—tall, handsome, a little bored, and, Emmy judged, somewhat taken aback at the presence of a fellow countryman who was also a delegate at the very conference on which he was working. He soon relaxed, however, and expounded at some length and over many whiskies the complex structure of Genevan society.

"The Genevois keep to themselves," he said, "and I can't say I blame them. The place is infested with foreigners, and if they once started inviting them to their homes, there'd be no end to it."

Annette looked uncomfortable. "I am Genevoise, *mon cher Jean*," she said.

"You're different," said John, with a quick, attractive smile. "I'm generalizing now. And in general the Genevois keep to themselves. *D'accord?*"

"I suppose so," said Annette.

John went on. "Then there are the expatriates. The American business people have their own society which overlaps with that of the English, but only just." He poured himself another drink. "The elite of the expatriates are the writers and film stars and exiled royalty and other rich men who come here because of the tax laws. They usually spend only a few months of the year here, and they talk only to each other and God."

"Some of them," said Annette, in a slightly clipped voice.

"You know very well what I mean," said John. "I'm talking about the gold-plated lot. Then you have the floating foreign population—the diplomats and people attached for a year or so to international organizations. No sense in making friends of them. They come and go too fast. At the bottom of the ladder"—he took a gulp of whisky—"are people like me. There aren't very many of us. We're foreigners living and working here permanently, of our own free will." He paused. "Personally, I try to cut across the strata, and make friends with people I like in each group, and ignore the rest. It can be done, but you have to be damned careful, or one or other of the tight little groups will suck you in. Still, it's worth it. This is such a bloody wonderful place. Skiing in the winter and sailing in the summer, and good food and drink and . . ."

"For some people," said Annette. The sharpness in her voice

was more pronounced now.

John glanced at her, annoyed. "You go skiing every winter, and you could sail if you wanted to," he said.

Annette gave him a long, serious look. Then she said crisply, "*Jean, chéri,* you know that's not true. How could I afford it? Especially now."

"Things are certainly more expensive now than they were a few years ago," said John, in a conciliatory tone. Then he put his big hand over hers, and said, "*Je m'excuse. Ne sois pas fâchée, chérie.*"

"No," said Annette. "I'm sorry, and I'm not cross."

John turned to Henry and Emmy with his sudden, warming smile.

"Why don't we all go dancing?" he said. They did.

It was half past one in the morning when Annette dropped Henry and Emmy at their hotel. John Trapp climbed with some difficulty out of the front seat of the two-horse Citroën, and held the door open for them, while Henry marveled yet again that the toy-sized car could contain four adult people. They said their good-bys, Annette and Emmy arranged a rendezvous for the morning, and John climbed back into the front seat. As the door was shutting, Henry heard Annette say, "*Chez moi, chéri?*" John nodded and put his arm around her. The little car roared away through the empty streets.

"What a nice couple they are," said Emmy, as, a little later, she stifled a yawn and climbed into bed. "I wonder if they're going to get married."

"They seem perfectly happy as they are," said Henry. "Why are you always trying to marry people off?"

"I don't know. It's so much neater."

"And maybe less fun."

"Oh, rubbish. I adore being married."

"Yes, but look at the husband you've got."

"Conceited brute," said Emmy, and promptly fell asleep.

The next morning Annette called for Emmy in the tiny gray car, and the conducted tour began. They explored the old, ramparted city and had drinks in small, crowded bars full of students and reminiscent of the Left Bank in Paris. They went up Mont Salève in the cable car, and saw the lake and city laid out like a map at their feet. They took a paddle steamer and spent a whole day touring the lake from Geneva to Montreux and back, putting in at enchanting little towns like Coppet, Nyon, Rolle, and Morges on the Swiss coast, and returning down the French shore, touching at the glittering spa of Evian and the medieval fishing villages of Meillerie, Yvoire and Nernier.

One day they drove up into the Jura Mountains, through forests of wild yellow laburnum. The next, they headed southward into the French Alps to the lake of Annecy, climbed to Chamonix, and went up the highest cable car in the world, almost to the top of Mont Blanc, and into a white world of perpetual winter. Then there was a wonderful trip up the Rhône valley, through the ancient towns of Sion and Sierre, coming back by Gruyères—the perfectly preserved walled village in whose shadow is made the only true Gruyère cheese in the world.

In the course of all these excursions, Annette spoke at length and with enthusiasm about her job, her apartment and her hobbies, which were skiing and the study of Alpine flowers. Emmy noticed, however, that she hardly ever mentioned John Trapp, and on the occasions when Emmy tried to bring him into the conversation, Annette would reply in monosyllables, and change the subject quickly. Emmy, though blessed with her fair share of feminine curiosity, was tactful enough not to pry. Annette was an amusing and charming companion, and if she wished to keep her private life private, that was her affair.

Emmy sighed with contentment, and lay back in the warm water. Tonight there was yet another party. The thick white card was propped up on the dressing table. "Mr. and Mrs. Paul G. Hampton, At Home . . . 8 P.M. onwards . . . Villa Trounex, Genève . . ." It sounded fun.

She was roused from her pleasant reverie by the sound of violent rattling on the bedroom door. Guiltily, she realized that she had locked Henry out. She climbed out of the bath, wrapped herself in an enormous white towel, and padded, dripping, across the carpet to let him in. She opened the door, and Henry came in and took her in his arms.

Henry and Emmy Tibbet were a rare couple, although fortunately they were not sufficiently sophisticated to realize it themselves. They were both in their forties. Emmy was plump, black-haired and amiable. Henry was physically unremarkable. Their marriage had weathered fifteen years of happiness, of misery, of crises and reunions, and they had not been aware of growing any older. Consequently they were, if anything, more in love now than they had ever been—and this was the more remarkable since, through no wish of their own, they were childless. The greenest of amateur psychologists could have told them that they were at a dangerous stage in their relationship, but they would have laughed at him.

"I've had the most marvelous day, darling," said Emmy, disentangling herself and the towel from Henry's embrace. "Annette and I went up into the hills behind Nyon and took a picnic lunch. All the Alpine flowers are still out—gentian and wild orchids and the lot. She dropped me back at three, and I went swimming at the Lido."

"You're a brute," said Henry. "I've been in a dark brown conference room since nine this morning, and I'm tired and dirty. I need a bath."

"Have mine," said Emmy generously. "By the way, what is this party this evening? It just says Mr. and Mrs. Paul Hampton. I've never heard of them."

"Rich Americans," said Henry, taking off his jacket.

"Why on earth have they invited us?"

"Because I'm a member of the subcommittee on . . ."

"That doesn't seem much of a reason."

"It's good enough for Geneva," said Henry, and disappeared into the bathroom.

Two

The Villa Trounex was *en fête*. Every downstairs window of the great, beautiful house glowed and glittered with the dancing light of crystal chandeliers. Built at the turn of the century by a wealthy banker, the house had all the exuberant charm of Edwardiana, and resembled more than anything else an elaborate wedding cake with white icing. From the terrace, two graceful flights of steps curved down to the smooth green lawns, which in turn ran down to the lakeside, where Paul Hampton's white motor cruiser lay nuzzling her mooring buoy inside the little private harbor. The gardens were a precise study in calculated informality, for a highly paid landscape architect had placed each tree with consummate skill in exactly the right spot, improving vastly upon nature and yet avoiding any suspicion of symmetry.

Tonight the trees glimmered with tiny lights, and Paul Hampton's guests spilled out of the great drawing room onto the terrace, and down to the lawns below, where white-coated menservants dispensed champagne and *foie gras* with efficient discretion. It was the time of evening when the light has not quite faded, but the moon is already up—a full, yellow moon, hanging like a Chinese lantern in a bluebell sky, and throwing a pathway of restless gold across the calm silver water. Carefully concealed loudspeakers played Mozart softly; the music floated like thistledown on the warm air.

Paul and Natasha Hampton were famous for their parties, so their heavily embossed invitation cards were prized trophies on the mantelpieces of Geneva. The lucky recipient of such a card could look forward confidently to an evening of unostentatious luxury, of impeccable service, of elegance without stiffness, and of stimulating company. For Paul and Natasha had cleverly managed to cut across the rigid layers of society which John Trapp had outlined to Henry.

Financially speaking, Paul Hampton belonged to the category which John had cynically pigeonholed as rich tax-dodgers, and certainly one stood a good chance of meeting expatriate royalty and the even more sought-after film stars at the Villa Trounex. But his circle also included those of the Genevese aristocracy whom he found amusing, a fair smattering of the more intelligent diplomats, a selection of businessmen of all nationalities, and a number of other people who happened to be amusing or talented or just sympathetic.

So it happened that John Trapp stood on the terrace sipping his champagne in the company of an extremely pretty young French duchess, while Oscar H. Krumstein of Amalgamated Exports, Inc. (brought up in the Bronx, and proud of it) enlarged on the beauties of the lake to the firmly corseted wife of a Swiss banker, and Juan Moranta turned the full force of his Spanish charm on a young lady from Finchley whose great dark eyes had gazed soulfully, if without much animation, from every cinema screen in the world.

Paul Hampton moved serenely among his guests, a perfect, observant and considerate host. He was a tall, heavy man in his early fifties, gray-haired and blue-eyed, who walked with the springy step of an athlete: in fact, Paul had only one fear in life, and that was of putting on weight. He was justifiably proud of his body, and he took good care of it, treating it to massage and *sauna* baths, toning it up with water-skiing and squash, and bronzing it carefully in the summer sunshine. It repaid him by glowing with health, energy and well-being.

As he made his way from group to group on the lawns, Paul was keeping a sharp lookout for unfamiliar faces, for the only guests whom he did not know personally were the delegates from the International Narcotics Conference, and he was determined to watch over them with special care. So far, apart from his old friend Jacques Lenoir, he had located and made the acquaintance of Juan Moranta, Bill Parkington, and Konrad Zwemmer. Now he was in search of the remaining two—Alfredo Spezzi and Henry Tibbett.

As it happened, he was doomed to disappointment for the time being. Alfredo had met up with an old friend and compatriot, an internationally famous Italian athlete, and the two of them had wandered down to the little yacht basin, where they were deep in discussion about the finer points of water polo. Henry had not yet arrived.

It was not more than a few minutes later, however, that Henry and Emmy drove up to the Villa Trounex in a taxi. This put them at an immediate disadvantage, and as they watched the chauffeur-driven Bentleys and Mercedes circling the graveled forecourt, they instinctively glanced at each other for support and reassurance. This, they felt, was something altogether out of their class.

Their feelings were not helped by the infinitely superior, white-coated character who opened the taxi door for them. There was the inevitable, agonizing delay while Henry groped for the right amount of money to pay the cab driver, and added a very much exaggerated tip out of sheer panic. The gentleman in the white coat cleared his throat almost imperceptibly, indicating impatience. Henry pulled himself together. His resolution not to be impressed had weakened, and this had made him cross. Before the butler could put his inevitable question, Henry said irritably, "Mr. and Mrs. Henry Tibbett."

He took Emmy's arm firmly, and almost hustled her inside.

"Monsieur et Madame Henry Tibbett," echoed the butler, ringingly, with distaste and a faintly Italian intonation. Henry and Emmy walked into the house.

Instantly their feelings of inferiority and dismay were dissipated. A voice, charmingly un-English, said, "Inspector Tibbett —oh, we are so pleased—we thought you might have been too busy to come . . ." And Henry found himself looking into the largest pair of brown eyes he had ever seen. He felt his hand caught in a soft, cool one, and was aware of a whiff of Paris scent.

"And Madame Tibbett—this is more than we hoped for. You must be so tired, with all these Geneva parties . . . to think that you found the time to come to ours. Please come in. I am Natasha Hampton."

Natasha Hampton was the sort of woman who turns heads wherever she goes—tiny and blond, with a face whose exquisite bone structure takes the breath. This evening she was wearing a short, slim dress of pale gray satin, utterly simple and quite faultless. The diamonds at her wrist and the pearls at her neck seemed to have grown there, naturally. She exuded warmth and friendliness and simplicity, and both Henry and Emmy felt at once that they were among friends. The relief was enormous.

"Come out onto the terrace," said Natasha. "It is so beautiful this evening. You can see Mont Blanc—that is unusual so early in the year. And there are lots of your friends waiting for you."

Henry and Emmy crossed the parquet-floored drawing room and stepped out onto the terrace. At once, a waiter materialized with champagne, and at the same moment John Trapp said, "Hello, there. Nice to see you."

"My husband is dying to meet you," said Natasha. "I will go and find him." And she disappeared, a slim gray shadow under the Chinese lanterns.

"This is Sophie," said John, offhandedly. Henry and Emmy shook hands with the pretty girl, and it was not until much later that they realized her staggering social status. It did not seem to matter. At Paul Hampton's parties, such things were unimportant.

Henry said, "What a wonderful city this is."

Immediately the girl called Sophie said, "But isn't it? I have always said so. It is not only beautiful—it is symbolic of something so much more important."

"International friendship," said Emmy.

"That is exactly what I mean," said Sophie. "I know the nations are not always exactly friendly with each other, but at least here everyone can meet and talk on an equal level."

"Bloody nonsense," said John. There was a short silence.

"Here, at Paul's at any rate," said Sophie, with a quick, embarrassed smile.

"Geneva is a strange place," said John. "I told you so the other night. Don't be deceived by its beauty. All sorts of things go on here that . . ."

"You've stayed here voluntarily for quite a few years," said Emmy, smiling. "Why?"

"Because it amuses me," said John shortly. "I'll go and refill our glasses."

He picked up the four glasses expertly, and vanished into the house. At that moment Natasha reappeared.

"Paul is entangled with about a hundred people," she said. "Never mind. He will be over in a moment. I see you have met Sophie. And of course you know Señor Moranta."

Juan Moranta turned as he heard his name mentioned, and greeted Henry and Emmy. After the initial courtesies—somewhat prolonged in Moranta's case, and involving much flourishing and kissing of hands—the two men settled down to a discussion of the lighter aspects of the day's debate, and Emmy leaned against the gray stone parapet and let her attention wander over the general scene.

It was, she reflected, exactly like an episode from a film: an early Orson Welles or a middle-period Fellini, where, in a setting of great opulence, the camera moves leisurely but with a deadly observation, picking up a gesture here, a snatch of conversation there, a smile, a moment of anger. Pleased with this conceit, Emmy set her own eye to roving at random, like a searchlight beam. It was rewarding.

John had returned to Sophie, and Emmy caught for an instant the latter's pleading face as she said, "Please, John . . ." and John's rather too deliberate stubbing out of a cigarette as he said, not unkindly, "No, Sophie. It won't do. The best thing for you is to . . ." His voice was lost as he turned away, but the girl took a step after him and said, "Sometimes I think you are the most selfish . . ."

"Nobody will dispute that, Madame." The voice was Juan Moranta's, and Emmy was surprised to see that he had suddenly broken his conversation with Henry, and turned around to the French girl. "May I get you a drink?"

For a moment, Trapp and Moranta looked at each other, and Emmy could see the contempt on the Spaniard's face and the amused exasperation on the Englishman's. Then Trapp shrugged his shoulders very slightly and walked away, while from the other side of the terrace Bill Parkington said, loudly and dogmatically, "I don't agree. You can analyze the minutiae of any given particular case . . ." Emmy glanced around, to see Bill coming up the steps from the lawn with Konrad Zwemmer. As they passed her, Zwemmer was saying, "It is not the particular which interests me, Mr. Parkington. It is the general. Individual cases merely confuse the issue. To get a true picture . . ."

Emmy's camera-eye wandered again, caught by a burst of laughter from Natasha Hampton. She was talking to Jacques Lenoir on the lawn below the terrace—or rather, she was giggling like a schoolgirl, while Jacques indulged in some sort of mimed monologue. Emmy caught a stray phrase—"A wife and three Alfa Romeos to support . . . my dear lady, can you wonder . . . ?

"Oh, yes. It's very nice. The people, I mean." The accents of Finchley were unmistakable in Emmy's left ear. Not all the big guns of Hollywood could blow away their relentless respectability. Emmy turned and gazed with undisguised admiration and curiosity at the world-famous profile, which was at present dazzling Mr. Oscar H. Krumstein. "Well, Hollywood's just like anywhere else, really, I suppose. Only a bit bigger. If you like that sort of thing, I mean."

Henry's voice, suddenly loud, said, "If the expression had any meaning at all, I'd say it was a question of intellectual integrity. As it is . . ."

It was at that moment that Emmy heard her name being called, and she turned to see Alfredo Spezzi making his way up the steps, with his German wife, Gerda, in tow.

This was a delightful reunion, for Henry and Emmy had not met Gerda since her marriage. Their previous encounter had been on a murder case in the Dolomites, where the German girl had been for a time under suspicion. There she had exhibited all the reserve and prickliness of the persecuted, for Gerda was half-Jewish, and had survived the horrors of Nazism only to be suspected of murder in Italy. Now, married to Alfredo and sure of herself, she had blossomed. She still wore black, characteristically, but all the warmth of her personality had flowered and come to the surface. She kissed Emmy impulsively.

"Emmy!" she cried. "Oh, it is good to see you. And Henry. To think that the last time we met . . ."

"The last time we met," said Henry, smiling, "you didn't speak a word of English. When did you learn?"

"Alfredo has jobs all over the world now," said Gerda. "Without English, one can hardly survive these days." She looked out over the lake. "Is this not beautiful? Sometimes I never thought to see beauty again, and to enjoy it without fear. I owe you so much."

"You owe us nothing," said Henry.

"But when even Alfredo thought I was a murderess, and peddling drugs . . ."

"Drugs?" said a voice in Henry's left ear, and he turned to see Bill Parkington standing behind him. "Talking shop, even out here?"

"Not at all," said Henry. "Just ancient history."

"As a matter of fact," said Bill, "I wouldn't mind talking shop myself for a moment. Sorry to be boring, but with the committee meeting tomorrow morning . . . do you mind, Henry?"

"Not at all," said Henry. In the softly lit dusk, he saw that

Bill's normally cheerful face was strained and worried.

"Excuse us a minute," said Bill.

Alfredo looked up inquiringly, but Bill had already taken Henry's arm firmly in his iron grasp, and was leading him away from the group. Spezzi shrugged, and turned to talk to Emmy. Juan Moranta watched the two men go with a faintly puzzled expression.

Bill piloted Henry down the lawn until they reached the quay-side. There was nobody else in sight, and the sound of voices and music drifted faintly down on the light breeze. Bill sat down on the gray stone landing stage, lit a cigarette, and said, abruptly, "Henry, there's been a leakage of information from the conference."

For a moment Henry was silent. Then he said, "How do you know?"

"A coded cable waiting for me when I got in this evening. Today, the FBI finally caught up with one of our most notorious dope runners, a big shot. Guy we've had our eye on for some time. They made a good job of it, took him completely by surprise. On him, they found what amounts to a condensed but accurate report of last week's discussions on countermeasures."

"Where did this happen?"

"In San Francisco."

Henry whistled softly. "They haven't wasted much time," he said. "Must be pretty well organized. I don't like the sound of it."

"You're telling me," said Bill gloomily. "And there's worse to come."

"What?"

"He also had a copy of the agenda for our subcommittee. As you know, that's the really top secret part of the conference, because a countermeasure remains effective just precisely as long as we can keep our suspects in the dark about it. Now, nobody has access to that agenda except the six of us, our two interpreters, our verbatim reporter, and our secretary."

"That narrows the field," said Henry.

"It's damned impossible, on the face of it," said Bill. "The interpreters and reporters have been screened and rescreened until you could put them through a sieve. And one can hardly believe that a delegate . . ."

"So what do we do now?" Henry asked.

"That's what I wanted to talk to you about," said Bill. "My chiefs suggest we go ahead tomorrow with relatively unimportant matters—it'll mean changing the agenda slightly—and it's up to us to locate the leakage."

"Does anyone else know about this?"

"Not so far. You see the spot we're in. If it *should* turn out to be a delegate—which heaven forbid—we'd only put him on his guard by making it public. It's a darned tricky situation."

"We could always change our staff of interpreters and reporters," said Henry.

"Yeah, sure we could. And then if the leakage stopped, we'd never know which one of them it was, and either the culprit would be free to go on spying on other meetings, or three innocent people would lose their jobs along with the guilty one. No, the way I see it, we've got to run this thing down here and now. Besides, until it's cleared up, we're all automatically under suspicion. Not a pleasant sensation." Bill threw his cigarette into the lake.

"I appreciate the fact that you've told me," said Henry. "I hope that means you don't suspect me personally."

He spoke almost jokingly, but Bill's voice was perfectly serious when he replied, "I suspect everyone." There was a short pause. Then Bill went on. "I've told you for two reasons. First, because you're chairman of the committee. And second . . ." He paused again. "You know John Trapp socially, don't you?"

Henry felt slightly sick. "I have met him outside the Palais," he said. "How did you know?"

Bill smiled, but without amusement. "This is a small town," he said. "You and Emmy were seen out dancing with him and one of the Palais secretaries last week. The Moulin Rouge, wasn't it?"

"It certainly is a small town," said Henry. He was beginning to get angry. "Who saw us?"

"As a matter of fact, it was Mary Benson, the Australian girl. Our verbatim reporter."

"I'd be interested to know how the information got to you," said Henry dryly.

"Oh, hell," said Bill. "Don't start picking on Mary. She didn't mean any harm, just happened to mention it. We were having a drink together."

"I see," said Henry. "All right. So I know the man slightly. I don't see what that has to do with . . ."

"After I got the cable this evening," said Bill, "I went back to the Palais and did a little checking up on records. John Trapp belonged to the Communist Party in Oxford ten years ago."

Henry's anger surged up again. "When he was about eighteen," he said. "And in any case, what on earth have politics to do with dope running?"

Bill shrugged. "It's the only thread of subversive activity I could find against anyone."

"It's monstrously unjust to connect the two things," said Henry with some heat.

"The world tends to be unjust," said Bill.

"In any case, what do you want me to do about it?"

"You're a cop," said Bill. "I've told you the suspect. Now it's up to you. This is a serious matter, Henry. No good being sentimental about it."

There was a short silence. Then Henry said, "Very well. I'll see what I can do. If only to clear the man's name. I'll talk to him tomorrow."

"Attaboy," said Bill. He grinned, not very convincingly. "Now let's try to forget it, if we can, until the morning. Let's join the boys and girls."

They made their way up the garden in thoughtful silence. Henry was profoundly worried. Nobody realized better than he the gravity of the situation. Of all criminals, drug runners are probably the richest and the most highly organized. For a big international gang to get their hands on the details of all the latest countermeasures could annul years of patient work.

In his mind he considered the delegates and staff of his committee, one by one. Almost instinctively his thoughts turned to Zwemmer, the enigma. At once he reproached himself for unfairness. Each was equally suspect and equally likely to be innocent. One could at least rule out Spezzi and Parkington. Or could one? The fact that Spezzi was an old friend did not preclude the possibility that he might be susceptible to bribery on a large scale. He had Gerda and two children to look after now, and Italian policemen are no better paid than those of other countries. And Bill? He had told Henry the news, certainly, but then he could hardly have avoided doing so, being under instructions from his department in Washington. How significant was it that the leaked information had found its way so quickly to the States? Not very, for given an international organization, it was almost certainly distributed by now to selected people all around the world. Nevertheless . . .

Henry and Bill arrived back on the terrace just as Paul Hampton came out of the house. He paused on the threshold, while the intimidating butler murmured something respectfully in his ear. Henry saw him shaking his head impatiently, in a negative gesture. The butler melted discreetly away, and Paul Hampton stood for a moment in the open French window, surveying his guests with a smile. Gerda and Emmy were now chatting with Jacques Lenoir, who was entertaining them with a deliciously accurate imitation of one of the more venerable members of the Comédie Française playing Molière. Konrad Zwemmer stood with them, watching Lenoir with serious interest. John Trapp leaned on the balustrade, a little apart from the others, smoking and gazing down on the gardens. Spezzi had disappeared. Paul Hampton threw down his cigarette and stepped out onto the terrace.

Although Henry had never met his host, he knew at once that this must be he. The dark gray Savile Row suit, embellished by a single minature rose in the buttonhole; the slim gold cigarette holder; the gray hair, neither too long nor too short, framing the still-youthful, sun-tanned face—all these added up irresistibly in Henry's mind to the formula of the hidden persuaders. Men of Distinction drink (or eat or smoke or drive) Somebody's Scotch (or cornflakes or cigarettes or automobiles); therefore, by a dubious leap of logic, if you, dear reader, will only drink or eat or smoke or drive likewise, you will soon grow to look like Paul Hampton. Henry had never, even in his more gullible days, been deceived by this spurious reasoning. He knew that what set Paul Hampton apart from his fellow men was the magical aura of money, which surrounded him like a cellophane casing. This reflection did not depress Henry. On the contrary, he was delighted to see wealth in the hands of somebody who so clearly made excellent use of it, and he knew that, contrary to folklore, rich men are frequently as good if not better company than poor ones.

Paul spotted Bill Parkington, and went across the terrace to him.

"So you were the culprit," he said, with mock severity.

"Culprit?" Bill sounded a little taken aback.

"For half an hour," said Paul warmly, "I have been trying to meet Inspector Tibbett. Only to hear that you had spirited him into some dark corner to talk shop. Shame on you."

"Sorry, Paul," Bill apologized awkwardly. "Something came up that . . ."

Paul held up his hand. "Not another word," he said. And then, to Henry, "I'm Paul Hampton. I'm extremely pleased to know you, sir." He lowered his raised hand, and held it out for Henry to shake. "An old Swiss custom," he added, "which we new Swiss have adopted. I find it civilized."

Henry, a little overpowered, murmured politenesses, and complimented Mr. Hampton on his beautiful home. At once the older man's face lit up with very real pleasure.

"I guess I'm like a child with a new toy when it comes to this place," he said. "Not that the Villa Trounex is new, not even to us. We've been here nearly five years now. But we've worked hard, Natasha and I, to make it the sort of place we enjoy, and that we hope our guests enjoy, too."

"You've certainly succeeded," said Henry.

"I hardly like to suggest this," Paul went on, almost diffidently, "but would it amuse you to see a little of the house?"

"It would indeed," said Henry. Emmy, overhearing, begged to be allowed to come too. In fact, the idea was taken up enthusiastically by the whole group.

"This way for the conducted tour, then," said Paul gaily. "Natasha—where is the girl? Never mind. She can look after the party for a few minutes. Are you joining us, John?"

For a second, John Trapp did not answer; indeed, he seemed not to have heard. Then, as if coming out of a reverie, he stood up straight, put his empty glass down on the balustrade and said, "I won't, Paul, if you don't mind. I've seen the place before—remember?"

"O.K., O.K. Stick to boozing if you want to," said Paul, good-humoredly. "Now, ladies and gentlemen, here we have the main drawing room. There's quite a story attached to those chandeliers. Four years ago, when we were in Paris . . ." Still talking, he stepped inside, under the soft, brilliant lights.

The little group followed him, for all the world like sightseers at a country mansion open to the public. Emmy and Gerda walked together, chattering excitedly. Konrad Zwemmer kept to himself, observing and listening with studious care; Henry felt that he was longing to take notes, and was only prevented from doing so by the fact that he had no notebook with him. Juan Moranta was escorting the young lady from Finchley, to whom he was paying extravagant court in what seemed to Henry a slightly mocking manner. He had little time to spare for the beauties of the house, for he was fully occupied not only in charming the doe-eyed sex symbol, but also in disengaging her from the wiles of Jacques Lenoir, who, greatly smitten, walked on the other side of her, exuding gallantry. The situation was complicated by the fact that Moranta spoke very little English. The object of their admiration having volunteered that she learned French at school, the conversation was being conducted in that language, of which she understood perhaps ten words, if spoken slowly. Consequently, the rapier exchanges of wit, the thrust and parry of nuance and the delicately flicked compliments escaped her completely. She walked gracefully between the verbal duelists, serene and uncomprehending, rewarding now one and now the other with a ravishing smile. All three were enjoying themselves immensely.

Henry and Bill Parkington kept together, in somber silence. Bill's disclosure weighed heavily on Henry, and it seemed to be having the same effect on the big American. He walked slowly, apparently more interested in the toes of his shoes than in the rooms they were seeing; every so often he shook his large, shaggy head, as if in depressed chagrin.

So the little procession wended its way through the elegance of small drawing rooms, through the long dining room with its Louis XV furniture and *trompe-l'oeil* walls decorated with painted pillars and urns of flowers. They visited the ferny greenness of the big conservatory and the leather-and-gilt tranquillity of the library, stopping frequently to admire some special piece of furniture, valuable picture, or amusing knickknack.

Paul Hampton was a fascinating guide. With excellent taste, considerable knowledge, and a lot of money, he had chosen each piece himself, scouring the shops and markets of Europe. Emmy, crying out with pleasure at the sight of a cabinet full of antique Waterford glass, was not only privileged to handle some of the precious pieces, but was pressed, embarrassingly, to accept a fragile bowl for herself. ("I can get another one. . . . I know the guy. Has a little shop in a back street behind Merrion Square, you'd never find it unless you knew it.") Jacques Lenoir, seduced for a moment from the film star's side, lolled at his ease in a chair which Le Roi Soleil had kept for his especial use at Versailles, a new acquisition, it seemed, since Lenoir's last visit. Henry and Juan Moranta simultaneously spotted a dagger of superb Toledo steel hanging on the library wall. Paul insisted on taking it down and making each of them handle it to get the feel of the fine, sharp blade and the delicate inlay of ivory on the hilt.

Reluctantly returning the weapon to its owner, Henry, a trifle light-headed from champagne, said, "If I had money, Mr. Hampton, I'd try to spend it just as you have."

To which Paul Hampton replied seriously, "That is a very great compliment, Inspector."

It was only when the party found its way upstairs that a hiatus occurred. A manservant, in black trousers and starched white coat, materialized from nowhere and whispered to Paul. Henry noticed that Hampton's face changed almost imperceptibly, hardened, became businesslike. One could see why he was a rich man.

"Please excuse me," he said, with a charming smile. "I have to take a telephone call from New York. And I was the one who was complaining about Bill talking shop. I apologize." To the manservant he said, "I'll take it in my room." And then he added, rather surprisingly, "Natasha and I are old-fashioned; we have separate bedrooms, even in this day and age. Excuse me. You'll find all the fixings downstairs."

He walked off down the corridor, and the party dispersed. Alfredo Spezzi arrived from nowhere and bore Gerda away. Lenoir and Moranta, still arguing brilliantly in French, escorted their uncomprehending quarry downstairs in search of a drink. Bill Parkington wandered off with Konrad Zwemmer, who was remarking earnestly, "In Germany, it is the old-fashioned married couples who share the same bed."

"Sure, sure," Bill answered reassuringly.

"And in America?" Zwemmer persisted. "This is a social question of some significance."

"In America," said Bill ponderously, "we share the same room, but we have separate beds and separate lives."

"Ah, so?" Zwemmer was fascinated. "Just what do you mean by separate? For example, Mr. Parkington, in the average American family, in a heavily industrial area such as Pittsburgh, how many times per year would you imagine . . ." Their voices were lost down the corridor.

Henry and Emmy, left alone, grinned at each other.

"I'd like to explore this place a bit further," said Emmy.

"Better not," Henry said prudently. "Come on downstairs."

"There must be another flight of stairs at the far end of the corridor to balance the one we came up," returned Emmy. "Let's look."

"No. It would be rude. We hardly know the Hamptons."

"I don't mean I want to pry into people's bedrooms," Emmy replied with spirit. "I just want to see the general layout. I'm sure there's another staircase."

"You do what you like, then. I'm going down to join the others." Henry always felt helpless in the face of one of Emmy's fits of stubbornness.

"Go on then. I'll see you later." Emmy gave him a smile in which he detected a certain amount of affectionate mockery, and walked away down the passage, her golden silk dress rustling gently as she went.

"For heaven's sake, don't get lost," Henry called after her. Which was foolish of him, for, as it turned out, he was the one who missed his way. Probably because he was irritated with Emmy, worried about the leakage of secret information, and preoccupied with the thought of the committee meeting in the morning, he forgot that, to reach the staircase, it was necessary to turn off the corridor and into another. Realizing his mistake, he tried to rectify matters by taking a right turn, which led not to the stairs he was seeking, but to another, smaller flight.

Deciding that, at all events, his general direction of progress should be downward, Henry descended the staircase, to find himself not on the ground floor, but on a mezzanine story with no apparent facilities for getting any further down. In every direction, royal blue carpeted corridors stretched away from him, studded with padded white leather doors. Henry felt ridiculous and trapped, like a man lost in a Kafkaesque luxury hotel with no way in or out. From below, the music and babble of the party was just audible. Otherwise, everything was completely quiet.

It was perhaps because of this muffled silence that the sound of a door opening somewhere behind him gave him a sudden shock, and prompted him to react untypically. Furthermore, he had an instinctive revulsion against appearing foolish in this great house where he had been so kindly welcomed, but where he felt fundamentally out of place. In any case, for whatever undefined motive, at the click of the door-latch Henry stepped quickly into an alcove, where, under the protective arms of a white marble goddess standing on a small pedestal, he was out of sight of the opening door.

Instantly he regretted this move. For immediately following the opening of the door came Natasha Hampton's voice. It was low and ardent, and it said, "No. There's nobody. Please go now."

And then it said, "Oh, my darling. My darling . . ." several times over and indistinctly, blurred by passion or tears or perhaps just because Natasha's golden head was half-buried in somebody's shoulder. Then distinctly but quietly, she said, "It was a risk. Go now, quickly."

An undistinguishable masculine voice murmured something, and then Natasha said, very softly, "All right. Just for a minute then. One minute." The padded door closed with a gentle click, and the corridor was silent again.

Henry stepped out of his hiding place, hating himself. It was nothing to him one way or the other if Natasha Hampton cared to have a lover, but, since his job necessarily involved a great deal of prying into other people's affairs, Henry was a great respecter of privacy whenever possible. The Hampton façade was smoothly flawless, and it made him cross and unhappy to think that he had, by sheer chance, discovered a rift in it. Besides, he had a feeling that he recognized the man's voice.

Henry walked back along the corridor in the direction from which he had come, deciding that the only sensible way to find the main staircase was to retrace his steps and start again. He had just begun to climb the short flight of stairs to the next floor when another of the white leather doors behind him opened, and Paul Hampton came out.

"Hello," remarked Paul, dryly. "Lost your way, Inspector?"

Henry felt himself reddening. "Yes, I'm afraid I have," he said, lamely. "I must have taken a wrong turning, and . . ."

"Easy to do, in a rabbit warren like this. You've got yourself into our bedroom wing." Paul smiled. "Come on down and I'll . . ."

It was at that moment that the door of Natasha's room opened again, and John Trapp stepped quickly out into the corridor. Henry felt his stomach muscles contract in an agony of embarrassment. He stood there, as helpless as a spectator in the cinema, while for a long moment the two other men looked at each other in silence. Clearly both of them were shaken off balance and could find no words.

Hampton recovered first, and his voice was light and friendly as he said, "Good God, John. Where did you spring from?"

"Natasha's room, of course," said John. A tiny pause. "I've been telephoning. I hope you don't mind. The downstairs line was busy."

There was another pause. When Paul spoke again, his voice

was harder. "My dear man, why should I mind? It was Natasha's room you invaded, not mine. Where is she, by the way?"

"I don't know. Downstairs, I suppose."

"Well, I trust you got your call through."

John smiled slightly. "No, as a matter of fact I didn't. But it doesn't matter. My time wasn't wasted. There are better things to do than talking on the telephone." There was a definite, lilting challenge in his voice.

Is the man mad? Henry thought. And then, glancing from one to the other, it flashed through his mind with the clarity of lightning that the shocked silence, the tension, the pathetically thin story about telephoning, were all on his account. Hampton knows, he thought. And John knows that he knows, and everything is managed discreetly and in a civilized manner. If Hampton is angry with John, it's because he has been careless enough to encounter a stranger. If John was taken aback, it was to see me, not Paul. I'm the one who ought not to be here, who has caused an awkward situation. It was not until some days later that Henry realized that this assessment was not quite accurate. At the time it seemed certain.

"C'mon downstairs, then, both of you," said Paul. He took John's arm. "Can't have my guests wandering all over the house at this hour of night."

The party downstairs was drawing to its close. Many people, including Bill Parkington, had already left, while others were looking for their host and hostess to say good-by. Natasha, gay as ever, appeared a few minutes later. She and Paul did not even glance at each other, and Henry noticed that she avoided John Trapp rather too carefully.

Henry found Emmy with Alfredo and Gerda. Zwemmer was talking earnestly to a disinterested Moranta who, it appeared, had finally been worsted by Lenoir. The latter had departed some minutes earlier, in company with the celluloid beauty, and headed for a night club. Moranta had clearly been drowning his sorrows in whisky. He tried to persuade Henry and Emmy to go on with him and sample the night life of Geneva.

"It is not yet of midnight," he announced, in his jagged, heavily accented English. "Is early. Come with me. I know many places."

Henry and Emmy declined politely. Whereupon Juan, sad but unsurprised, offered at all events to drive them home in the car which he had hired for the period of the conference. There would also be room, he said, for Alfredo and Gerda. In the dwindling group, his pointed omission of John Trapp from his invitation was conspicuous.

"What about you, John?" Paul Hampton asked quickly. "Have you a car?"

"You know very well I haven't. I'm just a common working man."

"I'll call a taxi for you, John," said Natasha. With so few guests left, she could no longer avoid him completely, but Henry noticed that she kept as far away from him as possible.

"I will drive you home in my car, Mr. Trapp." Zwemmer, already in his overcoat, rapped the words out, like an order. But Paul Hampton intervened.

"Natasha." Paul spoke lightly, with only the faintest edge on his voice. "Why don't you drive John home, darling? You can put the new Renault through her paces for him." He turned to Henry. "Natasha just got this jalopy last week. She's pleased as punch with it." And then, to John, "Forgive me if I don't come with you. I'm catching a plane for Paris at half past six in the morning, and I haven't started packing yet."

Natasha said, "Paris, Paul? You never told me."

"There are plenty of things I don't tell you, my sweet, but it so happens that this isn't one of them. I told you last week."

"Oh, so you did. I'd forgotten." There was a tiny pause, and then Natasha went on. "But I dare say John would sooner take a taxi, darling. He knows how badly I drive."

"No, no." Paul sounded impatient. "I want to know what he thinks of the Floride. You take him."

Natasha shrugged. "Very well. If you want me to."

Henry caught Paul Hampton's eye for a moment, and saw in it an amused challenge. "You see?" it seemed to say. "Doesn't this prove that there is nothing between my wife and this man?" He could not help admiring the gesture.

The Spezzis and the Tibbetts said their farewells and went out to Juan's car. While they were still settling themselves in, Zwemmer drove off in his black Volkswagen, and Natasha and John came out of the house together. Natasha had thrown a dark sable coat over her pale dress. John, deliberately, had chosen to wear an old and crumpled mackintosh. Henry watched them with a mixture of sympathy and irritation as they got into a small pale green Floride and, with Natasha at the wheel, swept away down the drive and out of sight. He wondered, too, about Annette Delacroix and the girl called Sophie; and decided that John

Trapp's life must be rather more complicated than most.

On the terrace, in the gardens, in the reception rooms, the lights went out, one by one, as the butler made his final rounds, locking windows and bolting doors. The Villa Trounex slept under the moon, slept, that is, except for three tired Italian boys who were washing up glasses in a basement kitchen, and Paul Hampton, who was packing monogrammed silk shirts in a small leather suitcase in his bedroom.

Three

The telephone by Henry's bed rang insistently. Cursing it, he rolled over and stretched out a hand automatically. He had been in so deep a sleep that he had already picked up the telephone before his mind had fully registered the fact that he was in a hotel bedroom in Geneva and not in his own London flat. Consequently, it was with a sense of shock that he heard the bright, polite, female voice saying, *"Monsieur Tibbett? Bon jour, monsieur. C'est sept heures et demi. Vous voulez du thé . . . du café . . . ?"*

"Deux cafés complets, s'il vous plaît," he muttered. *"Merci, mademoiselle."*

"Service."

That word brought him back abruptly to Geneva. As a reply to "thank you," the French as a rule say *"C'est moi qui vous remercie,"* although their current passion for truncated expressions often turns it into a mere *"C'est moi"*: but the Genevese, without exception, say *"Service!"* with a particular, pert, uprising intonation which is unmistakable. This is better than the English, however, who say nothing at all.

Henry lay on his back and contemplated the ceiling with some gloom. Memories came flooding back, most of them unpleasant. The opening session of the subcommittee today. The leakage of information. Bill Parkington's insinuations about John Trapp, and his own reluctant promise to "see what he could do." What, for heaven's sake, could he do? Approach John as one Englishman to another? "I say, old man, we rather think you may be in the pay of a gang of dope runners. Do tell us about it, there's a good chap. Don't want any unpleasantness, you know." Henry smiled to himself wryly. There was, of course, another classic line of attack. "Trapp, I know your secret." To which, he reflected, John might well reply, "Which one?"

Henry lit a cigarette, and blew a thin column of smoke toward the ceiling. Beside him, Emmy stirred. She was sleeping on her face, and her head of thick black hair looked like a golliwog's on the white pillow. She made a little moaning noise, yawned and rolled over.

"Gosh," she said indistinctly, "is it morning already? What a gorgeous party that was. I feel awful."

"You shouldn't have drunk so much champagne."

"I know. Never mind, it was worth it. Have you ordered coffee?"

"I have."

"You're an angel and I adore you," said Emmy. She sat up, kissed Henry, and then collapsed onto the pillow again. "I could sleep forever."

"There's no earthly reason why you shouldn't, at least till midday," said Henry. "I've got to be bright and early, worse luck. I promised our verbatim reporter I'd be in at half past nine sharp to go over the transcript of the speech I made yesterday, and then there are changes in the agenda for today . . ."

Emmy giggled. "I can't imagine you making speeches."

"I'm very glad you aren't there to hear them," said Henry.

"Anyway," Emmy went on, "I've got to get up too, because I'm meeting Gerda at ten and we're going out to the country to have lunch."

"Lucky devils. Where?"

"I don't know exactly. Some little pub in a pretty village just outside the town. Natasha Hampton was telling Gerda all about it last night. She's got all the details." There was a discreet knock on the door. "Thank God. Coffee."

Henry reached the Palais des Nations at a quarter past nine, and by twenty-five past had found his way through a maze of green corridors to the suite of offices set aside for his subcommittee. In view of the "top secret" aspect of the agenda, they had been allotted one of the "closed" suites, consisting of a single passage leading to the conference room, with offices and cloakrooms opening off either side of it. The entrance to this passage was guarded by a large, melancholy gentleman, who wore a heavy mustache and the gray uniform of the Palais staff. He sat like a bored watchdog in his little glass kennel by the door, and admitted only such favored individuals as could produce the requisite pass.

"So if the security leak goes on," Henry thought, as he fumbled in his wallet for the precious scrap of paper, "it really does mean trouble in the nest. It must be one of us."

He found his pass. The watchdog scrutinized it sadly, nodded, made a note in a large book, and motioned Henry into the corridor.

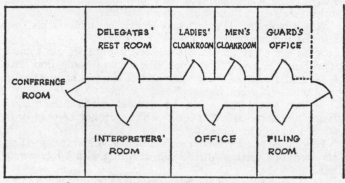

PLAN OF "CLOSED" OFFICE SUITE

To Henry's surprise, he was by no means the first to arrive, although the meeting was not scheduled to start until ten o'clock. The corridor was already alive with voices, and from the office a typewriter clicked busily. Through the open door of the conference room, at the far end of the passage, Henry could see Hélène Brochet talking to Konrad Zwemmer. She looked up, caught sight of Henry, and waved. He returned the salutation, and went into the men's cloakroom, on the right-hand side of the corridor. Here he met Bill Parkington coming out.

"Hi," said Bill. "Sleep well?"

"As well as could be expected," said Henry. Bill grinned encouragingly, and went off down the corridor and into the delegates' rest room. He was carrying a bulky sheaf of notes, and Henry guessed that he would be wanting to put the finishing touches to the speech he was due to make. Bill hated making speeches, and suffered from severe stage fright until he actually got going, when it was almost impossible to stop him.

In the cloakroom Alfredo Spezzi was combing his hair carefully in front of the mirror. As with many Italians, there was something of the dandy about Alfredo. His shirts were silk and monogrammed, his cuff links gold, and his shoes tapering and made of the finest suede. Indeed, he had always seemed to Henry to exemplify the saying that, whereas a Frenchman will cheerfully go around in rags in order to eat well, an Italian will starve sooner than appear badly dressed. At the moment, Alfredo was studying his handsome face with minute care, as the little tortoise-shell comb flicked through his fair hair.

"Good morning, Alfredo," said Henry. He took off his light raincoat and hung it up. "Ready for the fray?"

Spezzi smiled at him in the mirror. "I hope we can achieve something," he said. "This is not like a true investigation. This is talk, talk, talk and more talk—and at the end of it, what? A resolution on a piece of paper."

"Where would the world be without conferences?" asked Henry philosophically. "At least, neither you nor I would be in Geneva, so let's be thankful."

He glanced at his reflection in the mirror, found it depressing, and went out, leaving Alfredo still wrestling with a recalcitrant lock.

At the moment when Henry emerged into the passage, Annette Delacroix came out of the small filing room opposite. She looked very tired, Henry thought, and when she spoke, her voice was sharp and angry.

"Ah, there you are, Henry," she said. "Have you seen John yet?"

"Not this morning," said Henry. "Why?"

"He's apparently expecting you," said Annette. "He's in the office, typing away furiously at something, and he's given orders that he's not to be disturbed until you arrive, and that he must see you alone."

"Good heavens," said Henry. His heart sank. "What's it about, do you know?"

"I have no idea," said Annette icily. "I haven't seen him for several days. I can only tell you what he said this morning. It's extremely annoying of him. That's supposed to be my office and my typewriter."

"Oh, well," said Henry, "I'd better go and see what he wants. By the way, as soon as you can get in there, I've some urgent typing for you to do. There's a change in this morning's agenda."

"I've got my copy here if you'd like to mark it," said Annette, holding out the sheet of paper in her hand.

Henry took out his pen, and, holding the paper against the wall, made some rapid corrections, eliminating the more secret items and substituting innocuous ones. He was conscious of a dark sense of foreboding. Since his conversation with Parkington the night before, the pleasant, compact and relaxed atmosphere of this conference had disappeared abruptly, to be replaced by an oppressive feeling of suspicion. Henry was not given to emotional flights of fancy, but it was true that as he stood there in the bleak corridor of the Palais he felt an illogical impression of conspiracy around and against him.

He did not have much time to indulge in this fancy, however, for scarcely had he made the last correction when Mary Benson came out of the interpreters' room. Mary was a tall, auburn-haired Australian girl—quiet and competent, one of the finest verbatim reporters at the Palais des Nations. Henry had liked her from the beginning, and was delighted that she had been assigned to the subcommittee. Her work was highly professional and carried out with the minimum of fuss. She had a pleasant, low voice with only the faintest tang of an Australian accent to it.

"Ah, Inspector Tibbett," she said. "I was looking for you. I know you're very much in demand this morning, but we did have a date, didn't we?"

"We did," said Henry. "I'm right with you. Here you are, Annette."

Annette took the revised agenda without a word and walked off down the corridor and into the rest room. Henry followed Mary Benson into the interpreters' room.

"I understand," he said, "that John Trapp wants to see me."

"Oh, John." Mary dismissed him impatiently. "I don't know what's the matter with him. Shutting himself into the office like that. Anyone would think he had the plans of the H-bomb in there. Listen to him."

From the office next door, the typewriter, clicked, hesitated a moment, and then went on.

"He's been at it since about quarter past nine," Mary added. "He told me he had a date with you, but I said I had first refusal and he could jolly well wait. Now, I've typed the transcript, but there are a few things I'd like you to check before it goes into the final report. Here, on page three, for example, there's a reference to Interpol personnel, and I'm not sure if I have all the names spelled rightly."

"You've been very quick about getting it typed," said Henry, appreciatively.

"I stayed late and did it last night."

"You shouldn't have done that."

Mary smiled. "If I didn't, the work wouldn't get done at all, Inspector. As a matter of fact, I enjoyed doing it. It's such an interesting speech."

Henry took out his pen again and sat down at the desk. The typescript was impeccable and beautifully laid out, and contrived to make his speech, of which he had not been very proud, appear much more dignified and significant than it had on his scribbled notes.

He went quickly through the manuscript, checking a word here and there. Jacques Lenoir put his head in the door, and said, "Henri, why is there change for the agenda today? I do not understand."

"I can't explain at the moment, Jacques. I'm busy."

"Please, we must talk about it before the meeting. I shall be in the rest room."

Lenoir, who looked pale and had dark circles under his eyes, disappeared like a jack-in-the-box. Mary glanced at her watch.

"Twenty to," she said. "There's still lots of time. Don't hurry."

"I've finished," said Henry. "There you are. All done. Now I'll see what our friend Trapp wants with me."

"He's inclined to make mountains out of molehills, you know," said Mary briskly. She gathered up her papers, and, as Henry went to the door, suddenly added awkwardly, "Forgive me for saying so, Inspector, but I did want to tell you how pleased I am to be assigned to this committee. It's such a pleasure to work with somebody like you."

Henry felt unduly pleased. "It's mutual," he said. "I'm delighted to have you on the staff." They smiled at each other, suddenly both a little shy. Then Henry said, "Well . . . good-by for now."

"Yes," said Mary. "You'd better see John. He'll be livid at having been kept waiting so long."

As Henry stepped out into the corridor, he noticed that the typing had stopped. There was nobody in sight, but through the half-open door of the rest room Henry heard Helène saying in French, "I suppose we'll be able to get into the office before the meeting opens," and Lenoir replying, rather sharply, "I certainly hope so." The door of the ladies' cloakroom, opposite that of the office, was ajar, and Henry caught a glimpse of Annette's slender back as she combed her hair in the mirror. He opened the door of the office and went in.

John was sitting at the desk with his back to the door, bent over his work. Henry closed the door behind him, and said, "Well, John, here I am at last. What's it all about?"

John Trapp did not move, nor did he reply. Indeed, he would never move nor speak again. For he had been stabbed neatly in the back with the dagger of Toledo steel which Henry had seen the night before in Paul Hampton's library.

For a moment, Henry stood perfectly still. Then, very slowly, he walked around the desk and looked at the dead man's face. It expressed a mild surprise, but was extraordinarily tranquil. Henry turned his attention to the typewriter. In it was a plain sheet of white paper, and on the paper was written:

DEAR TIBBETT,

I am puzzled and disappointed that, for some reason, you have not seen fit to keep your appointment with me. Now other people are beginning to arrive, and it is clear that we shall have to fix another time and place for our discussion, which must obviously be strictly private.

I think you can guess without too much difficulty what I wish to say to you concerning Parkington's disturbing information. You can imagine that I am not looking forward to the interview with any pleasure, and I am sure that you are not, either. But, painful though it may be, I have come to the conclusion that I have no alternative but to bring the whole subject out into the open, and to tell you exactly what I know and what my position is.

As to the action which should be taken, I am naturally loth to use my initiative in such a matter, for obvious reasons. The ethics in a case like this are always infinitely more complicated than would appear on the surface. What right has one person to judge another? To what point can personal loyalty be invoked to justify the suppression of facts? These are questions which I should enjoy discussing with you on a hypothetical level, but unfortunately the matter in hand is far from hypothetical. I have my conscience and you have yours, and in the end it will come down to evolving a solution which satisfies both, as far as that can be possible.

All I know is that I have reached the point where it is impossible for me to hold my tongue any longer. As far as I am concerned, it is only a matter of what should be said, and to whom. I do not wish to take any irrevocable step without a full discussion with you, but I can tell you here and now that my mind is made up. I can see no alternative but to . . .

Here the typescript ceased abruptly. Henry read it over twice, without being able to make sense of a syllable of it. He had had no appointment with John Trapp. He looked around the office. Everything was orderly, in place, just as usual: the desk tidy and spruce, waiting for Annette to take up her secretarial duties, the empty, expectant wastepaper basket, the filing trays, the stacks of clean typing paper and fresh carbons, the newly sharpened pencils. The low shelves against the wall were stacked with bright-colored dossiers, notebooks and shorthand pads, and on top of them was the spare typewriter in its gray case, and the portable tape recorder. The wall calendar proclaimed, correctly, that it was the 8th of May, and the clock read twelve minutes to ten. Everything was exactly as it should be. The only monstrous incongruity was the dead man in the swivel chair.

Henry had had plenty of experience with murder cases in the past, but always these had been outside his own life. He had been called in—the outsider, the impersonal representative of the law. This was different. Now he found himself alone in a room with the body of a man whom he had known personally, and whom everyone else assumed to be still alive. Everyone, that is, except one person.

Henry pulled himself together. He realized that already he had stayed too long in the office without raising the alarm. He started for the door, but he was too late. Before he reached it, it was thrown open, and Juan Moranta came in, saying something in Spanish which Henry did not understand, but which was apparently addressed to John. He saw Henry's face, and stopped. There was a moment of silence. Then Henry said, in French, "Juan, John Trapp is dead. Murdered."

"Assassiné!"

Stupefied, Juan shouted the word back at Henry. It was enough. All down the corridor, doors were flung open and people came crowding into the office.

Henry stood there, motionless, while the crowd swirled and milled around him, and horrified voices cried out in a babel of languages. Annette Delacroix was in tears, kneeling beside the chair and repeating over and over again, *"Ah, non. Jean. Jean. Non, non . . ."* She put out her hand to take John's, and Henry heard himself saying automatically, "No, Annette. You mustn't touch him."

Bill Parkington, red-faced, was shouting instructions about telephoning the police. Nobody paid any attention to him. Jacques Lenoir, paler than ever, came hurrying out of the rest room and hovered in the doorway, asking endlessly, "What is it? What has happened?"

Konrad Zwemmer had arrived at a run from the conference room, his composure shattered at last. Sweat stood out in beads on his pink forehead, and ran down onto his glasses, so that he had to keep removing them and wiping them on a very white handkerchief. He made no attempt to speak to anybody, but pushed his way into the office and stood looking down at John Trapp with an expression of incredulity and something very like anger.

Alfredo Spezzi seemed perhaps less shocked than anyone else. He arrived last, and met Henry's eye with a quizzical expression and a resigned shrug. Helène Brochet was leaning against the doorpost, as white as a sheet, and looking as if she were about to faint. Mary Benson went quickly over to her, took her arm and led her gently out to the rest room. On the outskirts, the mustached doorkeeper fluttered like a hen trying to get into its coop: he was lost in the multiplicity of languages, and apparently could not grasp what had happened.

For a few minutes, everything was chaotic and disorganized and entirely natural. Then Mary Benson came back, went over to Henry, and said, "For heaven's sake, Inspector, get everyone out of here."

Her voice produced an immediate reaction in Henry. It had the competent timbre of an English nanny breaking up a rowdy party in the nursery. Recovering his senses abruptly, he said, "Yes, Mary. Of course." And then, raising his voice, he went on, "Please, everybody. You all know as well as I do that we must leave this room exactly as it is until the police arrive."

It sounded a ridiculous remark to make to a roomful of senior policemen, but it had its effect. Shepherded firmly by Mary, the delegates surged out into the corridor again, and by common consent made for the rest room. Only Annette stayed where she was. She was still kneeling on the floor beside John, making no attempt to touch him or even look at him, but weeping helplessly. Her hands hung limply by her sides, as if she had not even the spirit to lift them to cover her tearstained face. It was the most naked display of grief that Henry had ever seen, and it shocked him almost as much as the discovery of John's body.

Mary said, "Go with the others, Inspector. I'll manage Annette. She needs a sedative. I'll call the nurse."

"Thank you," said Henry, a little shakily. He went out into the passage and to the rest room.

A dead silence greeted his entrance. The delegates were standing together in a corner of the room, as if closing their ranks defensively against disaster. Helène Brochet lay back in an armchair, her eyes closed. The silence was broken by the small click of a lighter as Spezzi lit a cigarette. Then Bill Parkington said, "Well, we can't just stand here. What's the next move?"

"I think," said Henry, "that we should inform the head of the administrative division here at the Palais, and then the Swiss Police. In that order. As I found John, I suppose I had better do it."

As he walked over to the telephone and picked it up, he was acutely aware that every movement he made was being followed by five pairs of eyes. Wary, suspicious, unfriendly eyes. It was at that moment that the thought first penetrated his bemused mind, "My God. They all think I did it."

Four

When Emmy arrived at her rendezvous with Gerda—a lakeside café bright with colored umbrellas—she was surprised to find that Natasha Hampton was there, drinking a lemon tea with Gerda and chatting to her animatedly in German. The pale green Floride was parked on the opposite side of the road.

"What a lovely surprise," said Emmy, genuinely delighted. "I didn't know you were coming with us, Mrs. Hampton."

"Neither did I," said Natasha. "It was an impulse. I hope you don't mind my inviting myself like this. And please, don't call me Mrs. Hampton. It makes me nervous. My name is Natasha."

Emmy sat down with them and exulted in the sunshine. "I bet it's raining in London," she said smugly.

"We are having *thé citron,* Emmy," said Gerda. "Will you join us, or would you like something stronger?"

"Heavens, no. Thé citron will be splendid," Emmy answered. And then, to Natasha, she added, "What a superb party that was. Henry tells me I drank too much champagne, but I don't care. I can't remember when I've enjoyed myself so much."

"Yes, it was amusing," said Natasha, but she did not sound amused. There was a little silence.

"I trust your husband got off to Paris in good order this morning," Emmy commented.

"Paul? Yes, I imagine he did. To tell you the truth, he left long before I was awake. I'm a lazy creature." Natasha stretched her brown arms languorously.

"We are spoiled today, Emmy. Natasha is going to drive us out to the country for lunch. I had been wrestling with bus timetables."

"Where are you taking us?" Emmy asked.

"To my very favorite place," said Natasha. "A little country restaurant about half-an-hour's drive from here. It's called Chez Marie." Her voice was warm and enthusiastic. "I am sure you will love it. The patron and his wife are very special people, and the *cuisine*—well, you'll see for yourselves. I only go there with . . . with very particular friends."

An hour later, the three of them were sitting at a gingham-covered table under a shady chestnut tree, on the terrace of the café which was officially called Le Restaurant des Trois Pigeons, but which everyone in the neighborhood knew as Chez Marie. Marie herself, a strong, smiling, attractive woman in her thirties, presided over a battery of stoves in the white-tiled kitchen. Her husband, Pierre, a genial mountain of a man in a spotless white apron, was adding the final flourish to the steak tartare which he was mixing at a nearby table. This done, he came over to Natasha, bubbling with welcome.

"*Ma chère madame,*" he cried, and then kissed her hand with a gesture of infinite gallantry. "It is so long since we have seen you. All goes well, I hope? And how is monsieur, your husband?"

"He is very well, Pierre. He is in Paris," said Natasha. "May I present Madame Tibbett from London and Madame Spezzi from Rome?"

When more hands had been kissed and compliments exchanged, Natasha got down to the serious business of the day. "And now, Pierre, what are you going to give us to eat?"

Pierre pondered. "Today," he said, at length, "I would advise the *plat du jour*. Marie has made a *coq au vin* which is truly sensational. Of course, if you prefer Chateaubriand or *filets des perches*, or *filet mignon à la crème* . . ."

"Coq au vin for me, please," said Emmy promptly.

Gerda nodded agreement, and Natasha said, "Three *coq au vin*, then. Now, what are we to drink with it, Pierre?"

"With coq au vin you may drink red or white, as you wish. A purist might insist on red. I refuse to be bullied."

Looking at his well-upholstered six-foot-three of solid flesh, Emmy did not find this hard to believe.

"Now, if you decide on white wine, I have an Aigle 'Fifty-Seven which is extraordinary." Pierre kissed his plump fingers to the sky. "The Johannisberg 'Fifty-nine is excellent, too."

"But maybe a little sweet?" Natasha asked.

Pierre's eyes twinkled. "Ah, Madame knows all the answers. It's true that the 'Fifty-nine contains more sugar because of the sunshine that year. But the bouquet—*formidable!*"

"We'll have a bottle of the Aigle," said Natasha. "Right away, instead of an *apéritif*. And a plate of *délices de Grisons* to eat with it, cut very fine."

Effortlessly, Natasha had assumed control of the party. It could not have been more charmingly done, but implicit in her attitude was the calm confidence of one who will, as a matter of course, pick up the bill. Emmy found herself slightly irritated. After all, Natasha had, strictly speaking, gate-crashed the lunch, and neither Emmy nor Gerda was a pauper. However, with the arrival of the wine, chilled to perfection in a metal ice-bucket, and the delicious, paper-thin slices of dried meat, the moment of annoyance was forgotten.

Gerda and Natasha were discussing the previous evening's party.

"Oh, yes, we have known Jacques for many years," Natasha was saying. "Ever since the old days, when we lived in Paris. Then we met him again in Madrid."

"Paris, Geneva, Madrid . . ." Emmy tried not to sound envious. "You've lived almost everywhere. Which do you regard as your real home?"

Natasha smiled a little wistfully. "I am a vagabond," she said. "I was born Viennese, but I have not seen Vienna for more than ten years. Now that I am married to Paul, I am an American, and yet I have never been to America in my life. As far as I have a home, it is here, in Geneva. But I was telling you about Jacques. He was always a charmer, but I see a great change in him now. He has developed into something more, a wit."

"He and Juan Moranta are an amusing couple," said Gerda. "Almost too good to be true. A pair of perfectly matched Latin temperaments."

"Yes, but Moranta cannot compare to Jacques when it comes to a turn of phrase." Natasha smiled reminiscently. "He is quite brilliant, even in a language not his own. His English idiom is really remarkable. He described that nice big American delegate as a bull in a talking shop."

"I dare say he had a more or less barbed epigram for each of the delegates," said Emmy.

Natasha laughed. "Perhaps," she said.

"Come on, tell us."

"Well," Natasha hesitated. "He was rather rude about Juan. He said he was an animal which defends itself only when safe from attack. But I understand they were rivals last night, which probably accounts for it. Curious how two such intelligent men should be irresistibly attracted to a bottomless void—that's Jacques's own description of the lady, by the way. And he called that poor little Zwemmer a sheep in sheep's clothing." She paused.

"Go on," said Gerda. "You can't stop now. What about Alfredo and Henry?"

Natasha threw up her hands in mock despair. "I should never have started this," she said. "Oh, well. Here goes. He said that Henry suffered from the regrettable flippancy of middle age, but that there was still hope he might grow younger and more responsible."

Emmy's eyes crinkled with laughter. "How very perspicacious," she said. "It's perfectly true. Henry will love that."

"Oh, don't tell him!"

"I must. He'll adore it."

"And what about Alfredo?" Gerda sounded a shade less friendly than before.

Natasha said easily, "I don't think he mentioned Alfredo."

"Of course he did," said Gerda sharply.

"Oh, well, if he did, I wasn't listening."

"I'm sure you were."

"Oh, all right." Natasha had gone slightly pink. "He said that Alfredo was so good-looking that he had no business here, but should be directing traffic in Rome."

Gerda and Emmy laughed politely, but Emmy, at least, realized at once that this was a hasty and not very clever improvisation, which lacked the bite and precision of Lenoir's other epigrams. Suddenly she remembered the chance phrase which she had overheard the previous evening. "A wife and three Alfa Romeos to support . . ." She wondered if that had referred to Alfredo Spezzi, and if so, exactly what it implied, and why Natasha would not repeat it to Gerda.

The coq au vin arrived, putting a pleasant period to the conversation. They ate and drank lavishly, lingering over coffee and sipping little vertical glasses of Williamine, the Swiss pear liqueur, while the sun slanted lower through the branches of the chestnut tree. At last Emmy looked at her watch and exclaimed in horror that it was nearly four o'clock and she really must go. She went into the café in search of her coat.

Inside, a card game was in progress. Pierre and Marie, together with two cronies from the village, were absorbed in the local variant of the game of "Aces." Pierre was bellowing imprecations against his wicked luck in the most good-humored way, while Marie, quietly and competently, amassed a large score. As Emmy put her coat on, the postman arrived with the afternoon mail and the local evening paper. Pierre threw his cards down on the table.

"An archangel could not play with such cards!" he cried. "Give me the paper. Perhaps I can at least read in peace."

He took the paper and opened it ostentatiously. Then suddenly he laid it down on the table; his face had grown very grave. He said something to Marie, who immediately stopped playing and transferred her attention to an item in the paper. In spite of herself, Emmy's curiosity got the better of her. She moved across the room and looked over their shoulders.

What she saw was shattering enough. A headline announced: "INTERNATIONAL FUNCTIONARY MURDERED. DRAMA AT THE PALAIS DES NATIONS." And underneath it, a large and unmistakable photograph of John Trapp. They all looked at it in silence. Then Pierre noticed Emmy, and said, "Please, Madame. It is better if we say nothing."

"But . . ." Emmy was almost too upset to speak. "But I know him."

"Ah, Madame. We all know him."

"I must tell . . ."

"Madame." Pierre laid a massive hand on Emmy's arm. "We can do nothing. Spare her the anguish."

Emmy looked at him, uncomprehending.

"I don't understand," she said.

"You know this gentleman?" Pierre indicated John's photograph with a pudgy forefinger.

"Yes, indeed I do. He's . . ."

Pierre jerked his head in the direction of the terrace. "Poor Madame. What can we say that will help her? It is better if she goes home quietly now, and finds out the truth there."

"But I must tell Natasha."

Pierre suddenly became angry. "You say you know him," he barked.

"Yes, I do."

"Then you must know," said Pierre more quietly, "that he is the husband of Madame Natasha."

It took several moments for this remarkable statement to penetrate Emmy's consciousness. Then she pulled herself together, and said, as composedly as she could, "Of course. I'm sorry. For a moment I confused him with somebody else. Leave it to me, Pierre."

She walked shakily out onto the terrace, where Gerda and Natasha were chatting lazily, unaware of impending disaster. In the ten seconds that it took her to come down the steps and across the terrace, Emmy considered ten different ways of breaking the news, and rejected them all.

Natasha looked up at her, and said, "Goodness, Emmy, are you all right? You look quite pale. I hope the lunch didn't disagree with you."

"No, I'm fine," said Emmy. "A little bit too much sun, perhaps. Let's go."

Emmy was very quiet during the drive back to Geneva. She was remembering John with Annette Delacroix in the little apartment overlooking the lake: and John with his ravishing French duchess. She still could not really comprehend the fact that Pierre thought John was Natasha's husband. And she remembered John himself, gay and ironic and tinged with unexplained bitterness, and she tried to imagine him dead, and failed. Above all, she thought of Henry.

The Swiss Police arrived at the Palais with commendable rapidity and lack of fuss. The personnel of the subcommittee were hustled smartly into the conference room; while the body was photographed from every angle; the typewriter, the desk, and the dagger were fingerprinted; and all the usual, melancholy rituals of violent death were enacted as smoothly and unobtrusively as possible. While the delegates and staff, with the exception of Annette who had been removed to the Sick Bay, sat gloomily and silently in the conference room, the gendarmes established themselves in the rest room, which they had commandeered as a base.

One by one, the occupants of the conference room were summoned. Henry was the last of all, and when his name was finally called, he found to his annoyance that his heart seemed to be beating at twice its normal rate. He himself had conducted God knew how many investigations of this sort, but to be on the receiving end of the interrogation was an entirely different matter. His conscience groped back to recall his own conduct in the past, and he hoped devoutly that he had done on those occasions as he hoped to be done by now.

He opened the door of the rest room and walked in. At the table sat a small, friendly-looking officer of the Swiss Police, who stood up and shook hands. ("Reassuring," Henry noted, mentally. "I must do that in future.")

"May I present myself?" this diminutive person asked in very good English. "I am Colliet of the Geneva Police. You are Chief Inspector Tibbett from London, I believe."

Henry admitted that this was true.

"Please sit down, Inspector. So. And smoke if you wish. I understand that you discovered the body."

"Yes."

"Did you notice the time?"

"Yes, I did. It was twelve minutes to ten by the office clock."

Colliet made a note. "Can you tell me what time you arrived at the Palais, or rather, at this suite of offices, Inspector?"

"I can't say exactly. I had an appointment."

"Yes. That we know. You were rather late for it, were you not?"

"No," said Henry. "I'm sure I was here before half past."

Colliet consulted a book which Henry recognized as the one kept by the doorkeeper. "According to the record, you arrived at nine twenty-six. Do you dispute that?"

"No, that sounds right to me."

"Tell me, please, what happened then?"

"I went into the cloakroom to hang up my coat."

"Did you meet anybody else?"

Henry told him, as accurately as he could remember, the events leading up to the finding of John's body. Colliet noted them down carefully. Then he put his pencil down, smiled at Henry, and said in the friendliest possible way, "But you say that you had no appointment with Mr. Trapp?"

"Certainly I didn't. My appointment was with Miss Benson at half past nine."

"I do advise you, Inspector, to search your memory," said Collict, sounding like a character from a second-feature crime film. "Perhaps you would care for another cigarette."

"I don't want a cigarette," said Henry crossly. "I tell you, I had no appointment with Trapp."

Suddenly and disconcertingly, Colliet became melodramatic. He had probably seen too many sensational movies. "Then how," he cried, "do you account for this?"

Triumphantly, he threw a small piece of paper down onto the table, and pushed it toward Henry. Henry put out his hand to take it, recalled fingerprints, and withdrew his hand again. Instead, he read it as it lay on the table. On it was written, in handwriting of a marked individuality, "My dear Henry, certainly I'll be there at nine, John."

Henry looked at it with a growing sense of nightmare.

"Where did you find this?" he asked finally.

"Ah, so you do recognize it?"

"I've never seen it before. I asked you where you found it."

Colliet smiled warmly. "In the pocket of your raincoat," he said.

"That's not possible."

"It is not only possible, Inspector, it is true. I tell you the truth, and I would appreciate it if you would do the same for me. You should know better than anybody how our job is impeded by witnesses who misguidedly suppress important facts."

"Anybody could have put that in my pocket," said Henry. "In any case, surely the fact that I didn't arrive until nearly half past nine is proof enough that . . ."

"That is just one of the many puzzling features of this case," said Colliet. "It is open to several explanations. I am hoping you will tell us which is correct."

Henry found himself growing more and more irritated. The man was behaving like a caricature of a fictional detective. Now he was leaning back in his chair, the tips of his fingers together, radiating sinister affability. The picture was somewhat spoiled by the fact that the legs of the chair began to slip from under him. Colliet sat up sharply and glared at Henry, daring him to smirk. Henry maintained a dignified silence.

"Well then," said Colliet crossly, "let us talk about the weapon. Can you identify it?"

"Yes," said Henry.

"Had you, in fact, seen it before? Before you found it this morning."

"I saw it last night in Paul Hampton's house. It belongs to him."

Henry ran briefly through the events of the party, culminating in the tour of inspection of the house. He agreed that, besides Hampton, he and Moranta had both handled the dagger.

"So." Colliet made another note. "Mr. Hampton was called away to the telephone, and the party went downstairs again. Is that correct?"

"In substance," answered Henry unhappily. He knew that he could not suppress the next part of the story.

"You went directly downstairs? You and your wife?"

"No," said Henry.

"Ah." Colliet gave a little grunt of satisfaction. "What, then, did you do?"

"My wife wanted to explore a little more of the house," Henry said uneasily. "I left her going off in the direction of the west staircase, and I attempted to go back to the drawing room."

"Attempted?"

"I'm afraid I took a wrong turning and got lost. The Villa Trounex is a very confusing house."

"For how long did you wander about in this confusing house on your own?" asked Colliet nastily.

"I can't tell you. About ten minutes."

"Did you meet or see anybody?"

Henry felt himself justified in a small white lie, a sin of omission, to safeguard a lady's honor. After all, neither John nor Natasha had seen him. "Not until I was rescued by Mr. Hampton," he said. He described his encounter with Paul, and John's appearance on the scene. He did not say which room John had come from, and Colliet did not ask.

"I am glad you have been frank about this, Inspector. What you tell me tallies with the stories I have heard from the others."

Henry said nothing.

"All the same, you must realize that you, of all people, had ample opportunity to return to the library and take the dagger, which could easily have been concealed in a sleeve or even an inside breast pocket. Please understand that I am not accusing you of anything. One merely remarks these things. Now, please tell me what you make of this."

He unfolded the piece of paper which had been in the typewriter. Henry saw that it bore traces of fingerprinting powder.

"I make nothing whatsoever of it."

Colliet sighed again, and lit an American mentholated cigarette. "Inspector," he said, "it is only fair to tell you that, apart from the note found in your pocket, we know from a witness that you had an appointment with Trapp today."

"You know *what?*" Henry asked incredulously.

"That you planned to speak to Mr. Trapp privately today."

"But . . ." Henry stopped dead. Could Bill Parkington have

repeated to Colliet the conversation about the leakage of information and Henry's promise to "see what he could do"? Henry realized that the Swiss Police would have to be taken into Bill's confidence sooner or later, but he and Parkington had agreed, in a monosyllabic conversation in the rest room, that Washington should be consulted by telephone before Bill handed over any information. It was obviously imperative to speak to Bill as soon as possible.

"Aha. So I have refreshed your memory, Inspector?" The inevitable cliché rolled out.

"Yes, you have refreshed my memory. I did intend to speak to John Trapp today, but I had made no appointment with him. It was merely an idea in my head."

"Perhaps Mr. Trapp was telepathic," suggested Colliet dryly. Henry began to like him rather better, and to forgive the clichés. After all, they are difficult to avoid in a foreign language.

"It looks like it," he said.

There was a short pause, and then Colliet asked, "And what did you want to talk to Mr. Trapp about?"

"Business connected with the conference," replied Henry promptly.

"Connected with 'Parkington's disturbing information'?" Colliet rapped the note with his hand.

"I am afraid I can't tell you that."

"You know what this information is?"

"Yes," said Henry, "but for the moment it is confidential."

Colliet let this pass without comment. He knew, and he knew that Henry knew, that any confidential business which bore on the murder would eventually have to be revealed. So he merely said, with a slight smile, "I presume that you can think of no possible connection between your confidential business and the murder of Mr. Trapp?"

"You presume correctly."

"Are you aware whether Mr. Trapp had any enemies?"

"I have no idea. I hardly knew him."

"You hardly knew him socially," said Colliet, "but you worked with him professionally. And this was a professional murder."

"Professional?" Henry sat up. "You're not suggesting a hired assassin, are you?"

Colliet smiled. "You misunderstand me. It is my English that is at fault. I meant that Trapp was killed in the course of his job, and by a professional colleague. Apart from Mlle. Delacroix, who

I am informed was a close friend of his, you are the only member of this committee, apparently, who knew Mr. Trapp away from business, and it is clear that your acquaintance with him was slight. This is no *crime passionel*, Inspector. Nothing to do with his private life. John Trapp was killed because of something to do with his work, something to do with Parkington's disturbing information, something he knew or guessed which made him dangerous. The note in the typewriter makes it quite clear that he was proposing to discuss this something with you at the interview which you claim was telepathetically arranged, and for which you did not turn up. It is the greatest pity, don't you agree, that he was killed before he could tell you what that something was?"

Colliet stopped talking and contemplated the shiny yellow pencil which he held between his small fingers. In the silence, Henry became acutely aware of the ticking of the big, white-faced clock on the wall. He said nothing. He realized only too well the position he was in, and his brain was working rapidly—planning, deducing, tabulating, above all remembering. He knew now that he alone would have to tackle this case, and that it would be stranger, more difficult and more important than any of his career; for this time, he would have to work independently of the police. In fact, he reflected wryly, he found himself precisely in the position of the amateur detectives of fiction, except that they were not as a rule suspected of the crime themselves. His only consolation was the thought that the arrest and accusation of a senior member of another nation's police force is not a thing to be undertaken lightly. He reckoned that he had a little time. Meanwhile, thinking of Colliet's position, he could even find it in his heart to feel sorry for the man. No wonder he fell back on clichés.

Colliet began to speak again. "Fortunately," he said, "we have a narrow field to work in. The doorkeeper was on duty the entire time, and there was no other way of getting in or out of these offices except for that one door. In fact"—Colliet raised his head and looked fixedly at Henry— "in fact, we can be absolutely certain that the murderer is in this suite at this very moment. Then, we can be very precise about the time of the murder. On your evidence, and that of others, Mr. Trapp was alive at twenty minutes to ten, and dead at twelve minutes to. That leaves just eight minutes, Inspector. It should not be too difficult a problem."

"I wouldn't be too sure of that," said Henry.

Colliet smiled again. "I am not down-hearted. If all the delegates and staff give me their fullest and frankest co-operation"—

he paused meaningly—"the case will soon be closed." He shut up his notebook and rose to his feet. "Well, Inspector, thank you for your help. That is all for the present. I trust you will not object to stepping into the filing room for a moment to have your prints taken. A pure matter of routine, you understand." Henry winced, thinking how often he had used this particular, sinister cliché himself. "You and your staff are all free to go now, so long as you give your addresses to us, and do not leave the city. We shall meet again soon for another little chat when things are . . . clearer."

Colliet shook hands warmly, smiled again—a grimace that was beginning to grow a little thin. Then he said to the gendarme who had been taking notes, "Please telephone and inquire whether Mlle. Delacroix is sufficiently recovered to speak to me."

Henry went out of the rest room, and into the filing room, where he submitted to the indignity of having his fingers rolled in ink and pressed onto a card. Then he went back to the conference room.

With the exception of Annette, all the staff and delegates were reassembled there. A sudden and complete silence fell as Henry walked in. He looked around at each face in turn, and wondered which of them was the face of a murderer: a murderer who had, what was more, apparently taken pains to pin the crime onto Henry himself.

Aloud he said, "Well, that seems to be that. We are free to go now, and I suggest that we do so. There's no sense in trying to work today. The subcommittee will start work at ten o'clock tomorrow morning."

He turned on his heel and walked out, fighting his way against the silence as if it had been a physical obstruction.

Then he took a taxi back to the hotel.

Five

The hotel dining room was almost deserted as Henry sat down to an unwanted lunch. He would dearly have liked to take the small amount of food he felt able to face in one of the more intimate little restaurants of the old town, but he felt that he must stay in the hotel, as he was more than half-expecting a visitor.

Hé missed Emmy sorely, and cursed the luck that should have taken her, today of all days, out to lunch in some entirely unknown direction. He longed for her comforting presence, and at the same time dreaded having to break the news to her, for Emmy had been fond of John, and Annette was her friend.

Henry tried to swallow another mouthful of what tasted to him like sawdust but was, in fact, an excellent grilled trout. On the table beside him lay a small notebook and a ball-point pen; he kept interrupting his meal to make an entry. He smiled a little grimly to think that Alfredo Spezzi, with his passion for time-tables, would approve of this activity.

The fact was that Henry's mind was working with less than its customary efficiency. Last night at Paul Hampton's party, and this morning before his gruesome discovery, there had been no thought in his head of recalling exactly who did or said what, and to whom, and when. People and places and voices swam mistily in his brain, merging and mingling in confusion. Hence the notebook, an attempt to sort out a coherent pattern from the chaos. As he wrote a pattern of some sort did indeed begin to emerge from the welter of unrelated facts, but it was vague and blurred in outline and full of gaps. In any case, Henry was not at all sure that he liked the look of the picture that was emerging.

So absorbed was he in his work that the waiter had to tell him twice that he was wanted on the telephone before this simple fact penetrated his consciousness. He closed the notebook and walked out to the phone booth in the hall.

"Henry? This is Bill Parkington." The American voice was jagged with worry, and had lost its normal, cheerful boom. "Are you busy right now, Henry?"

"No. I was hoping you might call."

"I think we ought to get together. Can I come to your hotel?"

"Of course. I'm just finishing lunch. Come and have a coffee."

"Be seeing you."

The line went dead, and Henry wandered thoughtfully back toward the dining room. The problem which was chiefly exercising his mind was that of the note in his raincoat pocket. Of course, anybody could have put it there, as he had pointed out to Colliet. Any of the men, that is. A woman would have risked exciting comment, to say the least, if she had gone into the men's cloakroom. No, how it got there was no great mystery, and everyone knew which was Henry's coat, for he had worn the same lightweight nylon raincoat each day since the conference opened. The mystery was how and when John was induced to write it, for Henry felt convinced that the handwriting was perfectly genuine. Both Annette and Mary, independent witnesses, agreed that John was under the impression that he had an appointment with Henry. This was confirmed by his last, unfinished note. Somehow, someone had made contact with John Trapp between last night's party and this morning, had conveyed a spurious message purporting to come from Henry, and had secured that damning note in return. There was, however, a brighter side to this dark speculation: whoever had contacted John might well have left a trail, and it would still be fresh. As soon as he had seen Bill, Henry decided, he would follow up this line of pursuit.

It was then that he remembered, with a stab of annoyance, that he did not know John's home address. He went back into the telephone booth and turned to the T's in the directory. It was not difficult to find. "Trapp, John S. Fonct. int. 5 Chemin des Chênes." Henry made a quick note of the address, and looked up to see Bill Parkington coming in through the revolving doors from the hotel foyer.

"Where can we talk?" Bill asked abruptly with no preliminary greeting.

"The coffee here is excellent," said Henry, "and I haven't quite finished my . . ."

Bill gave him a brief look. "We can't possibly talk here," he said. "We'd better go out of town somewhere, by the lake."

"Good heavens." Henry deliberately ironed everything out of his voice except a caricature of British imperturbability. "That seems rather melodramatic. And in any case, it'll take some time. Have you any idea when the trains go?"

"I have a car," Bill was clearly not amused. "Come on, for Pete's sake. Let's get out of here."

Henry made no further protest, but followed Bill into the street, where a blue Volkswagen with Geneva license plates was parked. Bill opened the door.

"Get in," he said. He could not have been more emphatic if he had been holding a gun to Henry's ribs. Henry got in.

Bill jumped in beside him and switched on the ignition, shifted gears, and released the clutch in what seemed to be a single movement. The little car roared away into the traffic, as inconspicuous as a couple of thousand exactly similar vehicles in the city.

"Where are we going?" Henry inquired.

"Near Belle Rive," replied Bill. This was the only remark he made until some twenty minutes later, when he drew the car to a halt at the end of a winding lane. Ahead, a small wooden jetty stepped shakily out into the limpid water of the lake. There was a little pebbly beach under the shadow of tall trees. The place was quite deserted.

"Now," said Bill, "we can talk."

"Yes," said Henry, and waited.

"First of all," Bill went on, "I think you ought to tell me about John Trapp."

Henry made a small, helpless gesture. "I know nothing whatsoever about him."

"Look, Henry," said Bill, with a kind of desperation, "I'm on your side. I mean that. I may be wrong, and I'm in a minority of one, but I don't believe you killed the man."

"Thank you," said Henry. "That's very kind of you."

"I've come here to try and help you, but I can't do a thing unless you'll be frank and tell me all you know."

"I've already done so."

There was a pause. Then Bill said, "Hell, Henry. Don't be this way. Look now. Nobody knew about the leakage of information last night except you and me. This morning Trapp knew about it. The note in the typewriter makes that clear enough. So, by a simple process of deduction, you must have told him."

"Unless you did, or he found out for himself."

Bill took no notice, but went on. "You told him, and you made a date to meet him this morning, as you had no chance to talk to him last night. It's perfectly clear from the note that Trapp knew who the culprit was." Bill paused. He was speaking slowly and deliberately, wrestling with each logical proposition in turn. "For some reason you didn't keep your appointment. Was that deliberate, or were you just late?"

"I suppose it's no use my telling you yet again that I had no appointment?"

Bill shook his head in slow exasperation. "You see," he said. "We get no place."

"Exactly."

"The guy's dead and I'm very sorry about it, but my concern is that security leak. I want to know what Trapp knew, and why he had to be killed before he could spill the beans. You're the only person who could help me, and you won't."

"I can't."

"By taking this attitude you're just simply pushing me into the other camp."

"Which other camp?"

"Lenoir and Moranta and the rest of them. I think you should know that they've got it all figured out, and God knows they may be right. This is the way they see it. You had a date with Trapp, and you didn't dare keep it. Why not? Because you had a guilty conscience."

"Wait a minute," said Henry. "Do they all know about the security leak now?"

"Sure they do." Bill looked a little uncomfortable. "There was that note in the typewriter, you see. I telephoned Washington from the Palais after I'd seen Colliet, and they said to go ahead and give the Swiss Police all the information they needed. So I reckoned the delegates should know. I told them while you were being questioned."

"I see. Well, go on. I have a guilty conscience because I myself am responsible for the leakage of information. Is that it?"

"More or less," admitted Bill, embarrassed. "The way they figure it, when you eventually did show up this morning, you decided to go in and bluff it out with Trapp. You're not even certain how much he knows. But as soon as you get into that office and read what he's writing, you know the game's up. So you kill him."

Henry laughed outright. "That's the weakest story I've ever heard," he said. "What about the dagger?"

"Precisely. The dagger." Bill slid around in the seat of the car to look directly at Henry. "They're puzzled about the dagger. They can only think you took it on impulse last night, knowing this interview was coming up. But of course, they don't know what I know, and I haven't told them."

"What do you mean?"

"I told you I was on your side. I still am. But you'll need to convince me. Look at it this way. Suppose—just suppose—their story was true. Suppose you *were* responsible for the security leak. As soon as I told you last night that the FBI were wise to it, you'd have known things were getting mighty dangerous. I seem to suspect Trapp, and that gives you a little hope. You talk to him last night, and from something he says you realize that he's wise to you. You make this date for the morning, and you decide then and there to kill him. You take the dagger. It's only later that you remember the security on our new suite of offices, and you realize that if you turn up at nine, with only you and Trapp checked in through the door, you'll have no hope of getting away with it. So you don't arrive until later, when the place is full of people. Then you walk in and kill the man. You meant, of course, to get the paper out of the typewriter, slip out of the office again, and let someone else find him. But Moranta comes into the office before you have time to do any of that. You're virtually caught red-handed."

Henry considered this statement in gloomy silence. Then he said, "You seem to have it all worked out. Perhaps you'd better go straight over to the other camp and have done with it."

"I hoped you wouldn't take that attitude."

"By the way," said Henry, "have you told Colliet about the security leak yet?"

"Not yet. I'm seeing him this afternoon."

"And will you tell him that I knew about it last night?"

Bill looked extremely awkward. "I was hoping I wouldn't have to," he said.

"And did you tell Colliet this morning that I was planning to speak to John Trapp?"

Bill looked away and lit a cigarette. "I didn't mention what it was about," he said. "Hell, I had to tell the guy." There was a long, oppressive pause. "Look, Henry, I deliberately came to see you before I went to police headquarters. If you'd just tell me all you know, we could maybe clear this thing up here and now, and I wouldn't have to . . . to make things worse for you."

"My dear Bill," said Henry, reasonably, "put yourself in my position. I didn't kill Trapp. I went into that office and found him dead. I also found a pretty ingenious scheme for putting the blame on me. That means that somebody in that suite of offices is not only a murderer, but has it in for me in no uncertain way. I don't know who that person is, and until I do, I'm bound to suspect everybody."

"You don't seriously mean"—Bill's ingenuous face under its thatch of red hair was comic in its shocked incredulity. "You don't think that *I* . . . ?"

"Well," said Henry, "just where were you when John was killed?"

"In the filing room. I was checking a point for my speech."

"Anybody with you?"

"Well . . . no."

"You see what I mean." Henry sighed. "I'm afraid this isn't a very satisfactory conversation we're having, or not having. I have a lot to do. Do you mind if we go back now?"

Bill suddenly smiled. "Gee, I'm sorry about all this, Henry. I guess I just hadn't thought of it from your point of view."

Henry smiled back. "I'm just as keen to catch the informer as you are," he said, "but I must catch the murderer first, from sheer self-preservation. I think they may well turn out to be the same person."

"Such as you," said Bill, with a grin.

"Or you," said Henry.

Bill started the engine, and roared the little car up the lane. As they approached the city on the lakeside road, Bill said, "Back to the hotel?"

"As a matter of fact," said Henry, "I have a call to make. Do you know where the Chemin des Chênes might be?"

Bill frowned. "This is my first time in Geneva," he said. "I known the Route de Chêne, but Chemin—that's a pretty small sort of street in these parts. I can't help you."

"Never mind," said Henry. "I'll find it."

"There's a gendarme on the corner," said Bill. "We could ask him."

"I think not," said Henry, "if you don't mind. Just drop me here. Thanks a lot."

Bill looked at him curiously, but all he said was, "O.K. So be it."

He drew the car into the curb and leaned across Henry to open the door for him. "See you in the morning."

"I hope so," said Henry.

The Chemin des Chênes turned out to be one of the small, steep streets which lace Geneva, climbing between one main road and the next. Number 5 was a small, modern block of flats, built of white reinforced concrete, with jutting balconies angled to catch the sun. There was a gendarme standing in the glass-and-marble hallway.

Henry walked over to the row of letter boxes and glanced quickly along it. It took no more than a flick of the eye to see the box marked "J. Trapp. 6 ième." At the same time, he noted mentally that the sixth floor was also occupied by M. et Mme. Zeigler, P. Hirt, and Dr. A. Mahoumi, Avocat. The gendarme, who had been contemplating without any apparent pleasure a large rubber plant in the corner of the hall, now strolled casually over in Henry's direction. Henry turned away from the letter boxes and went over to a door marked "F. Novari. Concierge." He rang the bell. The gendarme edged a little closer.

As the door of the concierge's flat opened, the wail of a small child filled the hall, and Henry was struck smartly on the knee by a large red rubber ball, which he retrieved expertly, and held out as if it were a peace offering to the woman who stood inside the door. She was young and dark and disheveled, and she wore bedroom slippers and her hair in curlers. Before either she or Henry could say a word, the owner of the ball, a black-eyed and obstreperous boy of three or four, made a dash along the corridor, yelling imprecations in an unidentifiable tongue. The woman, with the skill of long practice, put out a hand and caught the child, delivering an abrupt scolding in shrill Italian as she did so. Then she said to Henry, "Monsieur?"

They confronted each other, Henry holding the ball and the woman holding the child, who began to yell again. Henry smiled, and said in Italian, "Signora Novari? I think this ball must belong to your son."

"Yes, the little demon." The woman softened visibly, hearing her native tongue.

"May I come in?" said Henry.

The child was struggling and shouting.

"Yes, indeed, signore. Please do."

Henry stepped inside, and the door was slammed in the inquisitive face of the gendarme. Not for the first time, Henry blessed his facility with European languages.

Inside the flat, which smelled deliciously of garlic and olive oil and fried tomatoes, Madame Novari restored the ball to her son, cuffed him affectionately on the side of the head, screamed at him, and then propelled him firmly into the bedroom and slammed the door. Then she ushered Henry into the overfurnished living room.

"I'm afraid my husband is out," she said. "Can I help you?"

"I came to inquire if there might be an apartment vacant in the building," said Henry, lying shamelessly. He knew enough about the acute shortage of accommodations in Geneva to realize that this would be a commonplace enough excuse to disarm suspicion.

Madame Novari lifted her arms and shoulders in an exaggerated gesture of hopelessness. "An apartment? It is like asking for gold, signore. If ever we get an apartment free, it goes to friends of friends of . . ."

"Mr. Trapp's apartment will be free, of course," said Henry, conversationally.

"Free? Why should it be free? Is he going away?"

So she had not yet been told. Henry imagined that her husband might well be with the police now, and marveled at his good fortune.

"Someone told me he was leaving," he said. "Perhaps I misunderstood."

"I think you must have, signore. Mr. Trapp is one of our oldest tenants: he has been here since the block was built four years ago. He would certainly have told me if he was leaving. He is a charming gentleman. A friend of yours?"

"Yes," said Henry. "At least, a colleague. We're working in the same department at the Palais des Nations." He paused, thinking how to phrase his next gambit. Finally he said, "Of course, I realize that this wouldn't be a very convenient place to live, working at the Palais. It must be a complicated journey each day without a car."

"Oh, no, signore." Madame Novari rose beautifully to the bait. "All you need to do is to catch a tram as far as Rive, and change to a . . ."

"But it would mean leaving very early in the morning. Mr. Trapp tells me that he has to leave at half past eight every morning to be sure of getting in by ten."

Madame Novari looked puzzled, as well she might. "Half past eight?" she said. "No, no. I assure you. He must have made a mistake. He never leaves until nine thirty. Every morning I see him go. My husband says you could set your watch by him."

"That's very odd," said Henry boldly. "This morning I telephoned him at nine and there was no reply."

"Ah, you are right, this morning he left early. Half past eight. I was cleaning the hall, and I saw him go. But he had an early appointment, you see. I know because of the message."

Henry's heart rose. Steadily, he said, "I think you must be mistaken. He assured me he had to leave at eight thirty every morning."

Surely, thought Henry, I can't keep up this idiotic conversation much longer. She'll see through me in a moment, and then I'll be sunk. He had not reckoned, however, with the mentality of the wives of concierges. To Madame Novari, it was her greatest pride that she knew and observed, from vantage points in the hall and from behind the embroidered lace curtains of her sitting room, the exact comings and goings of every tenant. That her word should be questioned on such a matter hit her where it hurt most, and in her eagerness to prove her point, the incongruity of the subject matter was forgotten.

"This morning he had an appointment at nine, signore. I should know, for I took the message up to him at seven o'clock. Poor man, he must have been still asleep. 'There has to be a written answer,' I said. He was cross, I could see that. 'Inspector Teebeet must see you at nine in the office at the Palais'—that was the message. 'Why couldn't he have telephoned, the bloody idiot?' he said. But he went in and wrote the answer, all the same, and I brought it down to her."

"To her?" The words came out like bullets, before Henry could stop them. Madame Novari rattled on in full spate. "Why, yes, to the young lady who brought the message. It seemed silly to me that she wouldn't go up herself, but I suppose she was shy, it being so early in the morning, and Mr. Trapp a bachelor and . . ."

"Was the young lady Swiss or French or . . ."

Madame Novari suddenly stopped her chatter and looked at Henry suspiciously. He realized that he had overreached himself.

"She spoke French," said Madame Novari briefly. "My own French is not good enough to know what nationality she was. In any case . . ."

Outside in the corridor, the front door opened and closed and there was a heavy, masculine tread. A man's voice called urgently, in Italian, "Tilda! Where are you?"

"My husband," said Madame Novari.

"I must go," said Henry, quickly.

At the door he came face to face with a big, burly, dark-haired young man, who seemed to be excited about something; and small wonder, thought Henry, if he had just heard the sensational news from the gendarmes.

Ignoring Henry, Novari said to his wife, "Tilda, something has happened. Who is this man?"

"I just came to inquire about an apartment," said Henry. "Good-by, signora, and thank you."

He went quickly out of the flat and into the hall. There, under the eye of the gendarme, he got into the lift and pressed the button marked "6."

Six

There was no sign of a gendarme on the sixth floor, and Henry concluded that the forces of the law were probably installed inside John's apartment. He had little or no hope of getting in to take a look around for himself. His luck still held, however. As he had hoped, John's flat was one of the two that faced the front of the building, and his next-door neighbor was Dr. A. Mahoumi, Avocat. Had it been the Zeiglers or P. Hirt, Henry would have been hard put to it to think up an excuse for calling, but a lawyer can always be approached on business. He rang the bell.

There was a gentle shuffling sound from inside the apartment, and then the door opened a crack, and a soft, liquid voice said in English, "Who is it? What do you want?"

"I want to see Dr. Mahoumi," said Henry, and he added, "on business."

The crack did not widen.

"Have you an appointment?" the voice asked.

"No," said Henry.

There was a silence. Then the voice said, "What business?"

"A legal matter," said Henry deliberately. "Concerning money."

There was an audible hesitation. The door trembled slightly, and finally opened.

"I am Dr. Mahoumi. Please come in."

Dr. Mahoumi was a small, rotund man of obviously Middle Eastern origin. He was dressed in a tight-fitting brown suit and very pointed black kid shoes, and he appeared to walk permanently on tiptoe. His movements, which reminded Henry of those of a cat, were as liquid as his huge dark eyes, and he used his small plump hands like a dancer. He led Henry into the living room, which abounded in hand-worked leather poufs and camel saddles and woven raffia dishes. There were a couple of very beautiful Persian rugs on the parquet floor, and not even the fact that the long windows which led onto the balcony were wide open could dispel the lingering scent of Egyptian tobacco.

Henry walked straight across the room and out onto the balcony. Sunshine streamed down, over-hot in spite of the orange canvas canopy.

Henry said, "You have a beautiful view here."

"Yes, yes." Dr. Mahoumi danced out into the sunshine. "Very beautiful. Let us go inside."

"Can't we talk out here?"

"My dear Mr. . . . I did not catch your name."

"Smith," said Henry blandly.

Dr. Mahoumi gave him a melting look of reproach. "Can we not be honest with each other at the outset?" his eyes seemed to say. Aloud, however, he said, "Ah, yes. Mr. Smith. If we have business to discuss, it is better indoors."

"Why?" said Henry.

"Because . . ." Dr. Mahoumi danced a little. "Because it is better if all the world does not know our business, no? And here . . ."

"There seem," said Henry, "to be policemen in the apartment next door."

This fact was self-evident. The voices of the gendarmes in John's flat were clearly audible. They were obviously searching the place, and Henry heard one of them, as he passed the open window, saying, "Another lot? That settles the matter, I should say." It was plain that in warm weather there could be few secrets between neighbors in this building.

"Quite so. Just as you say." Dr. Mahoumi took Henry's arm lightly between his delicate brown fingers, and led him gently back toward the sitting room. "They have been there for some time. A burglary perhaps. I do not know. It's none of my business."

Having maneuvered Henry successfully indoors, Dr. Mahoumi sighed with relief and carefully closed the long windows. The voices of the gendarmes were cut off, but the heat grew oppressive. The lawyer motioned Henry to sit down on the divan, and then seated himself on a leather pouf.

"And now, Mr. . . . Smith. Your business?"

"Ah, yes. My business." Henry, who enjoyed romancing, launched into a complicated and extempore fiction concerning the will of a mythical uncle who had died possessed of untold riches which reposed in a numbered bank account in Geneva. Unfortunately, Henry explained, the uncle had been careless enough to allow himself to be run over by a tram without disclosing to Henry, his sole heir, the magic number which would open the door to his fortune. So Henry had come to Switzerland in an attempt to lay hands on his property. There would, of course, be a substantial reward for any lawyer brilliant enough to solve the problem.

As he talked, Henry was mentally registering the geography of the flat, which he guessed was a twin to the one next door. It was what is known on the Continent as a studio, that is to say, a one-room bachelor apartment with its own tiny hallway, off which led a box-sized kitchen and a dwarf bathroom. Its most attractive feature was undoubtedly the balcony, which was wide and sunny and commanded a fine view of the lake and the Jura Mountains. Henry could even pick out the cream-colored mass of the Palais des Nations, half hidden in trees on the far shore. He thought of the soberly interesting sessions of the conference which, until yesterday, had been his all-absorbing concern. A wild sense of unreality swept over him. What am I doing here? What *am* I doing here, sitting in the flat of an Arab lawyer in a Geneva back street, telling a series of monstrous lies, while the Swiss Police frame a murder charge against me? I shall wake up in a minute . . . Emmy . . . Where is Emmy . . . must see Emmy . . .

He heard his own voice saying, "I was strongly recommended to come to you by my friend Mr. Trapp."

"Trapp!" Dr. Mahoumi started, and looked at Henry accusingly, as though he had been bitten by a trusted camel. "You know Trapp?"

"Yes," said Henry. "I believe you have been doing some legal work for him."

"No. No . . . that is to say, just a few little routine details. To help a neighbor, you understand. What did he . . . ? That is, he should not have . . ."

"I not only know him," said Henry, "I also know why there are gendarmes in his apartment. Don't you?"

"I have no idea. No idea at all!" cried Dr. Mahoumi. "I hardly know the man. Only as a neighbor. It must be a burglary."

"John Trapp is dead," said Henry. "He was killed this morning."

For a moment, it looked as though Dr Mahoumi was going to faint. His face went a dirty gray, and he closed his eyes and swayed on his leather pouf. At length he said in a whisper, "Who killed him?"

"The general opinion," said Henry, "is that I did."

This remark had an even more dramatic effect on the doctor. He opened his eyes, disclosing an expression of abject terror, and began to gabble in an almost incoherent way. "I know nothing. I heard nothing. I shall tell the police nothing. Everybody has a right to his private life. Why should I interfere? I didn't interfere. I don't know what went on."

Henry tried to get a word in. "A girl came here this morning," he began.

Dr. Mahoumi cut him short with a wail. "I saw nobody. I heard nobody. Anyone may have a woman in his apartment. How could I know?"

A glimmer of light dawned on Henry. Taking a chance, he said, "It seems that this was a murder of revenge, like so many murders."

"Revenge . . . I don't understand."

"You are obviously a very clever man," said Henry. "Much too clever to take risks, I should have thought. I'm surprised that you let me in."

Dr. Mahoumi jumped up and backed toward the window. "There are gendarmes," he said. "You dare not . . ."

Henry grinned. "Don't worry. I didn't kill Mr. Trapp. That was just my little joke."

Dr. Mahoumi seemed to recover a little of his composure, but his voice was still shaking as he said, "Who are you?"

"My name is Smith," said Henry pleasantly. "Wilberforce Smith. And I have come to ask your advice on a legal matter. If you think it over and decide you can help me, contact me at the Hotel Étoile."

Dr. Mahoumi took a step toward Henry and looked at him almost defiantly. His courage seemed to be returning rapidly. "Mr. Smith," he said, "I am afraid I cannot handle your case. These numbered bank accounts are impossible to crack. Any lawyer will tell you so. I have no more to say to you."

"I see," said Henry. "How very disappointing. If you change your mind, ring me at the hotel."

He let himself out of the apartment and went down again in

the lift. The gendarme in the hall gave him a bored look. Henry walked quickly to the nearest stop and took a tram back to the hotel.

At the desk he paused to inform the porter that if anyone called asking for Mr. Wilberforce Smith they should be put through to him. The porter received this information without surprise, and made a careful note of it. He also told Henry the good news that Madame had already returned and taken the key.

When Henry entered the room, Emmy was lying on the bed with a copy of the paper, *Genève Soir*, on the floor beside her, and she was crying. A glance at the back page told Henry that he had no need to break the news to her. He went over to the bed and took her in his arms.

Characteristically, when Emmy learned the full gravity of her husband's position, she stopped crying and became practical. Certainly she clung to him like a child and sniffled at intervals, but the negative grief which she had felt for John and Natasha and Annette was miraculously transformed, passing through momentary panic to indignation and action.

She listened intently while Henry told her all that had happened, including his recent encounters with Madame Novari and Dr. Mahoumi.

"You were terribly lucky," she said. "That gives us a big lead. The girl with the message, she's the person to hang on to. Do you think Madame Novari would recognize her again?"

"I've no idea," said Henry. "I imagine so, but I had no time to ask her."

"Of course," said Emmy, "if we do find her, she may not help much. She was probably some little girl picked up from the street who wanted to earn five francs for delivering a message."

"I doubt it," said Henry. "Remember, it was a verbal message. One wouldn't trust just anybody with that. And then she had to bring back the written answer. It would have been too risky to involve a third person."

"A third person?"

"Yes. As I see it, we're dealing with a conspiracy of at least two people from the committee."

"How on earth do you work that out?"

"Well," said Henry, "let's assume that the mysterious message-bearer was one of the girls from our setup at the Palais. She must be deeply implicated, because everyone knows that I deny having an appointment with John, and she hasn't come forward with any statement about being asked to deliver a message this morning. She must know who the murderer is, and she knows that she's helping to frame me, and she's keeping quiet."

"Yes, but why shouldn't she be the actual murderer?" Emmy objected. "Do you mean that it would have been physically impossible for a girl to have . . .?"

"No," said Henry, "but for a start, neither Mary nor Annette nor Helène was at the Hamptons' party last night, so none of them had the opportunity of taking the dagger. Unless they burgled the house after everyone had gone home, which is highly unlikely. So there you have your first evidence of conspiracy."

Emmy opened her mouth to speak, then shut it again. "What is it?" Henry asked.

"I just thought, mightn't Natasha have taken the dagger?"

"Certainly, she could have. But why, for heaven's sake?"

"I don't know."

"Well, then, don't confuse the issue. Now, it would have been literally impossible for Mary or Helène to do the killing. Mary was with me in the interpreters' room, and Helène was with Lenoir in the rest room. I heard them talking. Annette was in the cloakroom alone, I admit, but—if you could have seen the way she broke down. I just can't believe she did it. Even if she did, she must have a partner. She wasn't at the Villa Trounex, and what's more, she was on leave last week, so she couldn't have been responsible for the leakage of information."

Emmy said slowly, "You say that she broke down completely when she found that John was dead. Could that have been because she realized too late that she'd helped to kill him?"

"It could be." Henry spoke thoughtfully. "On the other hand, anyone could see that she was desperately in love with him, so her breakdown was quite natural. Helène nearly fainted, but I suppose that's understandable. Mary was wonderfully calm and competent, but then she always is."

"Well," Emmy said briskly, "this isn't getting us anywhere. What we've got to do now is to get hold of photographs of all three of them and take them around to Madame Novari. I don't care whether she thinks we're mad or not."

"I expect the police will have been at her by this time."

"Never mind. The first thing is to get the pictures. I've got a snapshot of Annette, the one I took in Yvoire last week. Where can we get the others?"

"Heaven knows," said Henry. He felt helpless, bereft of the

streamlined organization of Scotland Yard, which could turn up a photograph of anybody in the world at the drop of a telephone.

Emmy's eyes went to the newspaper on the floor. "The local paper," she said. "Surely they'll have pictures of everyone in Geneva. Come on." She swung her legs off the bed, stood up, and took Henry's hand.

"I really ought to stay here."

"No. You must come with me because my French isn't good enough. And don't suggest that I stay here without you, because I don't intend to let you out of my sight for one moment."

Henry kissed her with enthusiasm, and, feeling much better, allowed himself to be bullied. In ten minutes they were in the offices of *Genève Soir*.

A polite and charming young woman listened gravely to their request, and referred them to a polite and charming young man, who in turn handed them over to a matronly woman in a white coat, the guardian of the paper's photographic library. An exhaustive search revealed that there was no photograph available of either Helène Brochet or Mary Benson. Henry and Emmy were then passed back to the polite young man, who had a brain wave.

"But there is an English newspaper here, with a famous social column," he exclaimed. "They will surely have the pictures you need."

He scribbled a note of introduction, and by half past five Henry and Emmy were wearily pushing open the door of the *Geneva Weekly Mail* editorial offices. Here, better luck was in store. It took an hour of searching, but eventually the helpful American girl assistant came up with two photographs. One showed Mary Benson in riding habit, receiving a blue rosette for show jumping at Morges. The other was of Helène Brochet, looking ravishing in a black dress with a cascade of white fox furs, attending a gala première at the Casino Theatre. It was not only the picture of Helène that was intriguing, however. Almost equally interesting was her escort, smart as paint in a neat dinner jacket, a carnation in his buttonhole. For it was none other than Konrad Zwemmer.

"When was this taken?" Henry asked.

The girl glanced at the caption pasted on the back of the photograph. "Last December."

"Five months ago," Henry remarked. He looked at the caption. ". . . Herr Konrad Zwemmer, a frequent and welcome visitor to

Geneva on his Government's business, but this time vacationing with old friends . . ."

When they finally got into the taxi which was taking them to the Chemin des Chênes, Emmy said, "Fancy the little Zwemmer man being mixed up with Helène Brochet. She looks stunning."

"It's very odd," said Henry. "They hardly ever speak to each other." Then he remembered something, and was silent.

It was with a sense of almost unbearable tension that, for the second time that afternoon, Henry rang the concierge's bell at 5, Chemin des Chênes. There was a different gendarme on duty in the hall, and he barely spared Henry and Emmy a glance. It was the hour when business people return home from work, and the foyer was busy with coming and going.

After what seemed an unbearable delay, the door opened.

"Madame Novari," Henry began, and then stopped dead. The woman who stood there was elderly and stout, and wore a flowered house coat and slippers. She was a complete stranger.

"Monsieur?"

"I want to see the concierge's wife," Henry began.

"Yes, monsieur. I am she. Can I help you?"

"But Madame Novari . . ."

"Ah, I am sorry monsieur. They left today. My husband and I have taken over. If there is anything . . . ?"

"Left?" Henry felt the nightmare closing in again. "When did they leave?"

"This morning, monsieur. They have gone back to Italy."

"That's not true. She was here after lunch," said Henry.

"Oh, well . . . this morning, after lunch, I don't know exactly, monsieur. My husband and I have only just arrived. You can see."

Sure enough, the passage was stacked with trunks and packing cases, and through the open sitting-room door, Henry caught a glimpse of an elderly man perched on a ladder, hanging chintz curtains.

"But"—Henry had the impression of struggling through cotton wool—"she didn't say anything about leaving."

"No, monsieur. It was very sudden. Monsieur Novari's mother had a bad accident, and they were forced to go at once. I told my husband it was ridiculous to expect us to move in at such short notice, and if you'd seen the state of the apartment, monsieur! Italians, of course. I said so to the agents, but you know what *they're* like, and one can't offend them, with apartments so hard to get and . . ."

Valiantly, Henry dammed the flood by almost shouting, "Did they leave an address?"

"No, monsieur. Any mail, I am to forward to the agents. Are you one of the tenants, monsieur? I have a list here of all the . . ."

"No, no," said Henry. He saw out of the corner of his eye that the gendarme was beginning to show interest. "No, I was hoping to get a flat here, and I had spoken to Madame Novari about it. Can you give me the name of the agents?"

"Of course, monsieur. Blanchard et Cie, Rue du Rhône. It is best to go direct to them if you want an apartment, though I can't see there's any hope of it, with things as they are. Of course, they'll be closed now, but you could go around in the morning."

"Thank you," said Henry.

"Service!"

The door closed. Henry took Emmy's arm. "Let's get out of here," he said.

Henry and Emmy did not go back to their hotel at once. Henry, saying firmly, "I think we both need a drink," took a taxi to the supermodern Hotel du Rhône, where they installed themselves in a discreet corner of the cocktail bar.

Around them flowed a tide of humanity as varied and haphazard as the occupants of an airport waiting room. Stately, dark-eyed Arabs in long white nightshirts strode purposefully through the foyer or conversed in eager, gesticulating groups over glasses of lemonade. American businessmen—dressed for the most part in London-styled clothes and distinguishable from their English counterparts only by their cameras, cigars, and haircuts—concluded million-dollar deals and planned their evening's entertainment, while their mink-and-diamond wives glittered, and wise-cracked over the driest of martinis. Small, neat Chinamen in large spectacles discussed international affairs with darkly hirsute South Americans. German, Dutch, Spanish, and French voices eddied in the rich atmosphere of scent and cigar smoke. Here, in a secluded corner, a quiet conversation could take place in the special sort of privacy that can be found only in a crowd.

"Well," said Henry, "so much for the girl with the note."

"I just can't believe it." Emmy was near tears. "Nobody should have such bad luck."

"I agree," said Henry. He took a sip of whisky. "Now, let's see where we've got so far. Going back to my idea of this being a joint operation between a man and a woman, we've established a connection of some sort between Helène Brochet and Zwemmer. Annette was involved with John. It's just conceivable, I suppose, that she might be involved with someone else as well. If she is, it's someone she knew before this conference, because she's been on holiday and only joined us today. That cuts out Bill Parkington, since this is his first visit to Geneva. All I've got on him is that he has had a drink with Mary Benson out of office hours, for what that's worth. There seems to be no connection between either Lenoir or Moranta and any of the girls, but who knows? I can't help feeling this thing may be easier if we try to hunt them in couples, as it were."

"But Henry, *why*?" Emmy shook her dark head in puzzlement. "Why should anyone kill John?"

Henry looked at her, surprised. "That's about the only thing that's reasonably clear. The security leak, of course. If John knew who was responsible . . ."

Emmy shook her head again. "Wait a minute," she said. "Let me think. I'm putting this awfully badly, I know. But you and Bill were the only people who knew last night that the leak had been discovered. That's one of the reasons it all looks so black for you, because whoever took the dagger had all this planned last night. As I see it, there are only two people who it's reasonable to suppose might or could have planned it then. Bill Parkington or . . ." She paused.

"Or me?" said Henry, with a rueful smile.

"Idiot. No, I meant Paul Hampton."

"Paul? Whatever made you think of that?"

"I haven't had time to tell you what I found out at lunchtime," said Emmy. And she told him.

Henry nodded somberly. "I knew about that myself," he said. "Never mind how. All the same, I feel absolutely sure that Paul wouldn't, and in any case he was never near the Palais. When John Trapp was killed, he was in a plane bound for Paris. No, he was already in Paris, come to that."

"How do you know?"

"I don't for certain, but we can check. But, darling, even if he wasn't in Paris, how do you suggest he got into that closed suite, past the watchdog on the door?"

"He could have had an accomplice, the girl."

"Annette? She's the only girl who could conceivably have done the killing. Apart from the fact that he almost certainly doesn't even know her, do you really think any man would get a girl to kill his wife's lover for him?"

Emmy sighed. "It does sound silly when you put it like that," she said.

Henry finished his drink. "Well," he said, "there's no point in talking in circles any longer. Let's try to forget it for tonight. Tomorrow we can get down to something more constructive. I'll be at the Palais all day, so I'm afraid you'll have to tackle Blanchard et Cie on your own. Don't speak to anybody who looks the least important there. Pick on the smallest office boy you can find, and say you want to send the Norvaris a little farewell present. But get their address at all costs."

"Oh, help," said Emmy. "Supposing the office boy doesn't speak English."

"This is Geneva," said Henry. "He will."

Seven

As things turned out, Henry and Emmy were not, after all, able to forget the whole thing that evening. When they got back to the Hotel Étoile, they found a message that Signor Spezzi had rung three times, and would like them to call him as soon as possible.

Henry telephoned Spezzi's hotel at once. Alfredo sounded worried. "Can we meet this evening, Enrico? As soon as possible?"

"Of course. Why don't you and Gerda come around here?"

"Gerda is not with me."

"Oh." Henry did not inquire any further, and merely said, "Well, come around yourself then."

"Thank you. I will."

Alfredo arrived twenty minutes later. His newfound composure was cracking somewhat, and he seemed to Henry to be young and vulnerable. He also showed a tendency to lapse back into his Italian weakness for melodrama. He came into the bar, where Henry and Emmy were waiting for him, and seized one of Henry's hands in both his, saying, "Enrico. *Caro* Enrico," with such a hint of tears that Henry could not help smiling.

"It's not as bad as that, I hope," said Henry.

"Enrico, if you could have heard what they were saying today, those others at the Palais. I could not . . ."

"Oh, to hell with them," interrupted Henry. "Have an apéritif, and we'll go and dine somewhere."

"Enrico," said Spezzi, as if making a dramatic confession, "I have a car outside."

"Good," said Henry. "Then we can drive out to . . ."

"We are going to the Villa Trounex."

This did take Henry aback somewhat. Alfredo explained.

"Gerda is there already. She has been there all the afternoon."

It appeared that, after dropping Emmy, Natasha had stopped to buy an evening paper, had seen the report of John's death, and promptly become hysterical. Gerda had been obliged to drive the Renault perilously back to the villa, whence she had telephoned Alfredo. Since then, it seemed, Natasha had refused to let Gerda out of her sight, and was morbidly insistent that not only Alfredo, but also Henry and Emmy, should come out to the villa as soon as possible. She had sent a chauffeur-driven car for them, which was at the moment breaking all parking regulations by standing, throbbing gently, immediately outside the entrance of the Hotel Étoile. Since it was a brand new Rolls-Royce, nobody seemed to mind very much.

The three of them got into the car and drove out to the Villa Trounex in silence. Once or twice Henry was tempted to make a remark, but each time he was restrained by the sight of the back of the chauffeur's head, with its young, pink ears protruding on either side of the smart livery cap. One could never be sure how many languages anybody understood in this city.

The same lofty major-domo who had greeted them the night before was standing at the front door. This evening his manner was very different. He almost hurried to greet them.

"Madame has asked that I serve an apéritif in the *salon* to Signor Spezzi and Madame Tibbett," he said. "She would appreciate it if Monsieur Tibbett would go up to her room."

So Alfredo and Emmy were ushered into the stupefying elegance of the big drawing room, while Henry found himself, for the second time in twenty-four hours, confronted by the leather-covered door in the blue-carpeted corridor. This time he was accompanied by a maid, who knocked discreetly. At once the door opened, and Gerda came out. The maid vanished silently.

Gerda said, "Oh, Henry. I am so glad you are here. I have had a terrible time with her."

"Tell me," said Henry.

"There's nothing to tell. She won't talk to me, but she wouldn't let me go. She keeps weeping and threatening to kill herself and every sort of nonsense. You are the only person she seems to want. You'd better go in. I'll be downstairs."

With that, Gerda slipped away silently. Henry pushed the door a little further open, cleared his throat nervously, and said,

"It's Henry Tibbett. May I come in?"

There was no reply. Henry opened the door wide, and walked in.

He found himself in a room which appeared at first sight to be a sort of spider's web of frothy white tulle and lavender ribbons. The carpet was thick and pale mauve, and every available object, including the dressing table and its stool, was draped in waterfalls of crisp white muslin. Here and there a mirror glittered, reflecting still more frills. The centerpiece of this shrine of femininity was the bed, a small four-poster which appeared to have exploded in a riot of soapsuds. On it, through the translucent draperies, Henry could just see the outline of a dark, recumbent figure. Tentatively he stepped up to the bed and pulled back a curtain.

Natasha lay prone, her face buried in a beribboned lace pillow. She was still wearing the dark brown linen dress which she had chosen for lunching at Chez Marie, and she had not even taken off her sharp-heeled brown shoes. Her honey-colored hair was tousled and splashed carelessly over the pillow. She did not move.

Henry said awkwardly, "Mrs. Hampton, I believe you wanted . . ."

Slowly, Natasha raised her head and turned her face to him. The mascara had run in muddy brown rivulets down her cheeks and her nose was pink and shining and her lipstick had transferred itself to the lace pillow slip, but she was still beautiful. She said shakily, "For God's sake, my name is Natasha," and then began to cry again.

Henry's pity got the better of his shyness. He sat down on the bed and said, "Look here, Natasha, you'll have to pull yourself together. Nobody can help you if you carry on like this."

Natasha stopped sobbing, as if considering this remark, and then suddenly turned over and sat upright. "Yes," she said. "You are quite right. Have you got a handkerchief?"

Henry held one out to her, and she blew her nose loudly and pushed her damp hair back off her forehead. Then she said, "I suppose I'm a fool to trust you, but I do. You saw John coming out of my room last night, didn't you?"

"Yes," said Henry.

"I heard your voice," said Natasha. She opened a mother-of-pearl cigarette box on the flounced bedside table, took out a cigarette with a silver tip, and lit it. Her hands, Henry noticed, were far from steady.

"What," said Henry, "are you frightened of?"

Natasha looked straight at him. "Paul, of course," she said.

"I don't believe it," said Henry.

Natasha's eyebrows went up. "What do you know about it?" she asked.

"Very little," admitted Henry, "but I'm reasonably sure that you're not afraid of your husband finding out about you and John. I think he has known all about it for some time."

Instead of answering, Natasha kicked her shoes off onto the floor, drew her slim knees up under her chin, and took a long pull at her cigarette. She blew the smoke out in a white plume, which hovered uneasily among the frilly white curtains. At last she said, "I suppose I had better tell you everything, from the beginning."

"If you want to," said Henry.

As though talking to herself, Natasha said, "I've always been desperately in love with Paul. When he asked me to marry him, I just couldn't believe it. I was only twenty, and I had just left school in Vienna. It was soon after the war, and we were very poor; everybody was in those days. The big house on the Ring was shut up, and we lived in three rooms, my mother and I, with only one servant."

"How terrible for you," said Henry heartlessly. He could not help reflecting that he and Emmy had never had more than two rooms and a char once a week.

Natasha paid no attention. "Then Paul came along. He had some business in Vienna, and he was staying in a suite at Sacher's. I met him at a party given by some wealthy people, old friends of my family who had escaped to America before the war and made even more money there. I shall never forget that party. A girl friend of mine worked for a *couturier,* and she sneaked a dress and a mink stole out of the collection for me to wear. I spent the whole evening in a state of panic in case somebody spilled wine on the dress or burned a cigarette hole in the mink. When Paul asked me to lunch with him the next day, I nearly cried. I had to say I was busy. I couldn't tell him that I couldn't accept because I had nothing to wear. When I got home, I did cry. It wasn't just that Paul was rich. I really had fallen in love with him, and I thought I'd never see him again."

"But you did."

"Yes." Natasha smiled. "He found out my address from the people who gave the party, and a couple of days later he turned up at our apartment laden with roses. It was terrible. I was in old trousers, washing my hair in the kitchen. You see," she added, with a trace of mischief, "I haven't always been spoiled."

"I'm glad to hear it," said Henry, and grinned at her. "Go on."

"Well, Paul swept into our lives like a sort of jet-propelled Santa Claus. He proposed to me that very day, and of course I said yes. Then he took a smart new apartment for us—my mother lives there still—and he whirled me around to hairdressers and jewelers and couturiers. I felt exactly like Cinderella, and we both had the time of our lives. I shall never forget it. We've never been so happy as we were then."

"So," said Henry, "what went wrong?"

Natasha stubbed her cigarette out and lit another. She spoke hesitantly, considering each word. "It was never right," she said. "Never, from the beginning. I was so thrilled and excited that it didn't occur to me to wonder why Paul wasn't more . . . demonstrative in his affection toward me. Anyway, I was very young and inexperienced. I thought once we were married . . ." She broke off and looked straight at Henry. "It was only afterward I realized that I hadn't married a man at all. I'd married a . . ." She shrugged. "I don't know how to describe him without being unjust. I know what you're thinking, and I may as well tell you that I don't think Paul is even homosexual. Sometimes I wish he were; then he might feel something for somebody. But the passion of his life is possession. Not just money; things. Beautiful things. His whole life is one exquisite façade, and there's nothing behind it."

"I wonder what made him marry you," said Henry.

"That's easy. He had just bought the house in Paris, and he needed a wife. A hostess. Someone to be decorative and organize his parties. Another possession. Oh, dear, now I've put it far too strongly. Please don't think he's an unpleasant person. You know he isn't. He's charming and brilliant and the greatest fun to be with, so long as one stays on the surface. But he's cold as ice physically and inaccessible mentally. And the terrible thing is that I still love him as much as I did that day in Vienna." Natasha looked at Henry and wrinkled her pretty nose. "It doesn't make sense, does it?"

"Real people very seldom do," said Henry. "Anyhow, it explains a lot. Have you really stayed with him all these years for love alone?"

Natasha looked embarrassed, then caught Henry's eye and

grinned. "I *do* love him," she said, "but let's face it, Henry, I like the good things of life, too. I've grown accustomed to them. Paul made his terms quite clear, almost from the beginning, without ever actually putting them into words. So long as I stay with him, I can have anything I want that money can buy. He won't give me actual cash, but I can run up any sort of bill I like, anywhere. He pays them without question. And more than that. He leaves me completely free in . . . other ways."

"Like John Trapp, for instance."

"Yes." Natasha spoke coolly, with no embarrassment. "The only condition is absolute discretion. No breath of scandal. My job is to be part of the façade that is Paul's life, and I've always known that if I slipped up there I'd be finished. Out. Divorced and broke. He'd play the injured, unsuspecting husband, and then find someone to take my place. Another Cinderella. You see, no woman who was independent would stand for it."

"Now I see why you are frightened," said Henry.

"It's much, much worse than you think," said Natasha.

"I'm afraid I didn't help matters by getting lost outside your door last night," said Henry contritely.

"That started it," said Natasha. "I knew from his voice that he was terribly angry. You wouldn't be able to tell, but you don't know him as I do. But the real trouble was when he made me take John home. Deliberately. You heard him. I can't think why he did it. A sort of perverted revenge, I suppose."

"Surely," said Henry, "he did it entirely for my benefit—to plaster over the hole in the façade, to demonstrate to me that there was nothing between you and John. I would have been quite convinced by it if I hadn't unfortunately overheard you talking the first time you opened your door. I'm really very sorry about that. I wasn't eavesdropping deliberately."

"It doesn't matter," said Natasha, wearily. "Anyway, I was upset and maybe a little drunk. And I am—I was—really rather fond of John. I knew Paul was leaving on the early plane for Paris, and wouldn't expect me to be awake in the morning. I need hardly tell you that there was no risk of his coming to my room during the night." She smiled bitterly.

Henry said softly, "So you stayed all night at John's apartment."

"Yes." It was little more than a whisper.

"You've done that before, haven't you?"

Natasha looked really scared for the first time. "Only once.

How did you know?"

"I guessed. Does Dr. Mahoumi handle any of your legal affairs?"

"My God," said Natasha, "is there anything you don't know?"

"Plenty, I'm afraid," said Henry, sadly. "The things I do know are relatively unimportant. I suppose you used Mahoumi as an excuse to go to the Chemin des Chênes."

"I had to," said Natasha. "You've no idea what people are like, concierges and so on. I didn't dare visit John openly, and I could only ask him here with other people, because of the servants. So I used to go in and out through Mahoumi's apartment. His balcony adjoins John's, you see, with only a thin metal partition separating them. We cut a little door in it for me."

"Your ideas of discretion seem a little elastic to me," said Henry. "What about Chez Marie?"

"What about it?"

"The patron and his wife apparently assumed that John was your husband."

"I can't help that," said Natasha. "We used to lunch there quite a lot. It's not the sort of place Paul would ever go to. And anyhow, it's not a crime to lunch with someone, is it?"

"That rather depends," said Henry. "You were taking a risk."

"A very little one," said Natasha. "That doesn't bother me. No, everything would have been all right if it hadn't been for this awful thing. How was I to know that John would go and get himself murdered?"

"So what do you want me to do about it?"

"It's Mahoumi. Naturally, he knows I was with John last night. I came out through his apartment this morning. Normally he's perfectly reliable; I pay him well, and he keeps his mouth shut. But suppose the police start questioning him? Will he have to say he saw me?"

"Of course, if they ask him."

Natasha grabbed Henry's arm. "You've got to stop him," she said. "I'll do anything, anything at all. You've got to go and see him and stop him from telling the police. I'll give you a thousand francs to take to him. No, two thousand would be better. Will you go and see him and give him the money and make him promise not to talk, about seeing me, or about . . . about other things that he knows?"

"No," said Henry. "I won't. You should know better than to ask a policeman to do such a thing."

Two big tears rolled down Natasha's cheeks. "Oh, Henry," she said. "You must. You're my only hope. Isn't there anything you'd like for yourself? I'd be prepared to . . ."

Quickly, Henry cut her short. He had been offered many bribes in his time, but this was a particularly distasteful one, for he liked Natasha, in all her amoral honesty. He wanted to spare her the humiliation of being refused.

"I don't think you need worry," he said. "I have already seen Dr. Mahoumi, as it happens, and he has no intention of telling the police anything."

"Are you sure?"

"No, but I'm as sure as I would be if I'd given him two thousand francs."

Natasha gave a big sigh of relief. "Oh, that's wonderful," she said. "I knew I could trust you. Now everything is all right, except for . . . well, that can be arranged later."

"Everything," said Henry, "except for the fact that John is dead."

"Yes," said Natasha. "That is terrible." But the despair had gone out of her voice.

"And," said Henry, "that I am suspected of murdering him."

"You?" This brought Natasha up with a jerk. "What on earth do you mean?"

"Someone has taken great pains to make it look as though I killed him," said Henry. "I'm trying very hard to clear myself by finding out who really did. Will you help me?"

"Of course, if I can."

"I'm working on a process of elimination. For a start, I'd like to eliminate Paul."

"Paul?" Natasha was completely bewildered. "But Paul is in Paris."

"Are you sure?"

"Of course I'm sure."

"He's not here, but he could be anywhere."

"Well, it's easy enough to check." Natasha put out her hand and picked up one of the two white telephones by her bed. She held it to her ear for a moment, smiled mischievously, and replaced it. "Wrong telephone," she said. "That's the outside line. Very interesting, all the same."

"What is?"

"Household scandal. That awful sanctimonious Gamboni, our butler, was on the line, making a call from Paul's room, which he has no right to do anyway. And d'you know what he was doing?"

"What?"

"Making a date with a call-girl, by the sound of it."

Natasha giggled. Henry looked at her, tried to make up his mind about her, and failed.

Meanwhile Natasha had picked up the other telephone and dialed a number. In French, she said, "Is that the garage? This is Madame Hampton. Give me Golaz. . . . Golaz? You drove my husband to the airport this morning, didn't you? . . . He caught the plane all right? . . . Yes, I was just wondering. Thank you."

She rang off. "That was the chauffeur," she said. "He drove Paul to the airport, and waited until he saw him board the plane and take off. There's no doubt at all that he's in Paris."

"And in any case," Henry said, "Paul had nothing against John, had he?"

"Goodness, no. Nothing at all. He liked him."

"Did Paul know about . . . ?"

"Of course." Natasha looked amused. "He thoroughly approved. That made it all rather pleasant. Sometimes he hasn't liked the people I . . ." She stopped, and then added, "Are you terribly shocked?"

"No," said Henry. "I just think it's all rather sad, especially for you. Now about the dagger."

"What dagger?"

"Didn't you know that John was stabbed with the dagger from your library?"

"From our . . . ?" Natasha closed her eyes. "Oh, no. I can't bear it. That means we'll have the police here."

"I'm very surprised they haven't been here already."

"Henry," said Natasha faintly, "I don't feel very well. Could you get me a glass of water?"

"Of course," said Henry. "Where from?"

"The bathroom," said Natasha, with a vague gesture.

Henry got up and opened a door which lurked coyly behind yet another froth of muslin. The bathroom was also lavender, close-carpeted, and the sunken bath was fed by taps shaped like silver dolphins. Most intriguing of all was the lavatory seat, which was swathed in an outside rosette of white tulle, with a bunch of artificial violets in the center of it. Henry crossed the carpet gingerly, feeling that his uncouth masculine feet would surely leave bruises wherever they trod. He poured cold water into a cut crystal glass and took it back to the bedroom. As far as he could see, Natasha had not moved. She drank the water grate-fully, and then said, "I'm sorry. It was rather shattering to hear about the dagger. I don't understand it. It was there last night."

"I know it was," said Henry. "I saw it myself. The point is, when do you last remember seeing it?"

Natasha frowned. "I went through the library when I came downstairs after meeting John," she said. "It was there then."

"Are you sure?"

"As sure as I can be. I'd certainly have noticed," said Natasha, positively.

"Well, that's something. You didn't pass the library again when you went to get your coat?"

"No. My coat was downstairs."

"Oh, well. That seems to be that. Now, I'd like you to tell me if you noticed anything unusual in John's behavior, last night or this morning. Did he say or do anything peculiar?"

Natasha shook her head. "He was just the same as ever. The only out-of-the-way thing was the concierge's wife coming up at seven. I got a terrible fright when the doorbell rang."

"What happened?" Henry asked.

"I nipped into the bathroom," said Natasha, "and John got up and answered the door. I heard him say something about a bloody idiot. Then he took his pen out of his jacket pocket and a piece of paper from the desk and wrote something and went back to the door again. Then I heard the front door shut. I came out of the bathroom and got into bed again, and he said, 'Sorry, darling. Just some fool from the subcommittee wanting to see me before the session starts.' I said, 'What about?' and he said, 'I've no idea, but it can't be important.' "

"You're sure he said that?"

Natasha looked at him wide-eyed. "Of course," she said. "Why ever should I lie about it?"

"No reason," said Henry. "I'm just very relieved to hear that that was his reaction. Did he ever talk to you about his work?"

"Oh, yes, a lot." Natasha smiled reminiscently. "Chiefly about how much it bored him, and how he wanted to get away and do something worth while and make money. He had rather an ob-session about money, especially these last few weeks. He wanted me to leave Paul and go away with him, you see, but he knew he couldn't possibly afford it."

"If he'd been rich, would you have gone with him?" Henry asked directly.

Natasha gave him a straight, clear look. "Of course not."

"Not even if he'd been richer than Paul?"

"No."

"Why not?"

With no hesitation, Natasha said simply, "Because I love Paul. Because he's ten times as charming and witty and wise as John could ever be. He's irreplaceable."

"Whereas John Trapp isn't."

"I've told you the truth," said Natasha briefly. "Go downstairs now. I've ordered dinner for you, but I can't face any myself. I'm going straight to bed. Will you make my excuses to the others? And apologize to Gerda for me. She's a nice girl, and I've given her a hell of a day."

Henry looked at the small, beautiful face, now quite self-possessed and dry eyed. "I shall never," he said, "understand women."

Natasha gave him an impish grin. "I should hope not," she said. "By the way, if you do see Mahoumi or, if anything happens, ring me here. Not the number in the phone book, but our private line. Five-nine-seven-two. It'll come straight through to me here."

Henry made a note of the number, and then prepared to say his good-bys, but when he looked up, Natasha had already got up and the bathroom door was closing behind her. He shrugged, and went downstairs.

Henry did not go directly to the drawing room. He had been intrigued by Natasha's remark that she had passed through the library on her way back to the party the previous night, and at the risk of getting lost again, he decided to do a little exploring. Sure enough, after a few minutes he found what he was looking for. Hidden behind one of the leather-covered doors was a small staircase which led down to another door at the bottom. Henry pushed this open, and found himself in the library. It was beginning to grow dark, but the heavy red velvet curtains were still undrawn, so that the stone balustrade of the terrace outside glimmered whitely against the dark of the trees. The lake was not visible, for the library looked out at right angles to the lake-view rooms.

Henry was puzzled by the fact that the police had not yet investigated the Villa Trounex. In Colliet's place, it was one of the first things he would have done. He walked over to the wall where he remembered the dagger hanging, a million years ago. The wall, a space between well-stocked bookcases, looked naked;

the space which the dagger had occupied was as obvious and insistent as the gap left by a missing tooth. Natasha was quite right; she would have noticed. Henry shook his head in unhappy bewilderment, and walked slowly back to the window, where he stood in the half-light, gazing out at the gardens, and trying to reconstruct in his mind the scenes and conversations which had taken place on that very terrace the evening before.

He was jerked out of his reverie by the sound of a key turning in a lock. The door which led to the main hall opened, and instantly the library was flooded with brilliance as the electric lights were switched on. Henry wheeled around to face the door, and found himself confronted by Gamboni, the major-domo. The latter was obviously dumfounded to see Henry, and for a moment could find no words. Then he recovered himself and said in a voice of cold fury, "Did you require something, sir?" His English was excellent.

For the first time Henry had the opportunity of taking a really good look at this somewhat formidable character. Gamboni was a man of middle age, tall and spare, but with the wide shoulders and slim hips of an athlete. His hair was very dark, and his face now expressed an intensity of real anger which surprised Henry.

"I am afraid I must ask you to leave this room, sir," said Gamboni acidly.

"Leave?" said Henry. "Why?"

"Instructions from the police, sir. Had you informed me that you wished to use the library, I would have explained matters sooner."

"So the police have been here, have they?" Henry asked. Gamboni did not answer. Henry went on. "It's strange that Madame Hampton is apparently unaware of their visit."

Gamboni hesitated. He seemed to be debating whether or not to answer. In the end, he evidently decided that an explanation of some sort was called for. He said, "They arrived soon after Madame had left for her luncheon appointment. I dealt with them myself. When Madame returned she was distraught and ill, and I did not consider that she should be worried by such things."

"I see," said Henry. He paused awkwardly. It was a new and unpleasant sensation to realize that he had no legal right whatever to compel people to give him information. His only hope of finding out anything about Gamboni's conversation with the police was to attack the subject obliquely.

"It was very thoughtful of you not to trouble Madame Hampton," he said, "but of course, when one comes to think of it, it is natural that the police should have been more interested in you. After all, you were the last person to see the dagger."

"I beg your pardon, sir?" Gamboni was undoubtedly rattled.

"Well, I presume you made the rounds of the house after all the guests had left last night."

"I did not see the dagger."

"You mean, it had already disappeared?"

"It was not in its place when I came to draw the curtains at eleven thirty. I told the police so. I was not able to help them any further. And now, sir, if you don't mind. I have strict orders that nobody must enter this room. You will notice that it has been locked up since the police were here."

"One of the doors has been locked. Not the other."

"That is Monsieur and Madame's private door," said Gamboni, furious. "I naturally did not anticipate that anyone else would use it."

"I notice too," said Henry, "that you yourself are apparently exempt from police instructions."

There was a distinct pause before Gamboni answered, but when he did so, it was in a voice of angry defiance. All he said was, "Yes, sir."

"Oh, well," said Henry, "let's go." He walked out through the door which Gamboni held open for him. As soon as they were in the corridor, the butler relocked the door and put the key into his pocket.

Henry went back to the salon in a thoughtful frame of mind. Gamboni's attitude was strictly correct. He was obeying orders, and would naturally be shocked and displeased to find a stranger wandering in forbidden territory. All the same, the circumstances did not seem to warrant the degree of sheer anger that the man had shown. It was puzzling, and interesting. No less interesting was the definite information that the dagger had been missing after the party. It was, of course, only what Henry had expected, but this decisive testimony formed yet another small piece of the jigsaw which Henry was patiently assembling in his mind.

He found Gerda, Emmy, and Alfredo morosely drinking apéritifs. He was able to reassure them as to Natasha's condition, but did not feel that he could confide to the Spezzis the true cause of her earlier distress. Since they were both bursting with curiosity, the atmosphere was uneasy throughout the excellent dinner which was served to the four of them in the long, elegant dining room. It was typical of Natasha, Henry thought crossly, to use somebody like Gerda as a convenient shoulder to cry on, and then dismiss her without a word of explanation, throwing in a free meal as compensation, and leaving the unresolved personal situation to be handled by someone else. It was also typical that Gerda's very natural resentment should be directed at Henry rather than at the absent, languishing Natasha.

After dinner, however, when Emmy and Gerda had left the men to their port, Henry did manage to persuade Alfredo to give him his account of the events of the morning. This did not add much to what Henry already knew. Alfredo declared that he had arrived at the conference suite at about twenty past nine. He had not been the first. He could not say for certain who was there before him, but he had noticed Helène Brochet talking to Zwemmer in the conference room as he came in. He had gone straight to the cloakroom, where he had been followed almost immediately by Bill Parkington, who had hung up his coat, arranged his papers, talked a little, and gone out.

"That was when you came in, Enrico," Alfredo went on. "Then you went out, and just as I was leaving, Lenoir came in. I went up the corridor to go into the office, for I wished to get a new notebook, but Mary Benson came out of the interpreters' room and told me that Trapp was in the office—I could hear that for myself—and that he did not want to be disturbed. That was when you were talking to the secretary further down the passage. So I went on into the conference room. By that time it was empty; I don't know where Helène and Zwemmer had gone. I found my place at the table and sat down to arrange my papers. Then a few minutes later Zwemmer came in and made some remark about the agenda. I can't really remember what he said. I think he asked me if I knew whether there was to be a change in it or not, and I said I had heard nothing, but that he should ask you. We talked for a few minutes, and then we heard Moranta shouting murder. Zwemmer was standing near the door, and he rushed out in a panic. By the time I had got out to the corridor, everyone else seemed to be crowding into the office. That's all I know."

"I couldn't help noticing," said Henry, "that you seemed rather less taken aback than anybody else."

Alfredo shrugged. "A leak in security always creates an explosive situation," he said. "And people who deal in narcotic drugs are inclined to violence, as you know well."

Henry sat up very straight. "You already knew about the security leak this morning, when Trapp was killed?"

Spezzi smiled. "You are sometimes naïve, Enrico," he said. "Our friend Parkington is sincere and enthusiastic, but he cannot keep a secret, and his conversation is transparently easy to analyze. He did not tell me in so many words, but from what he said in the cloakroom this morning, I was in no doubt. Heaven knows how many of the others gathered the same information in the same way. Bill was worried, and he couldn't hide it. I suppose you think that you were the only person who knew, but I am afraid there may have been others." Alfredo twirled the beautifully cut wine glass in his long fingers for a moment, and then lifted it and drained it in a sudden movement.

"Ah, well," he said, "life is like that. Untidy. I wish you luck, Enrico. If I can help, you know you have only to ask me. Shall we go back to the salon now?"

Eight

The next day started with a dreadful parody of normality. Even a murder is no excuse for holding up an international conference, and the delegates and staff assembled as usual at the Palais in the morning. At least, almost as usual, but not quite; for the suite of offices in which John Trapp had died was now out of bounds and swarmed with policemen and plain-clothes experts, who could be glimpsed through the glass panels of the locked door as they went about their business of detection. The subcommittee and its staff were directed to another, similar suite on the floor above.

Henry got up early, and arrived at the Palais soon after nine. He was sad but unsurprised to be denied access to the scene of the crime, but somewhat consoled by the sight of the same lugubrious doorkeeper guarding the entrance to the new quarters. He produced his official pass and said, "Am I the first to arrive?"

"Yes, monsieur." The man was obviously bored and longing to talk. "What a terrible affair! I couldn't sleep all night, thinking of it. Poor Monsieur Trapp. We all knew him well. He was greatly loved." He blew his nose loudly. "My wife was distraught when I told her. Couldn't stop crying. Of course, she never actually met him, but she is sympathetic. And then the gendarmes. Questions and questions. Anybody would think they suspected me of murder. I told the Inspector, 'I've been eight years at the Palais, monsieur,' I said, 'Ever since I retired from the Post Office. I've got a trained memory. I don't make mistakes. In any case,' I said, 'it's all written in my book, like it should be. That cannot tell a lie, eh?' I had him there. Ah, well." The old man shook his head. "Now my little book has become important evidence, Exhibit A, I shouldn't wonder, and we start afresh."

With conscious self-satisfaction in a job well and accurately done, he looked up at the clock, and then wrote carefully, on the first page of a brand new notebook, "Tuesday, 9th May," and underneath, "0902. M. Tibbett."

"So the police have taken the book you used yesterday, have they?" Henry asked with exaggerated innocence. "I wonder what they want it for?"

"To see the times when people arrived, monsieur."

"But with your trained memory, you could tell them that without looking at the book, I'll be bound."

The old man reddened with pleasure but shook his head. "No, no, monsieur. Not the exact times, that would be too much. But I could tell them the order in which the ladies and gentlemen arrived."

"Will you tell me?" Henry asked. He saw no point in beating about the bush any more.

To his relief, the doorkeeper answered at once, "Of course, monsieur." He threw back his grizzled head and closed his eyes tight in an effort of concentration. "The first, of course, was poor Monsieur Trapp. That was just before nine o'clock. He was in a hurry, I thought. He asked me if you had arrived, and I told him no, he was the first. Then a few minutes later Mlle. Benson came. After her, a little gap, and then Mlle. Brochet and Monsieur Zwemmer, together. Then came Monsieur Spezzi. After that, people came quickly, one after the other. Mlle. Delacroix, Monsieur Parkington, yourself. A little gap again, and then Monsieur Lenoir. Last of all was Monsieur Moranta. He came in and walked straight from here up to the office, monsieur, and then we heard his cry of murder. That was how matters arranged themselves." He opened his eyes triumphantly. "You see, it is all there, in my head. I told the gendarmes."

"Did they not believe you?" Henry asked.

"Oh, they believed me in the end." The doorkeeper chuckled. "With the book, how could they argue? They have no sense. I shouldn't be surprised if they come from Neuchâtel, most of them. Can't tell who you're getting in the force these days. Figure to yourself, monsieur, they tried to tell me I had remembered wrongly, and that you had come in earlier and gone out again. I soon convinced them they were wrong. I'm not sure one of them wasn't from Saint-Gall."

"Thank you very much," said Henry. "You've helped me a lot." He walked down the corridor, unable to suppress a smile at the time-honored contempt which the citizens of any one Swiss canton have for those of the others. He was still smiling as he went into the office.

It bore an uncanny resemblance to the room in which he had found John Trapp dead. The layout and furniture were identical, and all the documents, files and equipment had been neatly transferred to their new quarters. The prim row of dark gray filing cabinets, the stacks of gaudily colored cardboard dossiers, the filing trays and the newly sharpened pencils were all there, exactly as they had been the day before. An identical typewriter stood on the heavy oak desk, with a virgin block of typing paper and a packet of carbons beside it. Henry looked around the room. For a moment it crossed his mind that there was something missing, but for the life of him he could not think what, and he dismissed the idea as nonsense. The only thing that was missing was John's large, limp body in the swivel chair.

The door opened, and a girl whom Henry had never seen before walked in, a short, dark, self-possessed little person in a navy blue cotton dress.

"*Bonjour,* monsieur," she said briskly. "I am Marcelle Dunant, the new secretary. I understand there are some changes in the agenda to be typed before the meeting opens."

"New secretary?" Henry repeated. "Where's Annette, I mean, Mlle. Delacroix?"

"She is ill, monsieur. I have taken over." Marcelle put down her handbag and made a quick, expert tour of the office, glancing at files, opening drawers, checking supplies. She reminded Henry of a small, efficient cat inspecting new quarters. Then she sat down at the desk, removed the cover of the typewriter, and said, "Everything seems to be in order. May I have the revisions now?"

Feeling slow and clumsy, Henry extricated the scribbled-over copy of the agenda from the file in which some unknown, business-like hand had deposited it. Marcelle glanced at it, nodded briefly, and inserted sheets of paper and carbon into the typewriter. The silence was ripped by metallic clicking. Marcelle had taken over. Henry wandered out into the corridor.

To tell the truth, he felt aimless and useless. Apart from a desire to speak to the doorkeeper, a procedure he knew would not take many minutes, he had had no very clear idea of why he had come to the Palais so early. The unacknowledged motive was probably a desire to escape from his own melancholy company, to get the day started at all costs. Now it was still only ten past nine, and it was unlikely that other people would arrive before half past at the earliest. Henry felt isolated and unhappy, standing in the empty passage with the insistent clicking of the typewriter behind him (another bitter echo of yesterday), and no sign of human company except for the doorkeeper, who was now sitting in his little glass box, half hidden behind a copy of *La Suisse*.

Consequently it was with great pleasure that Henry saw the entrance door of the suite opening. The watchdog lowered his newspaper and got up. Mary Benson came in.

Of all the delegates and staff, Henry could think of no more welcome arrival. Mary looked cool and crisp in her lime-yellow linen suit. Her auburn hair was coiled into a shining chignon which was impeccably neat without being in any way unfeminine. To Henry she seemed the embodiment of attractive, sympathetic common sense. He could not help contrasting her admirable qualities with the machinelike efficiency of Marcelle on the one hand, and the super-feminine, hysterical abandon of Annette and Natasha on the other. To do Henry justice, it never even crossed his mind that he might be falling in love with Mary. It was with the pure pleasure of seeing a friend that he walked down the corridor toward her, saying, "Mary. I'm so glad you're here. Come and talk to me."

Mary hesitated, and then smiled. "In a minute, Inspector. I'll just dispose of these." She indicated her shorthand typewriter and the trim portable tape recorder that she carried, and went into the interpreters' room. Henry followed her.

"Don't tell me you've been working overtime again," he said.

Mary began sorting the papers on her desk. In a light, steady voice, she said, "Working is better than brooding. Anyhow, there was a lot to do." She picked up a sheaf of papers and glanced through them. "I had a chance yesterday to catch up on a backlog of work. You'd be surprised how much talking you people do, Inspector. I had half-a-dozen tapes to type."

"I didn't know you worked from a tape recorder," said Henry.

"I don't. At least, I only use it as a check when I'm working on my own, as I am now. The tapes I mean come from this little brute." She gave an affectionate pat to the small shorthand typewriter on the desk, which was fed with narrow cylindrical rolls of white paper, reminiscent of those used in cash registers.

"It seems very hard that you have to take work home," said Henry.

"Home? From a secret conference?" Mary gave him a reproving look. "I certainly didn't take it home. I just came back here and worked in the afternoon, that's all." She saw Henry's eyes move toward the shorthand typewriter, and added, "I take my equipment home because it's my personal property and my livelihood. A verbatim reporter's typewriter is like a tennis player's racket or a musician's instrument; the two are never separated. But I can assure you it went home empty. All the tapes and papers from a secret conference have to be handed in here, and they're burned."

"Oh," said Henry, rather bleakly. He had, in fact, been toying not very optimistically with the idea that the leakage might have occurred through some charwoman getting hold of secret waste paper. Now this last hope disappeared. It had to be one of the delegates or staff. He sat down on the window sill and lit a cigarette. Mary busied herself with her work.

There was a long silence, during which Henry considered a number of conversational opening gambits. At last he decided to be blunt and to the point. "I suppose you know," he said, "that they think I killed John Trapp."

"Yes." Mary spoke quietly, without looking up.

"You heard them talking about it in the rest room yesterday."

"I could hardly avoid it."

"Who was doing the talking?"

Still with her back half turned toward him, Mary said, "Oh, Monsieur Lenoir and Señor Moranta, mostly. They said you were the only person who had the opportunity."

"Do you think I killed him?" Henry asked.

"Of course not, Inspector."

"That's very kind of you," said Henry. "As it happens, I didn't."

"I'm certain you didn't."

"Why do you say that?"

"Well, I mean . . ." Mary hesitated. "You're just not the sort of person to . . ." She stopped.

"Then who do you think did? I'd be interested to hear your ideas."

Mary did not answer at once, and Henry realized that she was deeply embarrassed. He did not blame her. This was the first time that he had spoken to her in any but a purely professional capacity, and the subject was, to say the least, a delicate one. He knew that she was hating the whole conversation, but his need for sympathy and information overrode his natural reticence.

"Who?" he asked again.

"I've no idea at all, Inspector. How could I possibly know?"

"I just wondered if perhaps you might have noticed anything. People often give themselves away by little things."

Mary made a pretense of sorting some documents, and then, suddenly and surprisingly, she burst out, "The whole place is buzzing with horrible rumors, and nobody really knows anything at all. You should have seen the way people looked at me when I came in to work yesterday afternoon, as if I were a criminal. This damnable atmosphere of suspicion is intolerable. I don't see how we can be expected to work like this."

"Nor do I," said Henry. He felt unaccountably elated at having broken down her reserve. "But the only way we can be rid of it is to find out the truth. That's what I'm trying to do. Will you help me?"

"Of course, Inspector, if I can."

"I wish you'd call me Henry." Mary said nothing, and he went on. "First of all, can we go over your recollection of what happened yesterday morning?"

"Must we?"

"Please, Mary."

"Very well. I can't tell you much. I got here early, so as to have that transcript all ready for you to check. I thought I'd be the first to arrive, but when I went into the office, John was already there. He said he had a date with you, and I said that I had one, too, and that I considered I had a prior claim. I did notice that he seemed terribly nervous and on edge. He kept walking up and down, and then he looked at his watch and said, 'Well, if the bloody man isn't going to turn up . . .' and then he said, 'Mary, will you be an angel and see that nobody disturbs me until Henry comes? I'll have to write it down, and it's not for anyone else's eyes.' He sat down at the desk and put a piece of paper in the typewriter. I couldn't imagine what he was talking about, but it was none of my business. So I just said, 'All right,' and went out. He didn't answer. He'd started to type by then. So I came in here. I had the door open, and when people began to arrive I stopped one or two of them from going into the office. I think that's all. Then you came along and we checked the manuscript and . . . well, you know the rest."

"You mean," said Henry, "that you had the office door under surveillance from the time you left John until . . . when?"

"Until I came in here with you."

"And nobody went in or out?"

"Nobody."

There was a pause. Then Henry said, "Did you know John well?"

"No." Mary was quite definite. "We were colleagues here, and we worked together a certain amount. I never met him out of office hours. Quite honestly, he didn't interest me. He was mixed up in a social set that he couldn't keep up with financially, the Hamptons and all that lot. I always thought of him as a bit of a playboy. Not my sort of person at all."

"Not interested in show jumping, for example?" said Henry with a grin.

Mary looked really taken aback. "How did you know about that?"

"I'm a detective," said Henry. "You'd be surprised how much I know."

Mary smiled. "Yes, you're right," she said. "Riding is my one great weakness. I think horses are nicer than people." There was a short silence, and then she said, "Back in Australia I used to ride all day. Sometimes they let me ride the boundaries. I'd take a saddlebag full of food and a blanket roll and sleep rough, maybe four or five nights at a time. It was marvelous." She stopped suddenly and looked at Henry almost apprehensively, as if afraid of having overstepped the bounds of etiquette.

"I don't suppose you get anything like that here," Henry said.

"No, but show jumping is just as fascinating in its own way. Morges is a big center, you know. People come from all over the world, all the champions. It's the main reason I stay in Geneva."

"Do you have your own horses?" Henry asked, interested.

To his surprise, Mary blushed. "I . . . that is, yes, I have a pony of my own. But I ride for other owners, too." She paused, and then said, "We seem to have got rather far away from poor John."

"There doesn't seem to be much more to say about him," said Henry. "I suppose it's no use asking you the traditional question: Did he have any enemies?"

"No use at all. I'm pretty certain he didn't. That's what makes the whole thing so mysterious, the complete lack of motive."

Henry did not reply. He was thinking, of course, of the motive supplied by the security leakage, but Mary, not being a delegate, had evidently not been told about it. To Henry the motive was only too clear. John had known too much. But what had he known, and how had he found it out? The unfinished note in the typewriter nagged at Henry's mind. Evidence was beginning to pile up now, to make sense, and Henry was forced to admit that each new piece of information led with more and more certainty toward one suspect. Himself. He felt like a fly struggling in a spider's web, and he could not see the spider's face.

He became aware of the sound of voices, and of Mary's sympathetic smile. "The others are arriving," she said. "The working day begins, whether we like it or not." And then, softly, she added "Truly, I don't believe you did it, Henry. And I really am terribly sorry about everything."

"Thank you," said Henry. "Well, here we go." He went out and down the corridor to the conference room, ridiculously happy because Mary had used his Christian name.

Lenoir and Spezzi were already sitting at the long table. Hélène Brochet was also in her place, next to a small, sharp-faced Scotsman called Mackay, who had replaced John. Marcelle had distributed the closely written pages of the new agenda, one to each delegate, and filled the glasses of water which stood like sentinels beside the snowy blotters and sharpened pencils.

Juan Moranta came in, in conversation with Zwemmer. Bill Parkington drifted into the conference room, slumped heavily into his chair without greeting anybody, and began to study the new agenda. Henry took his place at the head of the table, and glanced instinctively over to the small desk where Mary was now established with her shorthand typewriter. He looked at his watch, took a deep breath, and said, "Well, gentlemen, it is still only ten minutes to ten, but since we are all here, I think we should start at once. You will notice that the agenda has been slightly changed. In place of Item One, 'Identity Checks at Customs Posts,' we shall now be discussing the statistical analysis of relative quantities of narcotic drugs illegally introduced into the countries of Europe and North American during the period of . . ."

He heard his own voice droning on. In fact, at that moment, his mind was far away from the subcommittee. Among other things, he was wondering how Emmy was getting on.

Emmy was angry and exasperated. Full of hope, she had climbed the two steep flights of stone stairs above a furrier's shop in the Rue du Rhône, and pushed open the heavy door marked "Blanchard et Cie." Inside she had found herself facing a solid wooden counter, behind which typewriters and adding machines clicked busily. A slickly groomed young woman in a pleated skirt and white cotton blouse greeted her pleasantly.

"*Madame désire . . . ?*"

"Do you speak English?"

"Yes, madame. Can I help you?"

"It's only a small thing," said Emmy. "I wonder if you could let me have the address of Madame Novari. Her husband used to be the concierge at Five, Chemin des Chênes."

The girl's eyebrows went up a trifle. "The address of a concierge?" she repeated disdainfully.

"They left rather suddenly yesterday," said Emmy, smiling in what she hoped was an ingratiating way. "Because of an accident in the family, I understand. I would like to send them a little present."

"I see, madame. You are a tenant of Five, Chemin des Chênes?"

"No," said Emmy. She realized in time that this could be checked too easily. "No, I have been staying there with friends, and Madame Novari was always so kind and helpful. I had intended to give her something before I left."

"Would you wait a moment, madame? I will inquire."

The girl smiled encouragingly, and disappeared through a door marked "*Direction*" in gold letters. Emmy waited nervously. She was uncomfortably aware that she had not worked out her cover story in sufficient detail. Suppose they asked the name of the friends with whom she was supposed to be staying? The only residents she knew by name were the late John Trapp and Dr. Mahoumi, neither of whom seemed opportune.

Almost at once, the girl returned, smiling. "If you would care to send your gift to this office, madame, it will be forwarded directly."

"I would prefer to send it to Madame Novari in Italy," said Emmy stubbornly.

"I am afraid we never divulge the private addresses of employees, madame. It is part of the company's policy. I can assure you that your gift will be sent straight . . ."

"I see no reason to make such a mystery of it," said Emmy. In the face of the girl's relentlessly bland good humor, she felt herself growing ruffled and angry. "Why shouldn't I have the address?"

"One moment, madame."

The girl disappeared again, this time for several minutes. When she came back, her smile was as smooth as ever. "If you would give me your name, madame, and that of the friends with whom you are staying . . ."

Something prompted Emmy to counterattack. "Do you intend to give me the Novaris' address in return?" she demanded.

The girl hesitated. "Well, as a matter of fact, madame . . ."

"Do you or don't you?"

"Monsieur le Directeur would prefer to send it in a letter to you."

Emmy was cornered, and she knew it. Quickly, she said, "Oh, for heaven's sake, it's not worth all this fuss. I'll send my letter here."

The girl said again, "Your name, madame?" but Emmy was already out of the office and clattering down the spiral stone staircase. She could not make up her mind whether or not there was anything sinister in the sudden disappearance of the Novaris and the unhelpful attitude of the house agents. On the whole she was inclined to think not. The accident to Signor Novari's mother was probably one of those infuriating coincidences which happen in life, and the agents' point of view was, after all, a reasonable one. Nevertheless, this did nothing to alleviate Emmy's miserable sense of failure.

She came out into the sunshine and turned down to the riverside walk. The day stretched before her, empty and full of shadows. To shop or go to the cinema was out of the question. The very sunlight seemed hateful, and the butterfly abandon of the summer visitors, with their bright cotton dresses and happy, excited voices, was a cruel mockery of her wretchedness. Wandering by the river with no clear idea of where she wanted to go, Emmy found herself at the Jardin des Anglais, where the floral clock marked twenty-eight begonias after ten. Beyond, at the Quai Anglais, a white lake steamer was about to set off for its morning tour of the Petit Lac. On a sudden impulse, Emmy decided to board it. The fresh wind and open water seemed an attractive alternative to the claustrophobia of the city.

As she reached the gangplank, the crew were already preparing to cast off and called to her to hurry. She ran up the shaky gangway, only half aware, as she did so, of a voice behind her calling,

"Emmy! Emmy!" There was a clatter of high heels on the plank behind her, and yet more urgent shouts from the sailors. Emmy, safely on board, turned to see Annette, panting but triumphant, jumping onto the deck just as the the gangway was raised.

"Ah, Emmy, I have been looking everywhere for you. I've been to your hotel and telephoned and everything. I had quite given up hope when suddenly I saw you getting on the boat. Where are you going?"

"I've no idea," said Emmy. "It was just a mad, last-moment idea to come on board. I'm miserable and I don't know what to do with myself."

Annette nodded sympathetically. Emmy noticed how pale and ill she looked, with dark circles under her eyes. She wore no make-up except for a bright streak of lipstick, carelessly applied, and her normally immaculate hair was straggling and untidy.

"I feel just the same," said Annette. "I am supposed to be ill in bed, but I could not stay there all alone. Besides, I so much wanted to see you. This boat is a good idea. We can talk."

She took Emmy's arm and led her up to the bow of the boat, which was almost deserted, for it was a windy day. They were leaving the harbor of Geneva now, passing between the light-house and the immense white plume of the *Jet d'eau,* the huge paddles of the steamer churning the water into frothing whirl-pools. They could just hear the distant sound of laughing voices from the Lido as swimmers dived and ducked and splashed each other; in the Yacht Club harbor several small white sails scuttled busily about as a class of dinghies prepared for a race; a speed-boat screamed past with a nonchalant water-skier skimming dazzlingly in its wake. Leaning on the rail, Emmy could not help contrasting her present gloomy mood with the fun and excite-ment of her previous lake trip with Annette. She sighed and then said, "Why were you so anxious to see me?"

There was a long silence. The Swiss girl stood like a figurehead, with her long fair hair blown back from her face, gazing sight-lessly out over the deep blue water to the distant mountains. Two large tears rolled slowly down her cheeks.

"There's nobody else," she said. "I am so alone."

Emmy put an arm around her. "If you just want a shoulder to cry on," she said, "that's all right by me. I know how it some-times helps."

Without turning her head, Annette said, "I didn't think it would be so damned difficult to tell you. I'd better get it over quickly. I'm going to have a baby."

"John's?"

"Of course," said Annette quite steadily. Then all her composure suddenly drained away, and she collapsed, like a discarded marionette, onto the bench, where she buried her head in her hands and wept bitterly. Through the sobs, Emmy made out a few choked phrases in French: "What's to become of me? What will happen? What shall I do?"

At last, the paroxysm of weeping passed. Annette lifted her head, rubbed her eyes, blew her nose, and said, "I do apologize for that. It was the relief of telling somone, I suppose. I feel much better now."

"Good," said Emmy. "You poor darling. Do you want to tell me the whole story, or not?"

Annette sniffed a little, and then said, "I've been in love with John for more than two years. Ever since I first met him. We were going to get married, but then we decided to postpone it because of work. The Palais isn't keen on married couples working in the same department, and I am . . . I was going to transfer and become an interpreter. So we didn't marry. We just lived together. It was no secret; everyone knew. John kept his apartment at the Chemin des Chênes, but he hardly ever used it. Everybody knew." Annette paused, and then went on. "We were very happy. We agreed to continue the arrangement for as long as I was working, which really meant, until I became pregnant. We both wanted a child. We didn't do anything to stop it, but it never seemed to happen. Anyhow, everything was perfect until about four months ago."

"By the way," said Emmy, "what did your family think of all this? I mean, as old-established Genevese."

"They didn't know," said Annette. "My father is dead, and my mother lives in the South of France now. I've only got one sister, and she's married and in America. I'm completely on my own here."

"I see. Go on."

"Well, about four months ago, John met Natasha Hampton at a party. That was the beginning of the end. He started staying out till all hours, or not coming home at all. Finally we had a great row, and he moved back to the Chemin des Chênes. It was then that I found I was pregnant. Ironic, isn't it? The one thing we'd been hoping for all that time, and it happened too late. I told John, and I must say he was very sweet. He promised we'd get married, and that he'd never see Natasha again. But all the time I knew he was torn in half, between being happy and proud about the baby, and this other terrible thing, this witchery. It wasn't just Natasha, you see. The Hamptons took him up in a big way and introduced him into the sort of set that he and I had never dreamed of. It was a wicked thing for them to do. He couldn't keep up with them, but he hadn't the strength of character to break away. He was always short of money and he started to drink too much, and his work began to suffer. To do him credit, he did try to put a stop to it. That night when you and Henry came around and we went dancing, everything seemed to be back to normal, and I thought it would all be all right: but then a few days later we had our really monumental fight. It was about the Hamptons' party."

Annette lit a cigarette. By coincidence, the steamer was passing the Villa Trounex as she spoke. Instinctively both she and Emmy glanced across the water at the sweeping white façade of the house. The figures of two men were moving about on the terrace, but too far away for identification. Annette went on. "John hadn't told me about the party. He'd made up some excuse about having to entertain a business colleague for the evening. It was quite by chance that, after I'd dropped you that afternoon, I ran into a sweet, catty girl friend who asked me pointedly if John and I would both be at the Villa Trounex that night. It was a bitchy question, because everybody knows that I've never been there in my life. The Hamptons don't even know I exist. Anyhow, I was livid. I phoned John at the Palais, and in the end he admitted he was going there. He said he was too busy to talk, and rang off. So I went around to the Chemin des Chênes and waited for him to come in after work. I have a key to his apartment, you see. When he arrived, I delivered an ultimatum. Either he gave up this party, and Natasha, or I was finished with him. I told him not to worry about the child, I'd get an abortion. I didn't mean it. I was just mad. But then he said, 'All right. That's probably the best solution. I'm glad you're being sensible about it, because I may as well tell you that Natasha is going to divorce Paul and marry me.' "

Here Annette's voice trembled on the brink of tears again, but she pulled herself together and went on. "That was the very end. I'm afraid I got a bit hysterical. I even"—her voice dropped to a whisper—"I even said I'd kill him if he did that to me. And the awful thing is that somebody heard me."

"Mahoumi?"

"How on earth did you know? Yes, John grabbed hold of me and said, 'Shut up, you little fool. Don't you know Mahoumi can hear every word—and he's there, I came up with him in the lift.' I said I didn't care who heard, but John went and slammed the windows and then bundled me downstairs and into a taxi. I never thought that I wouldn't see him alive again."

Annette stopped talking, and looked down at the water foaming out from under the paddles. "Oh, Emmy," she said, "what am I to do?"

"The first thing," said Emmy briskly, "is to stop worrying that you'll be accused of killing John. Do you know what the weapon was?"

"He . . . he was stabbed. I didn't look. I was too upset."

"He was stabbed with a dagger from the Villa Trounex."

Annette gave a little cry. "Not . . . not the one from the library? I never recognized . . ."

She stopped suddenly and looked away. Quietly Emmy said, "Annette, I thought you said you'd never been to the Villa Trounex." There was a long silence, and then Emmy went on, "I'm not the police, Annette. I'm on your side. But I think you're silly to tell lies."

Eventually, in a small voice, Annette said, "All right. I'll tell you the truth. I did go there once. That evening. After John threw me out, I was completely distraught. I wandered about the city and had a few drinks, and then I went home and had some more, and then I thought of this crazy plan. I thought that if I went and told Paul Hampton all about John and Natasha, he'd put a stop to it, and John would have to come back to me. You can see how lunatic it was. I must have been drunk or I'd never have done it. Anyhow, I drove out to the Villa."

"What time was this?" Emmy asked. "Try to remember, because it's important."

Annette shrugged her shoulders hopelessly. "I haven't the faintest idea," she said. "It must have been fairly late. The party was in full swing. I just haven't any idea of the time."

"Oh, well," said Emmy, "never mind. Go on."

"I rang the bell and told the butler I wanted to see Mr. Hampton privately. He was pretty furious, but he couldn't actually turn me away. He showed me into the library. I was there alone for what seemed hours, though I suppose it was probably only about ten minutes in fact. I had plenty of time to study the décor,

I can assure you. That was when I noticed the dagger. The longer I waited, the soberer I got, until at last I lost my nerve completely. All I wanted to do by then was to get away, but I didn't dare go back through the house in case I met somebody. So I slipped out through the French windows into the garden. There were still quite a few people wandering about outside, but it was pretty dark, and I'm sure nobody noticed me. I nipped round to the front again, got into my car and drove home. That's all. Do you think that awful butler has told the police?"

"Did you give your name?"

"No. I refused. That didn't please him either."

"Well," said Emmy, "he's almost sure to have told the police that a strange young woman called that evening. But it seems that nobody except me knows who it was."

"Nobody must ever know," said Annette. "Nobody. Ever."

Nine

The morning session of the subcommittee dragged interminably on toward the midday recess. The atmosphere in the conference room was strained and uneasy, and anger flared like spurts of magnesium flame around the table. Bill Parkington became engaged in a bitter wrangle with Jacques Lenoir on a complicated point concerning the legal powers of excise authorites, and, when Lenoir attempted to relieve the tension with a mild witticism, accused the Frenchman of not taking his job seriously. Zwemmer, who was known to have strong Left Wing views, made a reference to Secret Police methods ("happily long since outlawed in my country, but still prevailing in some more southerly parts of Europe"), which Moranta chose to interpret as a slighting reference to the political system of his own country. Spezzi, who had no love for Zwemmer, championed Moranta and demanded an apology, while Lenoir showed signs of wishing to relate the whole discussion to the question of Algeria. The meeting began to assume a dangerously political air, and it was all that Henry could do to drag it back into more seemly channels. Even when he had succeeded in doing so, feathers remained ruffled and tempers frayed.

This was not surprising, considering the atmosphere of tension and suspicion engendered by the double menace of the murder and the security leakage. Henry found himself agreeing wholeheartedly with Mary's outburst that morning. It was impossible to work under these conditions. His own position was particularly unenviable, for he could not but be aware that a great measure of suspicion was directed against him. Both Lenoir and Moranta, it was clear, considered that he should be under arrest already. Parkington seemed to be making an effort to be impartial, but Henry could feel that all his tendencies were toward what he had called "the other camp." Only Spezzi supported Henry loyally. As for Zwemmer, he was as baffling and unreadable as ever.

By noon Henry felt exhausted. He closed the meeting, arranged for the delegates to reassemble at three o'clock, and walked out of the conference room, only to be told by Marcelle that Inspector Colliet wished to see him immediately.

Colliet was waiting in the rest room of the original suite of offices, to which Henry was admitted only after the most careful scrutiny. The Inspector looked tired and harassed, and Henry guessed that he had had little sleep since their last encounter. At his elbow was an ash tray piled high with cigarette butts, and as Henry came in he was lighting up yet another mentholated cigarette from a green and white packet. In front of him on the desk was a thick dossier full of typewritten sheets, the transcripts, Henry presumed, of Colliet's interviews of the previous day. Henry looked longingly at it, like a hungry dog in a butcher's shop. Colliet observed this, smiled a little grimly, and moved the dossier out of Henry's reach.

"I am sorry to have to take up more of your valuable time, Inspector Tibbett," he said, "but I think that our talk today should be more profitable than that of yesterday. For instance, we can now speak freely of this leakage of secret information from your conference."

"Yes," said Henry blandly.

"Please tell me what you know about it."

"I know nothing, except that Mr. Parkington told me about it, in confidence, as I thought, at Paul Hampton's party."

"Why do you say 'as I thought'?"

"Because it now appears that other people may have known. Parkington did not tell anybody else outright, but it seems that he was not very adept at concealing the truth from anyone who wished to dig a little for it."

"How do you know this?"

"From Spezzi, who tells me that he gleaned the information from Parkington in the cloakroom yesterday morning; but you must know all this."

Colliet smiled. "It is most interesting, coming from you, Inspector," he said. "Can we now go back to Mr. Hampton's party?

Parkington tells you of the leakage. What then?"

"Parkington implied to me that he suspected John Trapp, quoting as his only supporting evidence the fact that Trapp had belonged to the Communist Party as an undergraduate. This seemed to me to be irrelevant and unjust. However, I felt I could not refuse to make some further inquiries. I was chiefly concerned with clearing Trapp from suspicion. I agreed to speak to him the following day."

"One moment, Inspector. Could anybody have overheard this conversation of yours with Parkington?"

Henry frowned. "I don't think so," he said. "I suppose one can never be one hundred per cent sure, but we started talking down by the harbor, and then walked up the lawns, and there was nobody else near us. I would say you could rule out the possibility."

"So. You tell me all this, and yet you maintain that you had no appointment with Trapp?"

"I had no appointment."

"I see." Colliet took a deep pull on his cigarette, and leaned back in his chair. Henry waited for the inevitable cliché. Out it came. "Would it surprise you to know, Inspector, that we are now virtually certain that Trapp was responsible for the security leak?"

"Yes," said Henry. "It would."

"You think that he was killed because he knew the name of the traitor and was about to divulge it. We are convinced that he was killed because he was a traitor himself, and was about to confess. You should be pleased, Inspector. Our hypothesis makes your own position considerably easier."

"Thank you," said Henry. "I'm glad to hear it, but I can't agree with you. Would it be asking too much for you to tell me how you have worked out your theory?"

"Trapp," Colliet said slowly, "had been receiving large sums of money in cash recently, notably since the start of the conference. Clandestine money, evidently. We found it hidden in various places in his apartment, in notes of large denomination, whereas his bank account contained a mere three hundred francs. We also know that he was anxious to obtain money for personal reasons. The pattern hangs together and makes sense."

"To whom do you think he was selling his information?" Henry asked.

Colliet shrugged. "That is another matter. He was almost certainly approached by somebody in the social circle to which he had recently been introduced. You would be surprised how many impecunious aristocrats get involved as contacts in this sort of thing. Mostly women."

Henry suddenly remembered the girl called Sophie. The line of thought was disquieting. "Very well," he said. "Suppose, and I'm only supposing, that you are right so far. How do you explain what happened next?"

"It is easy enough for me to explain," said Colliet. "It is you, Inspector, who are being deliberately unhelpful, if you will forgive my saying so. Perhaps you have reasons of your own. I am hoping, however, that this may change your mind."

In his usual manner of the conjurer producing a hard-boiled egg from an unsuspecting victim's ear, Colliet whipped out a telegram and handed it to Henry. It was quite short, and merely stated that Inspector Tibbett should give all possible assistance to the Swiss Police, and place any information he had at their disposal. It was signed by the Assistant Commissioner at Scotland Yard.

Colliet gave Henry time to read and digest it, and then said, "Now, Inspector, will you not admit to me frankly that you know Trapp was selling information."

"No," said Henry.

"But why not?"

"Because it isn't true," said Henry wearily. "All right. Go on. Let's hear your version."

Colliet closed his eyes. "You found out that Trapp was responsible for the security leak," he said. "You arranged to meet him yesterday morning; there is little point in denying it. The note in your pocket, which is undoubtedly in Trapp's handwriting, makes it a certainty. I think myself that, as a fellow Englishman, you wished to give Trapp every opportunity of doing the honorable thing, and confessing. You made the purpose of the meeting quite clear. Whatever you said to him, it was effective. Trapp was not at heart a bad man, and was desperately unhappy about what he was doing; only the strongest possible emotional reasons had forced him into treachery. He resolved to take your advice and make a full confession. This explains a curious inconsistency in the note which we found in the typewriter. Apparently the interview had been of your seeking. Yet in the letter he wrote ". . . what I wish to say to you . . ." as though the initiative had been his."

"I wondered when you'd notice that," said Henry.

"You did?" Colliet blew a perfect smoke ring. "Well, that is my reconstruction of the situation at nine o'clock yesterday morning. But we are leaving out of our calculations another character. The murderer."

"I'm glad we're getting around to him at last," said Henry.

"The murderer," said Colliet impressively, dropping into the historical present, "overhears, or is told by Mr. Parkington, during the party at the Villa Trounex, that Trapp is under suspicion and will be questioned by you in the morning. He resolves that Trapp must die before he can open his mouth. The murderer steals the dagger, but finds no opportunity of killing Trapp that night, since Mrs. Hampton drives him home. So it must be done early next morning. The murderer arrives here at the Palais with the dagger, and stabs Trapp before he has a chance to speak to you."

"That's ridiculous," said Henry. "If your mythical murderer is a member of the subcommittee, then he or she can't possibly be the person to whom Trapp was selling information. Because the murderer has access to just as much information as Trapp, if not more."

"True," said Colliet. "Had it not occurred to you, however, that the security leak might have involved not one person alone, but a couple, working together?"

This came so close to Henry's own idea that he was momentarily taken aback, and said nothing. "Trapp may confess if he likes," Colliet went on with a fine sense of drama, "but if his confession is going to involve a delegate, what then?"

"It certainly sounds more plausible," Henry answered cautiously.

"It will almost certainly have been a double job," Colliet added. "Trapp was not on duty the entire time, nor, as an interpreter, did he receive complete transcripts of the meetings. He needed the co-operation of a delegate or a member of the secretarial staff. And this second person is the murderer." Colliet paused. "All this, Inspector, is what I should like to think, for it would exonerate you from any breath of suspicion. But"—he suddenly tipped his chair forward and glared at Henry out of his tired gray eyes— "but, Inspector, I do not believe for a moment that what I have just outlined to you is the truth."

"Really?" said Henry, taken aback and a little rattled. "I thought you said . . ."

"How can I believe this story," cried Colliet, "when you refuse to confirm it at any point? When you deny knowing about Trapp's treachery, let alone making an appointment with him? When, having made the appointment, you fail to turn up for it? Why should you behave in such a way? Why should you lie to us? And what is more, we have a most enlightening testimony here from Mlle. Delacroix." He opened the dossier and took out a piece of paper. "She was in the ladies' cloakroom combing her hair at the time of the murder. The door was slightly open, and in the mirror she could see the door of the office. She states positively that nobody went near that door until you went in there, just after Mr. Trapp stopped typing." Colliet leaned forward. "There is only one logical explanation for all this, Inspector. You must be the second person, and you killed John Trapp."

Now that the words were said at last, both Henry and Colliet experienced a curious sense of shock which made it impossible for either of them to speak. The accusation hovered in the air, ricocheted off the white walls, and spun mothlike, an inaudible echo, around the opaque glass lamp in the ceiling.

At last Henry managed to say, as steadily as he could, "Does that mean that you are arresting me?"

"No, no!" Colliet jumped up and took Henry's arm. "My dear Inspector, forgive me. I was perhaps carried away by my own thoughts. I should not have said such a thing. Nevertheless, you do see what I mean? I have done everything possible to avoid coming to this conclusion. I am still not at it, not by any means. Just a word from you, an explanation, a little frankness, and all would become clear, I am sure. Mlle. Delacroix may well have been mistaken. However, if by tomorrow things are not further elucidated . . ." He squeezed Henry's arm. "I am sure you have good reasons for your reticence. But I beg you to overcome them. It would indeed be a painful step if I were forced to . . . well, let us not even think about such a disaster. Consider, I beg you, Inspector. Reflect. Help me."

Colliet sat down again and mopped his brow. Henry felt genuinely sorry for the little man.

"Inspector Colliet," he said, "I don't envy you your position, and I'm sure you don't envy me mine. I assure you that I'm as eager to find the truth as you are, and that I'm not keeping anything from you. If the case against me looks black, it is because somebody has taken pains that it should. Why they picked on me, heaven knows. Perhaps just chance, or perhaps real animosity. In any case it's clear that I was chosen as what the Americans call the fall guy. You've swallowed it, hook, line, and sinker, and I don't really blame you. It's up to me to get myself out of this mess, and I intend to do so. May I go and have some lunch now?"

Colliet raised his hand in a tired gesture of acquiescence. At the door, Henry said, "Tell me just one thing. How long have I got?"

"What do you mean?"

"You know very well. How long have I got, before . . ."

There was a long pause. Colliet fiddled with his yellow pencil. At last he said, "All this is quite . . . the Chief of Police has not been . . . that is, no specific time . . . hm . . . that is to say . . . two more days."

"Thank you," said Henry. And, hoping he looked braver than he felt, he walked out of the suite of offices and took the lift to the restaurant.

There are two restaurants at the Palais des Nations. On the ground floor, the cafeteria runs the length of the central building, with a wall of glass giving onto green lawns and the great golden sphere which symbolizes the fellowship of the nations. Here polyglot queues of delegates and staff line up at the long counters to buy an excellent and inexpensive meal. Those feeling more affluent, however, can take the lift to the eighth floor, where a full-scale restaurant operates, with white-coated waiters and a roof-top terrace overlooking the city, the lake, and the mountains. Henry, who felt the need to pamper himself a little, took the lift to the eighth floor.

The restaurant was crowded. Over the cheerful clatter of cutlery, voices eddied in a clamor of tongues—precise French, measured English, emphatic German, melodious Italian, and the liquid flow of the Arab and Indian languages.

"Vous êtes seul, monsieur?" The *maître d'hôtel* hovered, apologetically. "I am afraid there is no table. If Monsieur would agree to share?"

At a table in the window, Henry saw Helène Brochet sitting alone. "I'll go over there," he said.

He walked up to the table, and said, "Do you mind if I join you, Mlle. Brochet? There doesn't seem to be a table free."

"Please do, Inspector." Helène looked up briefly, then went back to her copy of *Le Canard Enchaîné.* Henry, feeling snubbed, sat down and ordered rather too lavish a meal.

He ate in silence, considering Helène Brochet. It was appropriate, he felt, that she should be associated with Konrad Zwemmer, for both were people of reserve and a certain mystery. Her dark head was bent now over her paper, and if the witticisms of *Le Canard* appealed to her sense of humor, she did not show it. Her face was grave and unsmiling as she turned the pages. Henry sought vainly for a conversational opening, and was glad when Helène suddenly folded her newspaper, looked at him, and said, "This conference has turned out rather strangely, hasn't it, Inspector?"

"That's putting it mildly," said Henry.

There was a little pause, and then Helène said, "Did you kill John Trapp?"

The question was so direct and so unexpected that for a moment Henry felt at a loss. He hoped that he achieved the minimum possible hesitation before replying, "No."

Helène nodded slowly. "That's what I keep telling Konrad," she said.

"Does he think I did it?" It sounded to Henry's own ears a silly question, but it was the first of many that rose to his mind.

Helène considered it coolly. "He is just as much in the dark as anybody," she said. "He regards Trapp's death as a great nuisance."

"Oh, does he?" said Henry, nettled. "Not as a tragedy, by any chance?"

"No," said Helène. "A nuisance."

Henry controlled his temper with an effort. "You've known Zwemmer for quite some time, haven't you?" he said.

Helène smiled slightly. "Oh, yes. Many years now. Whenever he is in Geneva, he stays with my mother and me."

The thought of Helène Brochet living with her mother was somehow surprising. Henry said, "And I suppose you knew John Trapp pretty well too."

"We were colleagues," said Helène. "Outside the Palais I did not know him."

"You realize, I suppose," said Henry, "that I had no appointment with him yesterday morning?"

"You didn't?" Helène seemed genuinely astonished. "But Mary said . . ."

Stabbing in the dark, Henry said, "The appointment was faked by a girl who called on John Trapp early yesterday morning with a message purporting to come from me. Fortunately, the concierge remembers her."

"The concierge . . . at the Chemin des Chênes?" Helène was patently taken aback. She went very white and sat quite still. Then she said, "Excuse me a moment," got up, and walked out of the restaurant.

Henry's impulse to follow her was thwarted by the arrival of a *corps de ballet* of waiters, intent on preparing the elaborate *crêpes suzette* which Henry had rashly ordered. This was fortunate, however, for second thoughts dictated that, for the moment, it was better to sit tight and let events come to him. Without doubt, he had thrown a disturbing pebble into still, deep waters. The repercussions would surely follow. The waiters pranced and pirouetted around the sacred flame of the metho burner, the butter sizzled and the liqueurs flamed. Henry did not even glance toward the door.

He was digging appreciatively into his fourth crêpe when, without surprise, he saw Helène returning. She sat down.

"I had to make a telephone call," she said. She glanced at her watch. "It is still only two o'clock. Are you busy, Inspector, or could we have a talk, somewhere a little more private?"

"With pleasure," said Henry. He finished the last crêpe with regret. "Where do you suggest?"

"We could take a walk in the grounds," said Helène. "After all, it is a beautiful day."

Quite a few other people seemed to have the same idea. The green lawns were scattered with strolling or basking toilers for international friendship, their blandishments haughtily ignored by posses of splendidly strutting peacocks, who resented this noonday intrusion on their domain. Henry noticed Mary Benson walking by herself on the white marble terrace. Bill Parkington and Juan Moranta strode past, deep in conversation. Jacques Lenior, wasting no time, was steering Marcelle, the new secretary, down a leafy alley.

Helène led the way in silence until they came to a stone bench under a cedar tree. "This will do," she said. She sat down, a serious and shadowy figure in her severe black linen dress.

Henry sat beside her. "Well?" he said.

"Please," said Helène, "tell me all that you know."

"My dear girl, what a ridiculous request," said Henry reasonably. "I have no idea of your position, of whose side you are on, or of how much you know yourself. For me this is a very serious matter indeed."

"For me, too," said Helène. "But I appreciate your point of view. That is why I have decided to trust you. For a start, I will tell you that I know about the leakage of secret information, and I believe that John Trapp was responsible for it. May we talk about that?"

"Not," Henry said cautiously, "until I know just why you are so interested in it."

"I am afraid that is my affair."

"Then," said Henry, "this conversation is clearly pointless. You said you were prepared to trust me. With what?"

There was a little pause, and then Helène said, "Konrad is especially concerned with the security leak. He believes that certain acquaintances of Trapp's outside the Palais may have been bringing pressure to bear on him. Now that he is dead, the chances of finding out more are becoming very remote. We need every scrap of information we can get. Surely you see that?"

"I see several things. I see that you know very much more than one would expect of someone in your position, and I see that you are trying to pump me for information without giving anything away yourself. Let me ask you some questions for a change. For example, how did you know where John Trapp lived?"

"It is so unusual that I should?"

"You said you had never met him outside work," said Henry, "yet you knew his address, and his circle of acquaintances."

"Natasha Hampton and John—that is common gossip."

"I don't think so."

"What do you know about it?"

"John's friendship with the Hamptons, and his mixing with a rich and aristocratic circle—these were matters of common gossip, perhaps. But why did you specifically mention Natasha?"

Helène shrugged. "Rumors get around," she said. "Natasha is a dangerous woman, chiefly because she is silly. She also has some curious friends. This is a strange city, Inspector. A crossroads for many people, with many interests, both international and personal. It is always potentially dangerous for a naïve young man like John Trapp to dabble his fingers in those waters."

"And what about a naïve young man like Konrad Zwemmer?"

Helène was silent. She lit a cigarette slowly and deliberately. "You say that the concierge recognized the girl who brought the note to John Trapp?" she said, almost to herself.

"The concierge's wife," Henry amended.

"She identified her?"

"She would know her again."

"Who was it?"

"I am beginning to think," said Henry, "that it must have been you."

Helène looked at him sharply. "So you don't know?" she said.

"I don't know," said Henry, "because the concierge and his wife left suddenly for Italy before I had time to . . ."

For the first time since they had come into the gardens, Helène smiled. "The organization is very good," she said.

"That's what I think," said Henry.

"Nevertheless, Italy is not so far away. There must be some means of contacting . . ."

"I'm doing my best," said Henry. "The matter is in hand."

"Inspector Tibbett," said a sweet, clear voice above Henry's head, "could I bother you for a moment?"

Henry looked up, straight into Mary Benson's blue eyes. There was a movement beside him, as Helène stood up. She was patently furious. Henry had read in books of characters who smoldered with rage, but never before had he received that impression at close quarters. He drew back instinctively, as though scorched.

"I was just going," said Helène, in a voice that would have chipped granite. "I have work to do. I did enjoy our lunch, Inspector." She looked at Mary and simmered. "It is so seldom that one can find a moment of peace in this place. I will see you at three."

With that she turned and walked quickly away toward the Palais, her stiletto heels making tiny dagger holes in the soft path. Mary watched her go with exaggerated innocence.

"What's the matter with her?" she said.

"You know very well," said Henry. "You broke up a tête-à-tête, and you did it deliberately."

He grinned at her happily, feeling wonderfully relaxed and at his ease. Mary grinned back, and dropped on to the bench beside him.

"Guilty," she said. "I'm sorry. I haven't really anything special to talk to you about."

"I'm flattered," said Henry.

Mary's face grew suddenly grave. "The fact is," she said, "I know I've no right to say this to you, but I couldn't help overhearing a little, and . . . oh, please, Henry, do be careful. You've no idea . . . I mean, people aren't always what they seem, you know."

"I do know," said Henry. "The trouble is, you can't find anything out without giving away a certain amount in exchange."

"That's the hell of it," Mary said somberly.

"I gather that you neither like nor trust Helène Brochet."

Mary went slightly pink. "I've no business to say anything against her," she said. "I don't know her very well. It's just that . . ."

"That what?"

"Just something I feel, without any proof. I'm certain Helène isn't just an ordinary interpreter. I don't know what else she is, but in your position I think you should be careful."

"Don't worry," said Henry. "I'm almost excessively cautious by nature. Do you think," he added, "that we could persuade a peacock to accept that rather moth-eaten bun that somebody has left by the fountain?"

"I doubt it," said Mary, "but we could try."

At three o'clock precisely, the subcommittee resumed its session.

"I propose," said Henry, "that, in view of the very unusual circumstances surrounding this conference, we should agree not to meet tomorrow morning. This will give me time to rearrange the agenda in the light of certain recent developments. I feel sure, also, that delegates will welcome the opportunity of catching up on the heavy amount of paper work which has inevitably accumulated." Across the room, he caught Mary's eyes. She gave him the trace of a smile. She had already promised to meet him at eleven o'clock in the morning and drive out into the country for a picnic lunch.

"And now, gentlemen, I believe that Signor Spezzi has a statement to make on the analysis of the figures which we discussed this morning."

To Alfredo's surprise, Henry accompanied this remark with a broad grin, which he found himself quite unable to suppress. His heart was soaring like a gas-filled balloon, and, as far as he was concerned, Colliet and his merry men could go and jump in the lake, taking the murder, the Narcotics Conference, the Hamptons, and the security leak with them. In fact, he was in a very dangerous state of mind indeed.

Ten

Henry arrived back at the Hotel Étoile that evening still enveloped in the euphoric haze of the afternoon. Consequently it was with a sense of irritation that he listened to Emmy's dismal recital of her day of woe, beginning with her failure at Blanchard et Cie, and going on to the sad tale of Annette Delacroix. He was even less pleased to hear that Emmy had invited Annette to dine with them.

"She'd probably much rather be alone," he said. He was standing in front of the long mirror in their bedroom, wearing a red paisley dressing gown, and trying to convince himself he looked younger than his forty-five years. "Now I suppose we'll have her weeping into her soup all the evening."

"Don't be so mean," Emmy called from the bathroom. "How could we possibly leave the poor girl alone at a time like this?"

"I should have thought we had enough troubles of our own," said Henry.

Emmy came to the bathroom door, swathed in a huge white towel, and looked at him contritely. "Oh, darling, I'm sorry. Somehow this awful mess that Annette is in almost made me forget. Of course, I know you're worried and wretched, and I am too, but I thought it might take our minds off it."

Henry felt a pang of guilt. Since lunchtime he had hardly worried at all. He turned to Emmy. "You'll have to forgive me," he said. "I'm a bit on edge. I saw Colliet again today, and it seems we haven't much time. No, you're quite right. It'll do us both good to take Annette out."

Emmy smiled her relief. "I'm so glad you feel that way. And

anyway, I must confess that I wasn't entirely disinterested when I asked her."

"What do you mean?"

"Didn't you listen when I was telling you what she said?"

"Of course," said Henry untruthfully.

"You can't have, not properly. Henry, she has a key to John's apartment."

"By this time the police will surely have . . ."

"The police don't know. They didn't even ask her."

"You mean that we could . . . ?"

"Why not?" Emmy was bubbling with enthusiasm. "After dinner we'll get Annette to take us there. They surely won't have a guard on it still. It isn't as though John were killed there, and they must have taken away anything they need by now."

"That's the trouble," said Henry, "There won't be anything interesting left."

"You can't be sure. Maybe they're not looking for the same things as we are. They've been trying to find proof that John was selling information. We're trying to prove that he wasn't, so that we can find out who really was. Surely it's worth a try."

"I hope to God we don't get caught," said Henry, but in spite of himself he felt a rising excitement.

"Caught? At what? Annette has a key; she has a perfect right to be there, and to take us in if she wants to."

"I doubt if Colliet would look at it like that," said Henry. "Still, it's worth a try. You never know."

They met Annette at half past seven. Henry was relieved to find that, far from weeping into her soup, she had recovered herself remarkably well, and was making a great effort to be cheerful and natural. They had a delicious dinner in a dark-paneled restaurant in the old town, and over coffee Henry tentatively broached the idea of a visit to 5, Chemin des Chênes. To his surprise Annette agreed at once.

"I'm so glad you suggested it," she said. "You see, I want to go there myself, and I dreaded having to do it alone."

"You want to go there? Why?"

"There are some things . . . some purely personal things," said Annette mysteriously. She looked at her watch. "It's half past nine. That's a good time to go. With any luck the Novaris will be out watching television in the café next door."

"The Novaris aren't there any more," said Henry. And he explained about the concierge's sudden departure.

"Oh, well, so much the better," said Annette. "The new concierge won't recognize me."

"Do you know Dr. Mahoumi?" Henry asked.

"The little lawyer next door? Not really. I saw him once or twice. He moved in just about the time that John and I"—her voice quavered a little, but recovered—"that we quarreled. It would be better if he didn't see or hear us."

"Amen," said Henry fervently.

Luck was with them at the Chemin des Chênes. They parked the tiny Citroën in a small street at the back of the block, and walked around to the front door. The concierge's flat was dark, there were no gendarmes in sight, and the foyer was deserted. From the pavement outside, Henry saw a light burning in Dr. Mahoumi's apartment, but he reckoned that this was a risk which would have to be taken.

They went up in the lift. On the sixth floor Annette produced a key ring from her bag, selected a silver Yale key, and quietly opened the door of John Trapp's apartment.

"Wait here," she whispered. The door shut silently behind them, and Henry and Emmy stood quite still in the warm darkness of the hall. Emmy groped for Henry's hand. "It's creepy," she whispered.

Henry said nothing. He was watching Annette, as she moved across the living room, silhouetted against the pale glimmer of light from the window. Clearly she knew every inch of the apartment. Without a trace of hesitation, she went to the window and lowered the Venetian blinds, taking great care that they made no noise. Then, equally cautiously, she pulled the heavy blue curtains. The darkness was now complete, except for the faint rectangle of grayness which was the doorway to the kitchen. The shadow which was Annette moved into the kitchen, and there was a faint swish as the curtains there were closed, obliterating the last trace of light. In pitch blackness, Henry heard Annette moving again, quietly and surely, and a moment later the room sprang into sight as she switched on a darkly shaded table lamp in a far corner.

"I daren't put on any more light," said Annette quietly. "I don't think this can possibly show from outside. And all the windows are shut, so we can't be heard next door if we speak softly. Come in."

John Trapp's living room was in marked contrast to Dr. Mahoumi's. Where the latter was cluttered with Oriental knickknacks, this room was as austere as a Spartan hut. The only items of furniture were a blue-covered divan, a table and two upright chairs, a severe tallboy, a bookcase and a roll-top desk. The whole place had the air of a pied-à-terre, a hotel room rather than a home. This tallied with Annette's remark that John had virtually ceased to live there, and had only moved back within the last few weeks. Everything was spotlessly clean and tidy, evidence, Henry suspected, of the ministrations of a *femme de ménage,* who must have completed her work before the arrival of the gendarmes the day before. It was hard to imagine Natasha Hampton in this room; the thought was somehow distasteful. Henry dismissed it, and turned to look at the bookcase.

This gave the only available clue to the personality of the late tenant. Left-wing political books in English, French, and Spanish predominated, together with histories and biographies. There was a weighty selection of works on economics, several handbooks on the technique of playing bridge, and a half a shelf of back numbers of *Encounter.* The only light reading was a dogeared pile of detective stories in English and French.

Annette followed Henry's eyes, and smiled sadly. "Yes," she said, "he was always a serious one. Before, I mean. I don't think he ever read a novel. The detective stories don't count. He said he used them for mental gymnastics, like crossword puzzles."

"I do the same myself," said Henry with a smile. He went over to the desk.

"It's locked," said Annette. "I haven't got a key."

"Then I imagine we're wasting our time here."

Annette smiled. "Oh, no," she said. "You see, he didn't keep the most important things in the desk. He had a secret hiding place for them. I don't mean that he really had anything to hide, but he used to keep some emergency money there, and one other thing. That's what I've come to get. I hope the police haven't found it."

"They've combed the place pretty thoroughly," said Henry, "I can't believe they'd have missed anything."

"We'll see," said Annette, and she went into the kitchen and opened the oven door of the electric stove. "John never cooked at home," she said, "except to boil an egg or make a cup of coffee. He said this was a perfect hiding place."

As far as Henry could see, the oven was empty, but, as he watched, Annette took out the floor which covered the electric elements. Under it was a large Manila envelope. She gave a tiny sigh of satisfaction as she took it out.

Nobody spoke as Annette came back into the living room, opened the envelope, and spread its contents on the table, but Henry saw her eyes widen in incredulity. Hardly breathing, she counted out fifteen crackling thousand-franc notes, and stared at them unbelievingly. Then, in a whisper, she said, "But where did it come from? What does it mean?"

"That's a lot of money," said Henry. "Over a thousand pounds."

"It's not possible," said Annette. "He never had that amount of money. He was always hard-up. He used to keep two hundred francs there in the oven, in case of emergencies. But all this . . ." She seemed utterly confused, and near to tears.

"What," said Henry, "is the other thing that John kept in the oven?"

"His will." Annette could hardly speak. "He told me to come and get it if anything happened to him, and to take it to his lawyers. I don't know why, but he wouldn't keep it in the bank. It's here."

With shaking fingers she pulled a paper out of the envelope and handed it to Henry. It was an ordinary, printed will form, dated a year previously, and it directed, quite simply, that all his possessions without exception should go to Mlle. Annette Delacroix. That was not all, however. Pinned to the back of the will was another paper, written in John's characteristic scrawl, and this Henry read with increasing discomfort. For it was the draft of a new will. It was scribbled in pencil, with many erasures; clearly, John had had some difficulty in framing the exact provisions which he wished to incorporate into it, for it was more complicated than its predecessor. To Annette Delacroix, it seemed, he wished to leave the money in his current bank account, his furniture and personal effects and the proceeds from a small life insurance policy, as well as "any other objects [car? boat?] I may die posessed of." The draft then went on: "Any other monies whatsoever in my possession at the time of my death, I give and bequeath to Madame Natasha Hampton, of Villa Trounex, Geneva." Below this was scribbled, "See Mahoumi about this, 6 p.m.," and a date. The date of the day on which John had died.

Silently Henry handed this piece of paper to Annette. She looked at it in a sort of dazed incomprehension. "What does it mean?" she said. Her eyes were riveted to the pile of notes on the table.

"It means," said Henry, "That you are undoubtedly the legal owner of that money. That, and quite a lot more, I imagine. Colliet spoke of John receiving large amounts, and he didn't know about this little lot. It also means that if John had lived until today, you'd only have got the three hundred francs in his current account. All this would have gone to Natasha."

Annette said nothing, but closed her eyes and swayed, as if she would faint. Instinctively, Emmy held out a hand to her. The three of them stood there silently around the table in the half-light, like celebrants of some pagan ritual. The moment was shattered by the sudden, imperious ringing of the telephone.

For some reason Henry found this more macabre than anything which had gone before. There was something obscene about the shrilling of a dead man's telephone, especially in the presence of the living. Henry stepped quietly up to the phone. He let it ring until the moment when the caller might reasonably have given up hope of an answer. Then, between rings, he lifted it and held it to his ear.

Immediately a sweet, husky voice said in French, "Ah, John. Here is Sophie. Thank goodness I've found you. I've been trying to get you since yesterday. I did as you said, John, and I can't stand it. It's terrible out here in the country with nothing, no papers, no radio, no anything. I must come back. I have to see you. What are you doing tomorrow? John, I said . . . John, are you there? What's happening? John . . ."

Very gently Henry replaced the receiver.

Annette was still standing by the table, like a statue. She did not even ask about the telephone call. All she said was, "Henry, you must help me. What shall I do now?"

Briskly, Henry said, "Put all that stuff back into the envelope and replace it in the oven. First thing in the morning, go down to the lake and throw your key to this apartment into the deepest water you can reach. Then get hold of John's lawyer, the one who drew up the original will, and go with him to the police. Tell them about the secret hiding place, and come along here with them to find the envelope. Please God they don't fingerprint it. I'll do my best to wipe the papers clean, but both our prints must be everywhere. Then, if you have any sense, retain the lawyer to represent you, because you'll be in a very tricky position indeed."

Emmy said, protestingly, "Henry," but he gave her a sharp

look, and she was silent.

Steadily, Annette said, "Yes, Henry."

"Now let's go."

Swiftly and systematically, Henry wiped the notes and documents with his handkerchief, and carefully replaced them in the envelope. Then he said to Annette, "Now, put your gloves on and put this back where you found it."

"I haven't got any. I never wear them in the summer."

"Then hold it in your handkerchief, and wipe the handle of the oven door carefully and anywhere else where you might have left prints. Then turn out the light and pull back the curtains and we'll be off."

Like a sleepwalker, Annette did as she was told. In the darkness Henry listened at the front door. There was no sound from outside, except for the faint strains of a radio playing somewhere below. He opened the door gingerly, and they all stepped out into the rubber-floored corridor.

"Get the lift," whispered Henry. His eye was on Dr. Mahoumi's door. "Get into it and hold the door open for me. I can't close this wretched door without making a noise."

Again, their luck was in, for the lift was already at the landing. Emmy opened the doors, and she and Annette went inside. Henry pulled the door of John Trapp's apartment shut behind him. As he had foreseen, the lock made a loud and unmistakable noise as it clicked into position. Henry was down the corridor in two strides, but he had barely reached the lift before the door of Dr. Mahoumi's flat opened.

The lift door swung to, and Emmy's finger was already on the button, but in the seconds that it took the lift to gather speed, Henry had time to see, through the glass panel of the door, that Dr. Mahoumi was standing on the threshold of his flat, looking about him in inquisitive bafflement. This was not surprising. What was surprising was that he was not alone. Standing just behind him in the doorway was Konrad Zwemmer.

In the lift, Henry said to Annette, "Is there a way out of this building other than the front door?"

Annette thought for a moment, and then said, "Yes. We can go down to the basement and out through the garage."

"Good," said Henry. "We'll do that. Mahoumi will certainly be watching the front door from his window. Lucky we parked the car at the back."

They drove home in oppressive silence. As the Citroën drew

up outside the hotel, Henry said to Annette, "Now, remember what I told you. Tell the police the truth, for God's sake. Don't try to deny you were at the Villa Trounex. Tell them about the baby—they'll have to know sooner or later. Tell them you used to have a key to the apartment, but that you've lost it. By tomorrow that will be strictly true. If you can, be surprised at the amount of money in the apartment. They may believe you. Good luck, Annette."

"Thank you, Henry," said Annette.

Later, in their room, Emmy said, "Henry, why were you so beastly to Annette? The poor girl."

"I was beastly," said Henry, "because it was the only thing to be. Look at it this way. Annette is either innocent or guilty. If she's innocent, the shock of what she discovered this evening might easily have made her hysterical. The only thing was to be firm and a bit brutal. If she's guilty, well, not only does she deserve no sympathy, but she's been extremely clever. She's put me in one hell of a spot."

"How?"

"By deliberately arranging that you and I should be there, at our own request, when she opened that envelope. First, if she'd gone there alone and been caught, it would have been serious for her. As it was, she could have said truthfully that we'd asked her to take us. And then she may have wanted an audience for her little "Oh-help-what-have-we-here?" act when she found the money; not an impersonal, efficient audience of lawyers and policemen in broad daylight, but an emotional, suggestible audience in a dimly lit room. Then there's an even more sinister thought. How do we know she's not going to tell the police all about our asking to be taken to the apartment, and pretend that I found the money and will completely by chance? Or worse, by design? You notice how she handed the papers to me to get my prints on them? It's perfectly easy for her now to go to the police about that money, but still deny that she knew about it before John died."

Emmy sat down on the bed. "I can't believe it of Annette," she said. "After all, she didn't plan any of this. I asked her to dinner, and you suggested going to the Chemin des Chênes."

"Annette," said Henry, "made the most determined effort to find you this morning when she was supposed to be ill in bed. She carefully told you she had a key to the apartment. I'm prepared to bet she angled for the dinner invitation. Now, be honest.

Didn't she?"

"Well, yes, I suppose so. In a way."

"If we hadn't risen to the bait and suggested going to the flat, she would have, you can be sure. Of course, you may be right, and she may be as innocent as the air. But on the other hand, things do add up. What was she doing, alone in John's apartment, on the evening before he died? She knew the hiding place. She was furious with John, and she needed money for herself and the child. Supposing she had found the money and the new will draft? She wouldn't dare steal the money, for John would have known at once who had taken it. So she suddenly decides to go to the Villa Trounex and see Paul Hampton. It's far more plausible that her visit had to do with the money, rather than with John's physical infidelity. But while she was waiting for Paul, she saw the dagger, and had a much simpler idea. If John should die before he could change his will, she would get the cash he had hoarded up, presumably for his elopement with Natasha. And remember, Annette is one of the very few people who could have killed John. She was alone in the cloakroom."

"You told me," said Emmy, "that she was so distraught that you couldn't believe she'd killed him. Anyway, she was in love with him."

"Wait a moment," said Henry. "Remember my original idea of a conspiracy."

"What about it?"

"We've been considering a partnership over the security leak," said Henry. "But there are other kinds of partnership. Supposing this wasn't John's baby at all? Supposing Annette had another boy friend, and simply wanted John's money. The boy friend kills John, and Annette covers up for him by watching the office door and swearing that nobody went in there except me. But Annette only thinks that John is to be threatened, not killed. That's why she breaks down."

"That's all very well, but who could this boy friend possibly be?"

Henry considered. "Somebody on the subcommittee," he said. "Somebody who comes to Geneva often. Somebody . . ." Suddenly Henry sat up straight in bed. "I am a fool," he said. "Annette herself told us who it is."

"Henry," said Emmy, "you'd better go to sleep. You're imagining things. Annette's never spoken about anybody but John."

"Imagining, my foot," said Henry. "Just think back a bit. Use your head."

"Oh, I can't. Don't tease me. Tell me."

Henry told her.

Much later, lying sleepless in the warm darkness, Emmy said, "It's all very well to build up a case against Annette like this, Henry, but it simply doesn't work. She couldn't have had anything to do with the leakage of information from the conference, because she was on leave last week. And so why on earth should she go to all that elaborate business of faked notes to throw suspicion on you, of all people. And in any case"—Emmy propped herself up on her elbow—"in any case, she couldn't have been the girl with the note, because Madame Novari would have recognized her."

"That can cut two ways," said Henry. "Suppose Annette didn't know Madame Novari by sight. It was only when she heard that the Novaris had left that she told us they would have recognized her. That may have been done deliberately to make us think she couldn't have been the girl with the note. I agree with you that Annette had nothing to do with the leakage of information last week, but her boy friend may be the culprit."

"I hadn't thought of that. And of course, he was at the party."

There was a moment's silence, and then Henry said, "All the same, I agree with you. My nose tells me that the case I've worked out against Annette isn't true. I don't necessarily mean that she's innocent, but my reconstruction is wrong somewhere. I've got a niggling feeling at the back of my mind that I've missed the most obvious and important thing. I wish to God I could think what it was. Anyhow, we'll have a much better idea of Annette's motives when we find out what she tells the police tomorrow."

Emmy said sleepily, "What about those timetables you started to make out?"

"I'll finish them tomorrow. Maybe they'll help."

"It must be horribly late. Try to sleep now, darling."

"I'll try," said Henry.

Eleven

The next morning, for the first time in his life, Henry deliberately set out to mislead his wife. He was appalled to find how easy it was to do.

He had decided from the beginning that the best story to tell was the one nearest to the truth. To pretend to Emmy that there was a morning meeting when there wasn't, for example, would have been asking for trouble, for a chance remark from one of the other delegates could blow the fiction sky high.

So, while they breakfasted in bed, Henry said, "No meeting this morning. I can lie in for a bit."

"Darling, how splendid. You didn't tell me."

"Forgot," said Henry untruthfully. "I'm afraid that no meeting doesn't mean no work, though. I've got to go to the Palais to sort out the agenda and go through some stuff with the verbatim reporter." He took a gulp of coffee, and added casually, "I'll probably give her a bite of lunch somewhere. She's a nice kid, and she's been doing a lot of unpaid overtime for us."

"Yes, why don't you?" said Emmy.

"You could have lunch with Gerda."

"Don't worry about me. I'll be fine."

Henry felt guiltily pleased with himself. This way, even if he and Mary were seen together and recognized, it would not matter. In any case, what on earth was wrong with taking a feminine colleague out to lunch? The answer to this, of course, was that there was nothing wrong in it, and that Henry's sense of guilt came entirely from the fact that he had at last acknowledged to himself how powerfully he was attracted toward the Australian girl. He had no intention of doing more than having lunch and a swim with her. It was ridiculous, therefore, that his heart should be lodged flutteringly somewhere in the back of his throat, that he should sing for sheer joy in the shower and find it impossible to stop grinning at himself in the mirror as he shaved. "At your age," he admonished himself. But it had no effect.

Emmy lay in bed, idly turning the pages of *La Suisse*. "Is there anything you'd like me to do for you today?" she asked. "In the sleuthing line, I mean?"

With an effort, Henry refocused on somber reality. "Madame Novari is the key to the whole thing," he said. "I can't see that it would do any harm to send her the three girls' photographs, even if you have to do it care of the agents. Gerda could help you draft a letter in Italian explaining what we . . ."

"Henry!" Emmy gave a sudden cry. "Oh, it's horrible!"

"What is?" Henry put a lathered face around the bathroom door.

Emmy was sitting bolt upright in bed, with the newspaper in her hands. "Listen." She began to read haltingly, translating each word as she went along. "Tragic accident in the Tessin. A young family—father, mother and baby—all met their deaths yesterday evening near Ascona, when the car in which they were traveling left the road and plunged down a cliffside into the lake. The family, Antonio Novari, his wife Matilda and their three-year-old son Giulio were natives of Milan, but had spent several years in Geneva, where Signor Novari worked as a concierge. It appears that they were on their way back to the city after a short holiday in Italy when the accident occurred. A complete investigation has been ordered into the cause of the tragedy, which is believed to have been motivated by a fault in the steering gear of the automobile."

Emmy stopped, and looked at Henry silently. Then she said, "Is that a coincidence?"

"It can't be," said Henry. "It simply can't be."

"The little boy, too. Henry, this is really evil."

Henry nodded. "I never did have any pity for the person behind all this," he said. "But now . . ."

"What I don't see," said Emmy, "is how anybody in Geneva could possibly have . . ."

A phrase of Helène Brochet's came back to Henry: "The organization is very good." In spite of himself he shivered slightly. He was uncomfortably aware that the organization which had taken care of the Novaris was also watching him.

He kissed Emmy lightly. "I'll be back this evening," he said. "Try not to brood too much. Get out and enjoy yourself."

Once again Emmy said, "I'll be fine."

Outside in the street, Henry felt an exhilarating surge of liberation. He even managed to put the tragic fate of the Novaris out of his mind for the time being. Wicked and unethical it might be, he acknowledged, but nothing and nobody was going to spoil the next few hours. He hailed a taxi and gave the driver Mary's address.

She was waiting for him outside the block of flats where she lived, standing beside her little black Renault in the bright sunshine. As Henry climbed into the car, she said, "I've packed a picnic, as you said. Cold chicken, paté and salad, with lots of bread and butter and cheese and white wine. Will that do?"

"Marvelously," said Henry. "Where shall we go?"

"I thought we might go over to the French side of the lake," said Mary. "I know a beach there which is still relatively undiscovered. You can't drive right down to it, but it only means walking a few hundred yards from the road, through the woods. I go down there when I want to get away from everything, and just be alone. Will that be all right?"

"Anything you say," said Henry, settling himself happily back in his seat. "You're in charge."

The little car roared gaily through the city and out along the southern shore of the lake. As they passed the imposing wrought-iron gates that guarded the Villa Trounex, Henry had a glimpse of the dark green Rolls-Royce waiting to turn out into the road. He did not see who was in it, nor did he care.

As soon as the frontier post was passed, it became clear that the French shore was considerably less sophisticated than the Swiss. They turned off the main Evian road, and found themselves negotiating the cobbles of tiny gray-stone villages, where geraniums and petunias bloomed in window boxes, and dogs, cats, and cows ambled in happy unconcern around the women drawing water from the village pump. The lanes grew narrower and more unkempt, and through the trees they caught the silvery glint of water.

At last Mary stopped the car under a chestnut tree, at a point where the lane, now little more than a track, ended in the entrance to a farmyard. She got out and led the way across a field, a drift of white chickens at her heels, and then into a dense copse, where a mossy path ran downhill through ferns and brambles and wild roses. In a few minutes she and Henry emerged abruptly from the wood onto a deserted, gray-pebbled beach, lapped by the blue wavelets of the lake. Rugs and picnic basket were arranged on the shore, and Mary pulled off her green cotton dress to reveal a trim black swim suit underneath.

Henry retreated modestly into the woods again, and put on the swimming trunks which he had smuggled into his brief case before leaving the hotel. By the time he was ready, Mary was already swimming away from the shore, doing a strong, efficient crawl. Henry plunged into the fresh, clear water, which deepened with amazing rapidity a few yards offshore, and set out to join her. For ten minutes they splashed and laughed and dived. Then they clambered up onto the beach again, and lay down on the warm, smooth pebbles, staining them black with the dampness of their wet bodies. Mary pulled off her white rubber bathing cap and shook her bronze hair in the sunshine.

They spoke little, for there seemed to be no need for words. But after a few minutes, Mary, lying on her back with her eyes closed against the sun, said, "It seems wicked to be enjoying oneself so much with this terrible murder hanging over us."

"Life at the moment," said Henry, "would be intolerable if it weren't for moments like this."

"Do they . . . the police . . . do they really think that you . . . ?"

"I'm afraid they do," said Henry. "And I can't blame them. It's up to me to prove them wrong."

"And can you?"

"I'm doing my best."

"But are you succeeding?"

"I've got a few leads to follow," said Henry. "The girl who called at John's apartment with a message purporting to come from me—have I told you about her?"

"I heard you telling Helène," said Mary. "It all sounds very odd to me, insisting on an answer in writing, and all that. Aren't the police suspicious about her?"

"I doubt if they even know of her existence," said Henry. "I haven't told them."

"You said the concierge had left for Italy," said Mary. "What are you doing about getting hold of her?"

"Nothing," said Henry. "It's too late."

"What do you mean, too late?"

"She's dead."

Mary's voice was chilled with horror as she repeated, "Dead? But how?"

"She and her husband and their little boy were all killed in a car crash yesterday."

"But . . . it's impossible . . . they can't have been."

"They were," said Henry. "It's in this morning's paper."

Mary suddenly sat up. "Henry," she said, "do you think that was an accident?"

Henry sighed. "How do I know? I find it hard to believe, but it could have been."

"So," said Mary, "if you do tell the police about this mysterious girl, there's nothing to prove you're not making it up?"

"Nothing. In any case, they'd think it was some girl I'd hired to deliver the message."

Mary frowned. "Who on earth could it have been?"

"I have my own ideas about that," said Henry. "But as far as proof is concerned, it could have been anybody. It could have been you."

He spoke lazily, almost jokingly, but Mary answered seriously, "Yes, it could have been. It wasn't, of course, but I don't know how I'd ever prove it."

"For heaven's sake, Mary, I didn't mean that."

"I know you didn't. But it made me realize what a devilish position you're in. If one is suddenly called on to prove where one was at a certain moment, and what one was doing . . ."

"Tell me one thing," said Henry, suddenly. "Did John Trapp know how to use a typewriter?"

"Oh, yes. He was as good as I am. You could see that from the note he was writing when he was killed."

"Yes." Henry was remembering that and many things. "Oh, well, let's not talk about it. Let's eat. I'm ravenous."

Half an hour later, replete with food and wine, Henry said, "Do you know the Hamptons at all?"

"Me?" Mary laughed. "Hardly. They're way out of my class. I've met them occasionally through show jumping. I have ridden Paul Hampton's horses for him once or twice. Of course, he's very much the rich owner. He doesn't speak to humble people like me."

"And his wife?"

"She's very pretty," said Mary. "That's about all I know. Every so often she comes to the stables in an organdie dress and deigns to give a pony a lump of sugar. It's generally so saturated with perfume that the poor thing spits it out."

"You'd heard the gossip, though, about John Trapp?"

"John?" Mary looked puzzled. "What gossip? I mean, I know the Hamptons had taken him up lately, and that he used to go out to the Villa and so on. They're like that, they'll suddenly take a fancy to some quite ordinary person and make a great fuss of him for a bit, and then drop him. John wasn't the first."

"You don't like Paul Hampton very much, do you?" said Henry.

There was a perceptible hesitation before Mary said, "I wouldn't say that. I don't know him. I just don't like his type."

"What type do you like?"

"Oh, I don't know." Mary smiled. "I like simple people."

"Big simple Californians with red hair?" Henry suggested.

Mary laughed. "Just because I occasionally have a drink with Bill Parkington." But Henry noticed, with a distant pang of jealousy, that she was blushing.

"But you do like him?"

"Oh, yes." There was no hesitation now. "He's straightforward and very sincere."

"And he talks a lot."

Mary gave him a sidelong glance and then said, "What do you mean by that?"

"What's your theory," Henry said, "of why John was killed?"

"I don't know. I just don't know. Please, can't we talk about something else?"

Mary was obviously ill at ease, and Henry decided that she must know all about the leakage of information, but did not want to tell tales on Bill Parkington. Aloud he said, "O.K. Let's have another swim, and then I suppose we should get back."

It was the merest coincidence that Mary should have stumbled on a stone as she was coming out of the water, and that Henry had to take her arm to steady her. What happened immediately after that, he never quite knew, but somehow she was in his arms, and he was kissing her wet face, her neck, her hair, with uncharacteristic fervor. For a poised moment of time they stood there, ankle deep in the blue lake, clinging to each other and oblivious of the whole world. Then Mary said, almost with a sob, "No, Henry. No, no, no."

She broke away from his arms and ran up the beach. Henry followed her. "I'm sorry, Mary," he said. "I had no right."

"It was my fault, you idiot," said Mary. She turned to look

at him, and her eyes were shining. "It was wonderful, and I'd never have forgiven you if you hadn't. Now it's over, and we won't mention it again. Go and get dressed. Here's a towel."

They were both very silent on the drive back. At the entrance to the Palais, Mary stopped the car and said, "I'll drop you here. I have to go and park the car. I'll see you inside." She paused, and then added, "Thank you for a glorious day."

"I'll never forget it," said Henry.

"Nor shall I."

Henry put out his hand to take hers, but she moved it quickly away and put the car into gear. "Go now," she said. "Please, Henry."

Henry got out of the car and walked slowly through the beige marble arch and back to reality.

Marcelle, bright and bouncy as usual, came out of the office as Henry was being signed in by the doorkeeper.

"Ah, Inspector Tibbett. There have been some calls for you." She led the way into the office. Henry followed. "Inspector Colliet phoned. He would like to see you after the meeting. And Mrs. Tibbett rang."

Henry's heart sank. "Did she leave a message?"

"No." Marcelle consulted a notebook beside the telephone. "She rang at eleven thirty this morning. Apparently she thought you were here. I explained that you were not expected until after lunch."

"What did she say then?"

"She said that she had quite forgotten that you had an appointment outside the Palais this morning." Marcelle looked at Henry's damp hair speculatively. "I offered to take a message, but she said it was not important. She suggested you ring her in the course of the afternoon."

"Thank you, Marcelle," said Henry. He walked out of the office feeling wretched and trapped. Some people, he reflected bitterly, just can't get away with anything. Like me. Henry was a man who had lived for so long with a clear conscience that he found himself hopelessly inept at any sort of dishonesty.

The rest room was empty. Henry went in, picked up the phone, and asked for the number of the Hotel Étoile.

"Madame Tibbett?" The porter's voice was light and impersonal. "I do not think she has come in yet, monsieur. Just a moment." A buzzing noise intervened. "No, I am afraid she is still out."

"This is her husband. Did she say when she'd be back?"

"Inspector Tibbett? Ah, I have a message for you, sir. I believe you gave instructions that any calls for Mr. Wilberforce Smith were to be passed to you."

"That's right."

"A gentleman phoned this morning, asking for Mr. Smith. I put him through to Madame, but apparently she had no knowledge of the matter, so she transferred him back to me. He asked me to ask Mr. Smith to call at Dr. Mahoumi's apartment at seven o'clock this evening. He said it was important."

"Thank you," said Henry. "But about my wife?"

"I cannot tell you any more, sir. She left the hotel at noon with a gentleman. She gave me no instructions."

The door behind Henry opened, and Jacques Lenoir came in.

Henry said, "I see. Thank you. When she comes back, tell her that I called, and that I'll be back at . . ." He hesitated, and then amended, "Tell her I may be back late. If she likes, she can phone me at the Palais des Nations this afternoon."

Somewhat relieved at this postponement of a tricky interlude, Henry turned his mind gratefully to the business of the day. Apart from the fact that Moranta had telephoned Marcelle to say that he had had a sudden attack of flu, and would not be at the meeting, there was nothing exceptional about the afternoon session. The morning's respite seemed to have soothed the delegates, for the atmosphere was smooth, dull, and drowsy. Voices droned on; points were made, preliminary drafts approved, amendments considered. Mary's small machine tapped out its soft obbligato, as she bent her auburn head studiously over her work, carefully avoiding Henry's eye. Henry was very much aware that, with the security leakage still unsolved, he had been forced to postpone all the really important items on his committee's agenda. Nevertheless, even these routine matters were absorbing, and it was only when the hands of the clock were creeping toward five that he disengaged his attention from work and began to worry about his impending interview with Colliet. He felt convinced that it had to do with Annette. What story had she told the police? Henry began to wonder what a Swiss prison would be like. He knew that an arrested person could be held incommunicado until the police had prepared their case—a legal system which he found singularly unappealing from his present viewpoint. He supposed they would let him fetch a suitcase from the hotel and see Emmy, but he had serious doubts about whether Mr. Wilberforce Smith would be in a postion to call on Dr. Mahoumi at seven o'clock.

It was, therefore, with relief and surprise that Henry, pushing open the door of Colliet's room, saw the latter advancing with outstretched hand and a beaming smile, and heard him say, "Inspector Tibbett. My felicitations."

"Felicitations on what?" asked Henry.

"I must confess that there was a moment when even I was forced to conclude . . . but all that is over now. Please accept a cigarette."

"Thank you," said Henry, taking one. "I'm afraid I still don't understand. How has the situation changed?"

Colliet waved a hand. "I see you have not yet bought an evening paper," he said. "The case is solved. We have made an arrest."

Henry suddenly felt very cold. "Who?"

"Mademoiselle Annette Delacroix." Colliet pulled deeply on his cigarette. "It is a shocking story, yet understandable in human terms. She will get a light sentence, you will see."

"Inspector Colliet, I don't believe . . ."

"I had been worried all along," said Colliet in full spate, "by the thinness of motive. Two reasons for murder presented themselves. The murderer's fear of being exposed as the seller of secret information. Or, as an alternative, the jealousy of a deceived lover. Neither of these reasons seemed sufficient to me. It had not occurred to me before that the same person might have *both* motives. And when you add to them a strong financial interest, the picture becomes plausible for the first time. Mind you, one has sympathy for the girl. I can tell you in confidence that she is pregnant. It is a great tragedy, but in the circumstances the court will certainly be lenient."

"I find all this very confusing, Inspector," said Henry. "On what evidence have you arrested Mlle. Delacroix?"

Colliet sat back in his armchair. "She came to us this morning," he said, "with a story about knowing a secret hiding place where John Trapp kept his most important papers, including his will. We went to Trapp's apartment—she, I, and Trapp's lawyer—and found these papers hidden in the oven, of all ludicrous places. Of course, one realizes that the English care nothing for food.

"At all events, there was an envelope there, which contained a large sum of money in cash, a will in favor of Mlle. Delacroix, and the draft of a new will which made it clear that if Trapp had lived a day longer, the bulk of his money would have gone to Madame Hampton. Mlle. Delacroix made a pretense of being surprised to find the money, but it was not convincing. And then we found a curious thing. Neither the envelope, the money nor the papers had fingerprints of any sort on them. They appeared to have been wiped clean. Now, Inspector, you will agree that nobody draws up and signs his will while wearing gloves. No, Delacroix knew very well what was in that cache. She was driven to act by the fact that we inefficient gendarmes had not found it for ourselves, and she knew that the apartment would soon be relet. The first roast of meat in the oven, and pouf! Fifteen thousand francs gone up in smoke!"

Henry said nothing. Colliet went on. "She broke down under questioning, and admitted that she had a key to Trapp's apartment. She alleges that it is now lost. That is a matter for conjecture. At any rate, the matter was clinched by the fact that she was heard quarreling violently with Trapp the night before his death, and when Mr. Hampton's butler was called to the police station, he identified her as the mysterious young woman who arrived at the Villa Trounex during the party and demanded to speak to Mr. Hampton. The butler left her alone in the library, and when he came back to tell her that Mr. Hampton could not see her, she had disappeared."

"And the dagger?" asked Henry.

"The butler cannot be sure," Colliet admitted. "Since it hung on the wall beside the door, he would not have seen it in any case on that occasion. However, he is positive that it was not there when he locked up at eleven thirty."

Henry said, "Why are you telling me all this, Inspector?"

Colliet ignored this and went on. "The security aspect of the affair is more concern of yours than of mine, Inspector. It is clear, of course, that Trapp and the girl were working together. Who else should he have as a confederate? It is strange how often one overlooks the obvious. Yes, they were partners, and had been for some time, in more ways than one. Their romance was an open secret. Recently, however, they had split up, owing to Trapp's infatuation with Madame Hampton."

"How can you know that?" Henry asked.

Colliet spread his hands wide, and smiled. "The draft of the new will, the Delacroix girl's visit to the Villa Trounex—these things gave us grounds for suspicion. But, in fact, we have a witness. There is no doubt as to the situation. Naturally, we shall be discreet. We have said nothing to Madame Hampton at this stage. We have not even interviewed her. And we shall try to avoid any mention of the affair in court. On the other hand, regrettably, the defense may well drag it up. Inevitably, in fact. That is a matter outside our control. Now, where was I?"

"Mlle. Delacroix's romance had broken up," said Henry.

"Ah, yes." Colliet settled down into his stride again. "Here, then, is the situation. Mlle. Delacroix is becoming a serious nuisance to Trapp. She is pregnant. She is demanding money— her share, doubtless, of the payment for information. She has even threatened violence. Finally she commits the deadly sin of turning up at the Villa Trounex. We shall never know whether or not Trapp spotted her there, but it is perfectly possible that he did. The lights in the library were on, the curtains undrawn, and quite a few of the guests were still outside. Now, during the evening, Trapp learns that the security leakage has been discovered and that he is under suspicion. So he has a brainwave. He will save his own skin, and at the same time get rid of this troublesome woman. He will see you, and denounce Mlle. Delacroix. We can be sure he had enough evidence against her. He reckons he can cover up his own part in the affair, and any accusations she may make against him afterward will be disregarded. I see now that I interpreted wrongly the note we found in the typewriter. His reluctance, real or assumed, was not at the idea of confessing himself, but of denouncing a girl whom everyone knew to be his mistress. He wished to give you the impression that he was acting from a sense of duty, and against his heart. Unluckily for him, Mlle. Annette had had ideas of her own. It is possible that she took the dagger from the Villa Trounex merely to frighten him; but one glance over his shoulder at the note in the typewriter, and she knew she must silence him, or be lost.

"You see, Inspector, how every little detail fits in? Her nervousness that morning when she heard that Trapp was waiting to see you. Her anxiety to go into the office. Her insistence that she had kept the door under observation, and that only you had gone into it. Her collapse after the murder—perfectly understandable when you think of the experience she had just been through, and when you remember that, paradoxically, she still loved him. Yes, all the details fit, with the exception of a few small points in your own evidence. I do not know why you chose to be so mysterious with us, but surely now you can have no reason for concealing the truth. If you will just sign this, it will complete our evidence, and I need not bother you any further."

Colliet pushed a piece of paper across the desk to Henry. It was typewritten, and read:

> In addition to the statement of evidence approved and signed by me on May 8th, I wish further to affirm the following facts. During Mr. Hampton's party on the evening of May 7th, I arranged for a message to be conveyed to Mr. John Trapp, in which I asked him to meet me at the Palais des Nations at 9 A.M. the following morning. I made it clear that the interview would concern the leakage of secret information from the Narcotics Conference. He replied with a note to me (Exhibit H), indicating his willingness to meet me. In fact, I was delayed and did not reach the Palais des Nations until 9.26 A.M.
>
> HENRY TIBBETT, Chief Inspector.

There was a dotted line waiting invitingly for a signature. One stroke of the pen, and Henry's worries would have been over.

"If I have got any details wrong, Inspector, please correct the wording." Colliet, beaming, leaned forward over the desk and held out a black-and-gold fountain pen.

Henry stood up. "You've got everything wrong," he said. "I had no appointment with Trapp. I never sent him a message nor received a note from him. And I don't believe for one moment that Annette Delacroix is guilty of murder. Otherwise, your reconstruction is masterly, and I congratulate you. I'm going now, and if I can't produce the real murderer for you tomorrow, you'd better release Annette and arrest me. Good night."

He turned on his heel and walked out, leaving Colliet, open-mouthed, still tendering his expensive fountain pen to an empty chair.

I Twelve

"Dear Mr. Smith, how good of you to come. I feared my message might not reach you. Come in . . . come in."

Dr. Mahoumi grabbed Henry's arm and pulled him urgently into the apartment, closing the door rapidly and softly behind him. Then, somewhat to Henry's alarm, he locked the door and put the key into his pocket.

"Let me take your coat . . . ah, you are not wearing one . . . foolish of me . . . please sit down . . . may I give you a drink? A cigarette? Here, take this chair . . . it is more comfortable."

Henry looked around him. The doors to the doll-sized kitchen and bathroom were both open, and he was relieved to see that he and Dr. Mahoumi were alone, unless, that is, another visitor was concealed, like John Trapp's secrets, in the oven. It was evident that the little lawyer was in a great state of nervous agitation. Beads of sweat stood out on his dusky brow, which he mopped frequently with his handkerchief, and his tendency to dance had become more pronounced than ever. He hopped and pirouetted around Henry like a distraught jumping bean, making little, ineffectual darts toward the cigarette box, the bottle of wine on the sideboard, and the large, uncomfortable chair into which he was attempting to steer his guest.

Henry sat down on a camel saddle and brought out his own cigarettes.

"Here," he said, "have one of these."

He held out his case to Mahoumi, who made a grab for it and took a cigarette with trembling fingers.

"So kind, Mr. Smith. Thank you . . . I have been looking

forward to our little talk."

"Have you," asked Henry, "decided that you can handle my case after all?"

"Your case?" Dr. Mahoumi sat down abruptly in the big chair. "One never knows. Who can tell? Anything is possible." There was a long, nervous pause. "Yes, it is very likely that I can help you to obtain at least part of the money. How much did you say was involved?"

"I have no idea," said Henry blandly. "My uncle was a very wealthy man."

Dr. Mahoumi shifted uneasily. "If I could arrange for you to receive a part of the money, and if I took no payment for my services, that would be a good bargain, you agree?"

"Not from your point of view," said Henry.

"But I would do it from friendship, Mr. Smith. A friend in need is like a spring in the desert—is that not so?"

"Absolutely."

"A friend," said Dr. Mahoumi earnestly, "must help his friend." He got up and tripped over to the window, where he peeped behind the curtains, apparently to ensure that the room was hermetically sealed. Then he turned to Henry again. "I help you, you help me. That is friendship, is it not, Mr. Smith?"

"You and I," said Henry, "can hardly be described as friends."

Dr. Mahoumi bared his white teeth in a caricature of a smile. "*Touché*," he said. "*Touché*, Mr. Smith. But this evening could mark the beginning of our friendship, if you agree. I have offered to help you."

"As I understand you," said Henry, "you are offering me an unspecified sum of money in return for something which you wish me to do for you. Is that correct?"

Instead of replying, Dr. Mahoumi seized a red leather pouf, dragged it close to Henry, sat down on it, and thrust his face to within an inch of Henry's nose. Then in a confidential voice he said, "You told me that you were very friendly with poor Mr. Trapp."

"I knew him slightly," said Henry.

"Very, very friendly," repeated Dr. Mahoumi. "So friendly that you knew of his death almost before the police did. So friendly that you visited his apartment."

"What if I did?"

Mahoumi retreated a little, and sighed. "The law is a strange profession, Mr. Smith. Very strange. Situations arise in the life

145

of a lawyer which it is difficult for a layman to comprehend. Points of ethic as subtle as the bloom on a peach. Do you know the first, the fundamental rule that a lawyer must obey?"

"You tell me," said Henry.

"Loyalty, Mr. Smith," said Mahoumi, his voice vibrant with sincerity. "Loyalty toward his client. This law overrides all other laws."

"Does it indeed?"

"Only in certain circumstances, of course," added Dr. Mahoumi, rather hurriedly. "When such circumstances arise . . ."

"As I gather they have arisen now . . ."

"Ah, Mr. Smith, how well you understand. I knew you would be sympathetic."

"The picture," said Henry, "is slowly becoming a little clearer. You wish me to do something which a narrow-minded, unlegalistic person might consider to be against the law of the land."

"You put it very bluntly, Mr. Smith. Let us say rather, something slightly . . . unusual. Such a simple thing as a small pledge of our friendship."

"I wish you wouldn't go on about our friendship," said Henry, irritated. "It doesn't exist."

"Ah, but it does, Mr. Smith. More perhaps than you know. I have already proved my friendship to you, with no thought of recompense. I have been loyal to you, even though you are not my client."

There was an undertone of menace in Mahoumi's voice which Henry did not like. "Just what do you mean by that?" he asked.

Mahoumi took a deep breath. It was evident that the crux of the matter was at last in sight. "I did not mention to the police," he said, "that I saw you coming out of Mr. Trapp's apartment last night."

"Me?" said Henry. "Are you sure you're not mistaken?"

"No, I am not mistaken, Mr. Smith." Mahoumi's voice was strong and confident. "I am not the only one. I have a witness. A . . . a friend of mine who was with me saw you also. Of course, he does not know who you are, but I happened to ask him if he would recognize you again, and he said that he would. However, there is no need for you to worry. The police would not think of questioning him. However, they have been questioning me; all this morning I had them here. I told them nothing. Now, however, I have to make up my mind where my duty lies. Should I, as a good citizen, reveal to the police all that I know? Or should

I protect my friend?"

"Very nicely put," said Henry. "What do you want me to do?"

"Such a little thing, Mr. Smith." Mahoumi spread his hands wide. "Just a small loan."

"A loan? You want money?" Henry was genuinely bewildered.

Mahoumi tittered. "No, no, Mr. Smith. It is I who am to give you money; if I can break the secret of your uncle's account," he added hastily.

"Then what do you want?"

"The key, Mr. Smith. Just for ten minutes. The key to Mr. Trapp's apartment."

There was a silence. Henry could almost hear Mahoumi's heart beating. Then he said, "What do you want it for?"

"Ah, Mr. Smith, you are inquisitive. You wish to know all. Is that fair? You notice I have not asked you about the purpose of your visit last night. I am discreet."

"I'm not," said Henry. "Why do you want it?"

"I will tell you this much. It is on behalf of a client."

"To whom you are loyal?"

"Of course. Now you have grasped the heart of the matter. If you have the key with you now . . ."

Henry stood up. "I'm sorry to disappoint you, Dr. Mahoumi," he said. "I have no key to Mr. Trapp's apartment, and I never have had one."

Mahoumi jumped to his feet. He was shaking, though whether from rage or fright, Henry could not tell. "You are lying!" he cried. "You were there! The lock was not forced! The windows were bolted on the inside! You have a key!"

"I have no key," said Henry. "Now, if you'll unlock the front door, I'd like to go home."

"I shall tell the police!" Dr. Mahoumi was beside himself. "I shall tell the police, and my friend will identify you! I offered you good terms, more than fair. I offered you money as well as discretion, and this is how you repay me!"

"You are a very nasty little man," said Henry calmly. Suddenly many things had become clear to him. "You are a double-crosser and a coward. You don't even stick to your own miserable standard of ethics. Tell the police anything you like. Just open that door and let me go."

Suddenly, embarrassingly, Dr. Mahoumi collapsed, like a punctured balloon. He sat down on the red leather pouf and he began to weep. "The key," he moaned. "You must give me the key. He will kill me. I beg, Mr. Smith, just for ten minutes. It's not much to ask . . . he will kill me."

Henry walked over to him and shook him by the shoulders. "Pull yourself together, for God's sake," he said. "Nobody is going to kill you."

"You don't know him. He will kill me."

"He won't," said Henry. "You're not important enough. Let me out."

Mahoumi raised his head. In an awestruck whisper he said, "You know him?"

"Of course I do."

"I shall tell the police."

"You've already told the police all they want to know," said Henry. "And incidentally, even if I had a key, it would do you no good. The money has gone."

"Gone?" A light dawned in Mahoumi's eyes. "You took it! You stole it last night! Mr. Smith, I must formally protest, on behalf of . . ."

"I didn't take it," said Henry. "The police have it. So you needn't imagine that you'll ever lay hands on it now."

"Is this true?" Mahoumi could hardly get the words out.

"Yes, it is. You can ring Inspector Colliet and ask him, if you like."

The doctor moaned softly. "What shall I do? What shall I do?"

"I should take the next aeroplane back to wherever you came from," said Henry, "leaving no forwarding address." He held out his hand. "Give me the key. I'll let myself out."

Unprotestingly, as if in a daze, Mahoumi handed over the key of the front door. Henry let himself out of the apartment.

He walked back to the hotel, glad of the fresh air after the unsavory stuffiness of Mahoumi's flat. He was very thoughtful. A large part of the jigsaw which he was assembling in his mind had fallen into place, and he felt very close to the final solution.

The hall porter told him that Madame was already in. Henry found the bedroom door unlocked, and heard the bubble of splashing water coming from the bathroom.

"I'm back, Emmy," he called. Further splashing was his only answer. He went over to the bathroom door and tried the handle. It was locked.

Henry sat down on the bed in a mood of mingled guilt, despair, and exasperation. He felt lost and lonely, cut off from Emmy's loving reassurance. He knew that he deserved to be snubbed, and yet he felt that she might at least be magnanimous enough to make allowances for him in his present unhappy situation. He suffered pangs of guilt for having lied to her, and yet he told himself defiantly that not for anything in the world would he have missed his golden interlude with Mary. But now it was over, and he wanted Emmy, while at the same time being furious at her narrow-mindedness and lack of understanding. So his thoughts chased each other with a superb lack of logic. The splashing went on relentlessly. Henry stood up, sighed, went over to the desk and began working on his long-deferred timetables.

He was still deeply absorbed in this task when he heard the key turning in the bathroom door. He did not even look up. Emmy came in from the bathroom. It was the unexpected aura of expensive perfume which made him turn to look at her. She was fresh and pink from her bath, and she was wearing a white chiffon peignoir scattered with embroidered pink roses and edged with lace. She went over to the dressing table, sat down, and lit a cigarette which she extracted from a large, shiny, alligator-skin handbag. It was very beautiful and obviously expensive, and Henry had never seen it before. He put down his pen.

"Hello, darling," he said.

Emmy greeted this remark in ominous silence.

"That's a nice handbag," said Henry lamely. "Is it new?"

"I got it today."

There was a crackling pause. Then Henry said, "What did you do all day, besides shopping?"

"I went out to lunch."

"Who with?"

"I really don't see that it's any business of yours."

"I only asked."

Emmy put out her cigarette, and began rubbing cream onto her cheeks. "You may notice," she said, "that I am tactful enough not to ask you what you did today."

"Oh, for God's sake, Emmy."

Emmy did not take her eyes off her reflected face. "Mary Benson," she said, in a voice like a whiplash. "A very beautiful girl indeed, to judge by her photograph. Hardly my idea of the nice kid who's done a lot of overtime for you. Nor is a lakeside excursion starting at eleven o'clock in the morning exactly the same thing as taking the poor child out for a bite of lunch after a hard morning's work."

There was an endless pause. Then Henry said, "You're very

well informed."

"Thank you."

"How do you know all this?"

"Never mind."

After another silence, Henry said irritably, "Well, all right. I didn't tell you the exact truth. I apologize. But really, there's no need to make such a thing of it. It's perfectly true that Mary's been working overtime for me, and I took her out to lunch to say 'thank you.' I didn't explain it all to you in detail because I thought you might misunderstand. And how right I was."

Emmy started applying foundation cream to her face. "I suppose you were too busy to take any interest in the fact that Annette is under arrest?" she said.

"Of course I know about it."

"Fortunately the poor girl still has a few friends who don't spend their time philandering."

"Emmy," said Henry, really angry now. "I will not have you talking like that about . . ."

"Please don't shout," said Emmy. "There's no need to make excuses. I understand perfectly. Why shouldn't you take Mary out? Are you seeing her again this evening?"

"Of course not."

"Oh, dear, what a pity. I hope you won't be too bored on your own."

"What do you mean by that?"

"I'm going out."

"You're . . . ? Who with?"

Emmy did not answer, but applied herself to her make-up with loving care. Henry stood up, furious.

"Emmy, answer me. Where are you going?"

Emmy turned from the mirror and faced him. "You might still have time to ring Mary," she said. "In any case, don't wait up for me. I may be late."

"But . . ."

"I'm afraid I haven't time to talk. I'm being picked up in a few minutes."

"Emmy, are you crazy?"

"Yes, a little."

Emmy opened the wardrobe, slipped her golden silk dress off its hanger, and went into the bathroom again, slamming the door. A few minutes later she emerged. Henry was forced to admit that she looked extremely attractive. He was also delighted to notice that she had failed to do up the top button at the back, the one which he always did for her. The bedside telephone rang. Henry put out his hand to take it, but before he could do so, Emmy had picked it up.

"Thank you," she said. "Yes, tell him I'll be right down."

She put down the telephone, picked up her long white stole and her bag, and smiled brilliantly at Henry.

"Good-by, Henry dear," she said. "Enjoy yourself."

And with that she was gone.

For some moments after the door had closed behind Emmy, Henry stood quite still. Then he strode into the bathroom and tripped over the chiffon peignoir, which was lying in the middle of the floor. He kicked it crossly aside, and made his way over to the window, which, unlike that of the bedroom, overlooked the front entrance of the hotel. In the street below, traffic roared and flowed; hurrying, laughing, conversing, people moved quickly and purposefully along the pavements and up and down the steps of the hotel; but of Emmy and her escort there was no sign whatsoever.

For a moment Henry seriously considered ringing up Mary Benson. He was prevented from doing so chiefly by the conviction that she would refuse to see him, and a snub would have been more than he could bear. So, dogged and depressed, he returned to work.

The trouble with the job he was trying to do was its vagueness. There are few more exasperating pursuits than compiling a time-table in which every entry has to be marked "approx." Henry looked ruefully at his attempted tabulation of Paul Hampton's party, and cursed its inaccuracy.

9:00 approx.	Bill Parkington tells H.T. of security leak. Was he overheard? Do not believe it is possible.
10:15 approx.	Hampton takes his guests on tour of house. Dagger definitely in position on library wall.
10:20 approx.	Natasha and Trapp go upstairs by different routes for their rendezvous.
10:30 (sheer guesswork)	Annette arrives and is shown into the library.
10:35	Hampton called to the phone. Guests disperse. H.T. loses his way and overhears Natasha and Trapp.

10:40 approx.	Hampton comes out of his room and meets Trapp and H.T. They go downstairs. Annette leaves through the garden.
10:42 approx.	Natasha comes down through the library. Dagger still in position. Immediately after this, presumably, Gamboni goes to library to look for Annette and finds her gone.
11:00–11:15	Guests depart. First Parkington, then Lenoir. Moranta drives the Spezzis and Tibbetts home. Trapp leaves with Natasha.
11:30	Gamboni locks up library, and notices dagger missing.

Henry read this through several times, and then put it aside impatiently. On this reconstruction, certainly, it looked as though Annette could not possibly have taken the dagger, but nobody, not even Annette herself, had any idea of the exact times of her arrival and departure. Besides, there was another possibility as how she might have got hold of it. Henry sighed, and turned to his second timetable. This concerned the arrival times of the various people concerned at the office suite in the morning. It read:

8:58 approx.	John Trapp.
9:00 "	Mary Benson.
9:15 "	Zwemmer and Helène Brochet, together.
9:18 "	Spezzi. \
9:20 "	Annette.
9:23 "	Bill Parkington.
9:26	H.T.
9:30 approx.	Lenior.
9:50	Moranta.

The third and final sheet of paper was headed, cumbersomely, "Whereabouts of Suspects at Time of Murder." It was short and not very communicative.

Mary Benson and H.T. in interpreters' room.
Parkington in filing room (no witness).
Helène Brochet and Lenoir in rest room.
Zwemmer and Spezzi in conference room.

Annette in ladies' cloakroom.
Moranta, not yet arrived.

Henry studied this last document with great care, and deepening gloom, for the pattern was falling into place now, revealing a picture that was far from pretty. On another sheet of paper he wrote down a series of questions.

Why was John Trapp killed?
Who is Mahoumi's client?
How many words a minute?

After a moment of thought, he added a fourth question: "Who is Sophie?" It was the only one of the four to which he did not know the answer.

His next action was to pick up the telephone and ask for the number of the Villa Trounex, not the private number which Natasha had given him, but the one officially listed in the telephone book. The call was answered by Gamboni.

"Villa Trounex."

"May I speak to Monsieur Golaz?" Henry asked, in what he hoped was a a passable imitation of a Genevese French accent. He felt glad that Gamboni was Italian.

"One moment. I will connect you to the garage flat."

The receiver clicked and buzzed, and then a young voice said, "Golaz speaking."

"This is the police," said Henry, and then, without any warning, fired off two questions, and got his replies before the young man had had time to think. The answers were a surprised "No, certainly not" and an even more baffled, "Yes, once, for a minute or two." Then, recovering himself, Golaz said, "But who are you? Why do you want to know these things? Inspector Colliet did not . . ." Henry rang off quickly. Then, in a state of infinite depression, he went supperless to bed.

Thirteen

Henry woke with a start, to the sound of the telephone's imperious command. He fumbled for the switch of the bedside lamp, and, as the room was flooded with light, he registered two facts simultaneously: first, that it was nearly 3:00 A.M. by his traveling clock; and second, that Emmy had not yet returned. Suddenly wide awake, and not a little alarmed, he picked up the telephone and said, "Tibbett here."

"Henry." It was Emmy's voice, and she sounded desperate and very frightened. "Henry, I'm sorry about . . ."

"Where are you?"

"Henry, you must come here at once. We . . . I mean . . . I must talk to you."

"Don't talk nonsense. Come back to the hotel this minute," said Henry. His voice was harsh with alarm.

"You don't understand. I can't. You must come here."

"Where?"

"The Villa Trounex."

"Are you out of your mind?"

"No, I'm not. Please, Henry. You must come. At once."

"Emmy, are you all right?"

There was a tiny hesitation, and then Emmy said, with curious emphasis, "*I'm* all right. It's you that . . ."

There was a click, and the line went dead. Henry was left sitting up in bed in his blue-and-white striped pajamas, with the telephone receiver buzzing meaninglessly in his hand.

He jumped out of bed and struggled into his clothes, trying as he did so to come to some sensible conclusion. Obviously

Emmy was in some serious sort of trouble, and he must go to her. Should he telephone Colliet and ask for police protection? Protection against what? Nobody would take him seriously for a moment. Was he walking into a trap, for which Emmy was the bait? The word "trap" recalled John, sitting at the desk as though he were alive, with a knife in his back. It was not a reassuring thought.

He picked up the telephone, and when the night porter answered, said, "Can I hire a self-drive car at this time of night?"

The porter showed no surprise. "Certainly, sir."

"How long will it take?"

"I will telephone at once, sir. The car should be here in five minutes. There will be a few forms to sign, and a deposit."

"Geneva is certainly well organized."

"Thank you, sir."

"Meanwhile," added Henry, "will you get me an outside call?" And he gave the number of Spezzi's hotel.

Alfredo was obviously sound asleep when the call came through, and replied through mists of drowsiness. It took Henry some time to rouse him and make him understand what he wanted him to do. Alfredo, once awake, was half amused, half angry. He probably thinks I'm drunk, Henry thought.

"To the Villa Trounex? *Ma* . . . Enrico, at this hour? Is it a party?"

"Not as far as I know," said Henry. "In fact, it may even be dangerous. That's why I'm asking you to come with me."

"But who is there?"

"I have no idea, apart from Emmy. She was obviously frightened when I spoke to her. I don't know what's going on, and I don't want to go out there alone."

Even over the telephone, Henry was aware of Alfredo's shoulders shrugging. Finally Spezzi said "Well, if you insist."

"Bless you, Alfredo. I'll pick you up in about ten minutes."

The car was waiting when Henry got downstairs, and a dapper little man in a neat, dark suit stood by the desk with insurance forms to be filled in, as calm and chipper as if it had been three o'clock in the afternoon. Obsessed by the sheer unreality of the situation, Henry got into the gray Simca and drove off through the empty streets of the city.

Alfredo was standing, unshaven and shivering, on the steps of his hotel. He climbed into the car beside Henry, and said, "Gerda is not at all pleased, with you or with me."

"I'm terribly sorry," said Henry. "I wouldn't have . . ."

Alfredo grinned at him. "I think we shall enjoy this adventure, Enrico. What do you want me to do?"

"Nothing very exciting, I'm afraid," said Henry. "I want you to wait in the car outside the house. If I don't come back within a couple of hours, call the police. If anything else happens, use your own discretion."

"If I didn't know you so well," said Spezzi resignedly, "I'd think you were mad. As it is, I know it for sure."

"I quite agree with you," said Henry.

They drove on in silence. As they approached the gates of the Villa, Henry said, "Better get your head down now." Alfredo ducked down out of sight. Henry parked the car in a shadowy corner of the drive, and walked up to the front door.

There was a light burning in the hall inside, and hardly had Henry's hand touched the bell when the great door opened, and he found himself face to face with Paul Hampton. The American was as immaculate as ever. He wore his usual miniature rosebud in the buttonhole of a midnight blue dinner jacket, and he was smoking a very good cigar.

"Inspector Tibbett," he said, warmly. "This is splendid. We were so afraid you might not come. Please come in."

Henry went in. The door closed softly behind him. Paul led the way across acres of parquet to the salon. At the door he paused, and said, "I must apologize for stealing your wife from you this evening, but there was a reason. She will explain." He opened the door of the drawing room, and they both went in.

The huge room was shadowy, lit only by a pair of table lamps at one end. The heavy curtains were drawn, and, in the one small area of light, a sofa, two armchairs and a drinks table were assembled around the remnants of a log fire, which still smoldered in the elegant white marble fireplace. Henry was vividly reminded of a visit he had once paid to a film studio, where a tiny set representing a cosy sitting room had been isolated in a circle of bright light in the middle of a vast barn of shadows. Emmy and Natasha were sitting side by side on the sofa, each with a glass in her hand.

Paul said, "Henry has arrived," and both women looked up. Natasha's face was expressionless, a beautiful, blank mask of make-up. Emmy looked suspiciously as if she might have been crying.

"Now," said Paul, "the first thing is to get you a drink, Henry.

Whisky? Gin? Vodka? I hardly know what to suggest at this hour of the morning."

"Whisky, please," said Henry. The scene had such an air of normality that, but for the hour of the night and the strain on Emmy's face, it could have been a perfectly ordinary, informal gathering of friends. Paul poured out the drink, and only the clink of ice and the hissing of the soda siphon broke the silence.

"Say when?"

"Thank you."

Henry took his drink and sat down. He smiled at Emmy, who turned her head away. Then he said, "Good morning, Natasha."

Natasha smiled very faintly. "I'm glad you came, Henry," she said.

Paul poured himself a drink and walked over to the fireplace. He raised his glass, drank, and then said, smilingly, "I'm afraid we owe you an explanation, Henry."

"You certainly do," said Henry pleasantly. "I've come to take Emmy home."

"Oh, Henry, don't be silly," said Emmy impatiently.

Paul gave Emmy a quick, encouraging look. "You can't blame him for being annoyed, Emmy dear," he said. "I think I'd better explain, don't you?"

"Yes, Paul, I do."

"Well." Paul sat down and stretched his long legs. "When I saw you driving off with the Benson girl this morning, it occurred to me that Emmy might be at a loose end, and since Natasha was out and a business luncheon of mine had just been canceled, I took the liberty of calling her."

"Charming of you," said Henry. Paul ignored this remark.

"I'm afraid I was the bearer of bad news. Emmy didn't know until I told her that the Delacroix girl had been arrested. Of course, I had no idea you knew her. I've never set eyes on her in my life, but we knew all about it, because the police were here most of the morning, questioning Gamboni. It appears that, for some extraordinary reason, the girl came out here on the night of the party, demanding to see me. Gamboni let her in, and so he had to identify her this morning. Now, Emmy was very distressed to hear what had happened, and we discussed the case at some length over lunch. I began to feel more and more sorry for the Delacroix girl, and after lunch I began racking my brains to see if there wasn't any piece of evidence we'd overlooked that might help her. I came back here and had a talk with Gamboni, and suddenly I realized that I had the very bit of evidence in my hand all the time. Mind you, I wish now I'd kept my mouth shut, but believe me, Henry, I acted for the best. I only wanted to help that poor girl, and to please Emmy."

"Quite a little friend to all the world, aren't you?" said Henry.

Emmy raised her head and looked at him. There was agony in her candid brown eyes. "Henry," she said. "Please. Paul is trying to help you."

"I don't need his help, thank you."

"But you don't understand." Emmy shot a beseeching glance at Paul.

"Let me get ahead with the facts," said Paul. "As you probably know, one of the great difficulties the police have had in this case has been to establish reliable times for the various happenings, especially those on the evening of our party here. Nobody goes around at a party looking at his watch every five minutes, and time just slips by. The only thing I'm sure of is that it was just eleven fifteen when the last guests left, but before that . . ." He shrugged. "Gamboni is even vaguer than I am. He was naturally run off his feet, poor man. He couldn't give the police any definite idea of what time the Delacroix girl turned up here, and it seems that she herself doesn't know either. She was thoroughly wrought up over something or other, and she had been drinking." Natasha made the slightest movement of turning her head away from Henry. Paul did not glance at her, but went straight on. "When I spoke to Gamboni, I realized from what he said that the police had been assuming that the girl got here after we'd been on our tour of the house. Their case rests on the fact that she was left alone in the library and stole the dagger. But I can tell you quite definitely that Gamboni brought me the message that she was here quite some time before our little expedition. In fact, she had already been and gone before you and Juan Moranta had the dagger off the wall to look at it. I felt that this evidence was important."

"It certainly is," said Henry. "It virtually destroys the police case against Annette. What did you do next?"

"It just so happens," said Paul, "that the Chief of Police is a friend of mine. I thought that it would cut through a lot of red tape if I went direct to him. May I get you another drink?"

"Thank you," said Henry. Paul got up and went to the drinks table, still talking as he refilled the glasses.

"I saw him this afternoon. He agreed with me that this new

evidence makes it certain that Delacroix is innocent, and he told me that she would be released tomorrow. Now, he is a man of the greatest integrity and would never discuss the details of a case with an outsider like myself. Nevertheless, knowing my great interest—for I am in some measure involved—he did, as an old friend, let fall a really shattering piece of information. He told me that in the event of Delacroix's release the police would certainly arrest you."

He handed Henry his drink. "I only got back from Paris yesterday evening," he went on, "so I knew very little about the case. I had not the faintest idea that you were in any way involved. I presume, however, that this news does not come altogether as a surprise to you."

"You presume correctly," said Henry. His throat felt very dry, and he took a gulp of whisky.

"Naturally, I don't intend to ask you whether you're innocent or guilty," Paul went on. "It's none of my business. But the fact of the matter is that apparently the police have what they consider a watertight case against you. According to my friend, only you or the Delacroix girl had the opportunity of killing Trapp, and whereas in her case it would have been a question of split-second timing, in yours—well, it seems you went into the office, and would have had plenty of time to kill the man before you raised the alarm. They also found your fingerprints on the dagger, but not hers." He raised a hand to silence Henry's protests. "I know you'll say that they can be accounted for by the fact that you handled it here the night before. There are also some smudges which indicate that it was subsequently handled by somebody wearing gloves, but it seems that Mlle. Delacroix had no gloves with her at the Palais that morning. My friend told me in confidence that the evidence had pointed to you all along, but that naturally the Swiss authorites were not anxious to arrest a high-ranking officer of a foreign police force without incontrovertible proof. By an ironic coincidence, the final and damning piece of evidence came through when I was actually there at police headquarters. A confession from a drug trafficker in Germany that his information on the conference came from you."

Henry felt the hair on the back of his neck bristling. He was suddenly very cold. He looked quickly at Emmy. She sat with her head turned away from him, twisting a small handkerchief in her fingers.

Paul Hampton smiled pleasantly. "Now, I am a businessman, Henry," he said. "I am not the person to blame you for making a little money where you could. I have always maintained that so long as the police are underpaid this sort of thing is bound to happen. My own view, for what it is worth, is that you are innocent of the murder, which was probably committed for some quite different reason. Nevertheless, I have to admit that the police have a remarkably good case, and I think that your chances of acquittal are very small indeed. Let me freshen your glass."

"No, thank you," said Henry. His brain was racing. Desperately he told himself, "They can't make this stick"; and then he remembered John Trapp and the Novaris and the excellence of the organization, and was forced to admit that perhaps they could. His only consolation was the thought that his enemies must be desperate to make such a rash move. They must know that he was close behind them.

To Paul he said, "Thank you for telling me this."

"Don't thank me. You can imagine that I feel pretty bad about the whole thing. However innocent, I feel responsible. I tried hard to think how I could help you, and believe me, you need help. When the solution came to me, it was so obvious that I couldn't imagine why I hadn't thought of it straightaway." He leaned forward and fixed his bright blue eyes on Henry. "By a happy chance," he said, "Natasha is leaving tonight to visit friends in South America. She catches a plane for Brazil at half past five, in just under two hours' time. This plane is run by a private airline in which I have an interest, and I can arrange for you and Emmy to be on the same flight. At my expense, of course."

Henry looked at him, long and earnestly. Then he said, "Why are you prepared to do this for me? You hardly know me."

Paul looked down. "That's true," he said. "Put it down to my bad conscience, and to the fact that you have a very exceptional wife indeed."

"I see," said Henry. "Well, I'm very grateful, but the answer is no. To run away would be the last . . ."

Paul smiled ruefully. "I knew that you would instinctively refuse," he said. "You are the type of admirable, impractical Englishman who prefers to stay and face the music. That's why I asked Emmy to dine with me, so that I could put the scheme to her first and enroll her as an ally. Henry, I do beg you to consider this offer carefully. It is made in all friendship and quite disinterestedly. Of course, you are perfectly free to turn it down, but above all I ask you to think of Emmy." He paused. "I won't say any more. I realize that this is a shattering decision for you to make. Fortunately, there is still a little time left for you to think it over, and it is something that you and Emmy must decide together. Natasha and I will leave you to talk about it."

Natasha stood up without a word, and walked out of the room. Paul followed her. At the door he turned and said, with the gravity of a politician addressing his country in an hour of crisis, "Please be sensible, Henry. You are in a desperate position." Then he went out, closing the door behind him.

There was in interminable pause. Then Henry said, "Emmy, are you really a party to this idea?"

Emmy shook her head wretchedly. "I don't know what to think," she said. "I just feel numb. When Paul told me all this . . ."

Henry went over to her, and took her head between his hands, turning her face until she could no longer avoid his eyes.

"Look at me," he said. "Do you really believe that I have been selling secrets?"

"I don't know." It was a whisper. "When I found that you'd lied to me about . . . other things . . ."

"Do you think I am a murderer?"

"Of course not."

"Well, that's something," said Henry. He grinned at her, and was delighted to be rewarded by a tiny answering smile. "Poor darling Emmy. There's so much to say I can't say now. We've both been through our own kinds of hell, but it's nearly over now."

"Nearly over? But Henry, the police . . ."

"First of all," said Henry," get this into your head. I did not kill John Trapp. I have not been selling information, and there is absolutely no question of running away, however well-meaning Paul's offer may be. Is that clear?"

"But if they arrest you tomorrow . . ."

"Emmy," said Henry, "if they arrest me, it will be unpleasant, but I shall have a chance to prove my innocence. If I ran away now, it would be as good as a confession. Can you imagine what the rest of our lives would be like? Stranded in South America, virtually as fugitives from justice, with no job, no money."

"There would be money." They both turned at the sound of

Natasha's voice. She had come in quietly through a door at the far end of the room, and was walking toward them through the shadows, insubstantial as a ghost in her floating black chiffon dress.

"Ah, Natasha. I'm glad you came back. I want to talk to you."

Natasha opened a silver cigarette box, took out a cigarette and lit it from a slim porcelain lighter. "What is there to talk about?" she said.

"Plenty," said Henry. "For one thing, how long are you staying in Brazil?"

"That depends."

"On whether or not we go with you?"

Natasha blew out a cloud of smoke. "Henry," she said, "Paul really is trying to help you."

"And you," said Henry, "are trying to help yourself."

"What do you mean by that?"

"With Annette released, and with me virtually proved guilty by disappearing to South America," said Henry, "there will be no scandal, and you will be able to come back."

Natasha sighed impatiently. "You are so stubborn," she said. "We are all trying to help you. I will give you enough money straight away to . . ."

"It's very kind of you," said Henry, "but you have no money."

"Oh, yes, I have."

"You told me yourself that Paul didn't allow you any ready cash."

"That doesn't matter. I have a certain . . ."

"I'm sorry to disillusion you," said Henry. "You haven't. Mahoumi has let you down. He didn't get into John's flat, and even if he had it would have been too late, because the police had already taken the money away. As a matter of fact, it's probably safer with them. I think Mahoumi was planning to decamp with it."

Emmy was looking from Henry to Natasha in bafflement. Natasha showed no emotion. "It doesn't matter," she said. "When Annette was arrested, I naturally wanted both the money and the will out of the way. Enough mud would have been slung in court without that, and it was the only concrete evidence against me. Without it, I could have denied everything and Paul would have stood by me. Now, after Annette is released, I shall just have to wait for the will to be proved."

"That particular will," said Henry, "was never signed."

Natasha, in the act of raising her cigarette to her lips, froze into immobility. Then she said, "You're lying."

"I'm not lying. It's Mahoumi who has done that. I imagine he was too scared to tell you the truth."

"How do you know?" Natasha's voice rose slightly, with an undertone of hysteria. "How can you possibly know?"

"Because I saw the draft will myself, and so did Emmy. John was to have taken it to Mahoumi to be signed on the day he died."

Natasha turned to Emmy. "Is this true?" she demanded.

"It's true that I saw a draft will in your favor," said Emmy. "As for the rest, I haven't an idea what either of you is talking about."

"It's very simple," said Henry. "Natasha had a horror of poverty, and she realized only too well that Paul would throw her out without a penny if she got herself involved in an open scandal—and she was sailing close to the wind most of the time. So she decided to lay up a little nest egg in cash against a rainy day. Isn't that right?" he added to Natasha.

Natasha was trembling. "What happens to it then?" she said. "Who gets my money?"

"Annette Delacroix."

"That little bitch!"

"She's a nice girl," said Henry. "She may even give some of it back to you."

Abruptly Natasha sat down and began to cry.

"I agree, it's hard luck on you," said Henry. "I imagine it took some time and effort to get it together."

Natasha sniffed. "I dared not open a bank account," she said. "Not even a numbered one. Paul and I are too well known, and he'd have found out."

"So you used John as your bank."

"I trusted him."

"You let him believe that it was money you and he could use when you eloped," said Henry.

"He was completely honest. I knew he would give me the money any time I asked for it, even if I did throw him over. It was he who insisted on drawing up a new will, so that I'd get it back if anything happened to him."

"As a matter of interest," said Henry, "where did it come from?"

"It was so difficult." Natasha wiped her eyes. "I sold little bits of jewelry that Paul had forgotten about. I bought expensive dresses on account, and then took them back and got cash for them. I had to do it like that. Every time I collected a few thousand francs, I gave them to John to keep."

"That's what you were doing in your room on the night of the party, wasn't it?" said Henry, interested. "I thought it was a silly time and place for a romantic rendezvous. It was only afterward that I realized it was a business appointment."

"You are horrible," said Natasha. "It's true I had some money to give him, but . . ."

"All right," said Henry. "You gave him the money. What did he do with it?"

"He hid it in different places all over his apartment. I never thought the police would find the lot in the oven. They must be brighter than I thought. But that was less than half of the total. I had about thirty-five thousand francs altogether."

"Three thousand pounds," said Henry reflectively.

"I know it's miserably little," said Natasha, misreading his thought completely, "but it was all I had, and it would have seen me through for a bit. And now . . . now that miserable little cow gets it all. No wonder she killed him."

"You think she did?"

"It's obvious," said Natasha bitterly.

"If I were you," said Henry, "I'd keep that opinion to myself. It's in your best interests to decide that I'm guilty and persuade me to go to South America with you. Perhaps when you come back you can find another reliable banker who won't get himself murdered."

Natasha looked at him for a long moment. "You don't believe, do you," she said, "that I love Paul?"

"On the contrary," said Henry."

The big door from the hall opened, and Paul Hampton came in.

"Sorry to disturb you," he said, "but time is getting short, and . . ." He broke off as he saw Natasha. "What are you doing here?"

"Natasha has been adding another persuasive voice to get me to run away," said Henry. "I do appreciate what you're trying to do, Mr. Hampton, but . . ."

The revolver shot shattered the quiet unreality of the night with the brutal force of a street accident. Paul froze into immobility, his hands still upraised in what looked like a benediction; Natasha gave a little scream and dropped her cigarette;

Emmy clutched Henry's arm. Almost at once came the sounds of a struggle outside the window, in the dark, wild garden beyond the comforting curtains. Before any of them could reach the window, there was a crash of splintering glass, and Alfredo Spezzi stumbled into the room, clutching at the dark red curtains for support. With horror, Henry saw that the red of the curtains matched the stain that was spreading across Spezzi's white shirt.

"Enrico . . ." he gasped, every word an agony, " . . . gun . . . I tried . . ."

He fell clumsily onto the shining parquet floor at the exact moment when the curtains parted again, and Konrad Zwemmer stepped into the room, holding in his hand a small, evil-looking revolver.

Fourteen

There was a moment of incredulous silence. Then Zwemmer said, in English, "Please all stay quite still, and you will not get hurt." He looked down at Spezzi, and said contemptuously, "He is not dead." He addressed himself to Paul Hampton. "I apologize for this intrusion." Henry could not decide whether his voice was sarcastic or not. "However, it was necessary. You were beginning to interfere with my plans."

Before any of them could reply to this, the door leading to the hall was kicked open for the outside. In a split second, Henry had time to see that Gamboni was there, in the shadows outside, and that he had a gun in his hand. Then there was another shot, deafeningly close, and the revolver flew out of Gamboni's hand and crashed to the floor somewhere behind him.

"The gun," said Zwemmer, "will not be necessary." To Gamboni, who was nursing his hand with an expression of bewilderment and injured innocence on his face, he said, "Can you drive the Rolls?"

"Yes, sir."

Zwemmer nodded curtly to Hampton. "Throw him the keys of the car," he said.

Expressionless, Paul did so.

"Now," said Zwemmer precisely to Gamboni, "pick up this gentleman." He prodded Alfredo ungently with his foot. "He is not badly hurt. Take him somewhere where he will be looked after. Tell the other servants that there has been a slight but not serious accident, and send them back to bed. Then return here as soon as possible. Quickly, now. Don't waste time."

Unprotesting, Gamboni picked up the unconscious Spezzi as easily as if he had been a baby and carried him out to the hall.

"And shut the door behind you," added Zwemmer pleasantly.

Gamboni did so. Zwemmer went over to it and turned the key in the lock. Then, still with the gun trained on his four prisoners, he said, "Now perhaps we can talk a little in peace." The rimless glasses glinted, reflecting the lamplight. "You are a great nuisance, Inspector Tibbett. I presume it was you who stationed the inefficient Spezzi as an unarmed watchdog in the drive." Paul Hampton looked sharply and interrogatively at Henry. "It was a foolish thing to do," Zwemmer went on. He glanced with distaste at the gun in his hand. "I dislike having to use this thing. It is noisy and messy."

There was a pause. Then Zwemmer continued, "Before we get to the business in hand, there are one or two matters to clear up. For example, Tibbett, what were you doing in John Trapp's apartment last night?"

"Looking around," said Henry. "What were you doing in Mahoumi's apartment?"

Natasha drew her breath in sharply. Zwemmer said, "I am asking the questions. Did you find anything?"

"Nothing that would interest you."

"I see. Thank you. Now to the next point. You have known the truth for some time, I imagine."

"No," said Henry. "I suspected it, but it was only this evening . . ."

"I see that I am just in time." Zwemmer smiled without humor. "You see why I could not allow you to complete this visit undisturbed. I imagine you were planning a getaway."

"Something like that."

"It would have been very inconvenient for me."

In a voice which expressed more contempt than Henry would have believed possible, Paul Hampton said, "You really are a laughably clumsy villain, Herr Zwemmer. Gamboni will be back soon with every policeman in Geneva at his heels. I don't know how you intend to explain away this melodramatic intrusion."

Zwemmer smiled again, unattractively. "Please do not insult me, Mr. Hampton," he said. "I have my professional pride. Have you not yet realized that Gamboni is working for me?"

"For . . . ?" For the first time, Paul Hampton seemed utterly taken aback. He sought for words, but found none.

"Poor Gamboni," said Zwemmer. "I trust his hand is not hurt.

I had to deprive him of his gun, because he is inclined to be overenthusiastic, and might have used it foolishly. Also, it was necessary to dispose of Spezzi. Gamboni knows just where to take him and what to do with him." Still holding the revolver, he shot his cuffs. "I am sorry to have to keep you all waiting for so long. All will soon be over. What shall we talk about?"

"Let's talk about the security leakage," said Henry. "For example, who is Sophie?"

Zwemmer shrugged. "A silly Frenchwoman who was infatuated with Trapp," he said. "She has no part in this. The principals in this drama are all here, in this room."

"No," said Henry.

"What do you mean?"

"I mean the person who killed John Trapp."

Zwemmer looked piercingly at Henry for a moment, and then turned to Natasha, who was standing as though petrified, never taking her huge brown eyes off the dapper figure with the gun.

"You are very quiet, Mrs. Hampton. Have you nothing to add to the conversation?"

"I have no idea what you are talking about," said Natasha very distinctly.

"Oh, but I think you have. Poor Mrs. Hampton. I'm afraid you allowed your emotions to rule your head. You should not have trusted Mahoumi. In your position, you should not have trusted anybody."

Natasha, Henry thought suddenly, was in her small way not unlike Cleopatra. Foolish, self-indulgent, even wicked—in the final moment of despair she gained an unquestioned dignity. The movement with which she turned her small, beautiful head away from Zwemmer was at once doomed, decisive, and exquisite.

"Herr Zwemmer," said Paul Hampton. "you may say and do what you like to me, but I ask you to show some mercy to my wife, if you know the meaning of the word."

"Mr. Hampton, I am moved." Zwemmer turned slightly to look Paul Hampton full in the face. "I had no idea . . ."

It was at this moment that they heard the gentle scrunch of rubber on gravel as the Rolls came back into the drive. Henry felt a moment of sheer panic. It was impossible that Gamboni could have taken Spezzi to a hospital and returned so soon. What, then, had become of Alfredo? He thought of Gerda, and his spirit sank under the weight of intolerable responsibility. If only he had known sooner.

The front door opened, and banged shut again. Nobody breathed. Then the door of the salon opened, and Gamboni came in, with the gun in his hand once more. Zwemmer raised his eyebrows. Gamboni nodded.

Quietly Zwemmer said, "Paul Hampton, in the name of the Government of Western Germany, I arrest you for . . ."

Without warning, pandemonium broke loose. Paul Hampton made a rugger-tackle dive for the door, and all the lights went out. There were two earsplitting shots, and suddenly the room seemed to be full of people, struggling and breathing and cursing in the darkness. Henry grabbed Emmy's hand and began cautiously to steer her toward the window. They had almost reached it when the lights went on again, revealing a scene which remained etched in Henry's memory for the rest of his life.

Paul Hampton was lying on his back in front of the dying fire. Natasha was on her knees beside him. Gamboni and Zwemmer stood looking down at him, each with a gun in his hand. The background was filled in with the blue-gray uniforms of the gendarmes. As they surged forward, Zwemmer halted them with a short, decisive gesture.

There was a moment of dead silence. Then Natasha, as though unaware that there was anybody else in the room, said, "Paul. Darling Paul. Don't be afraid. You know I love you. I won't let them . . ."

The wounded man on the floor murmured something inaudible. Natasha slid down beside him, and laid her cheek against his. "Go to sleep," she said, softly. "My darling, go to sleep. I'm here. I won't go away."

Nobody moved. Paul lifted his right hand with a great effort and put it over Natasha's. Then he gave a great sigh, smiled at her, and died.

For a long moment, Natasha lay quite still. Then she stood up and said steadily, "He is dead. You can do what you like now." And she turned her back on all of them and walked out of the room. Nobody tried to stop her.

A hundred years later, it seemed, Henry was sitting with Zwemmer in the library of the Villa Trounex. Between them lay a pile of papers, each innocuous enough in itself, but, taken together, ample evidence that the greater part of Paul Hampton's fortune had come from the highly organized distribution and sale of narcotic drugs in almost every country in the world.

Henry lit a cigarette. He was almost too tired to raise it to his lips. Outside the sun was already turning the mountaintops to a glowing pink, and the clear sky presaged a perfect day.

"I haven't even said thank you yet," he said.

Zwemmer smiled coolly. "You have been a great trial to me, Inspector. I suppose I cannot altogether blame you. Hampton chose you as the scapegoat for this murder, and apparently did not reckon on the fact that you were capable of defending yourself. This last bid to get you out of the way was a very desperate stratagem."

"I realized that," said Henry. "I had my suspicions all along. It was clear that the brain behind the narcotics organization was somebody of ability and wealth, and Hampton fitted the part perfectly. He finally gave himself away this evening when he told me that the chief of the Geneva Police had informed him about the security leak, as well as other details of the case. No policeman would ever do that."

"I suppose he told you, too, that a German dope-runner had denounced you?"

"He did."

"That was quite true."

"I'm sure it was. Hampton was powerful enough to be able to arrange that without any trouble. If he had merely planted the evidence, and let things take their natural course, I would have been in a much worse position. As it was, he made one grave mistake."

"And what was that?" Zwemmer was interested.

"Never mind." Henry passed a hand over his forehead. "Tell me, what made you finally decide that I was not Hampton's agent?"

Zwemmer gave another of his humorless smiles. "I am still not completely sure that you are not," he said. Then, silencing Henry's indignant protests, he added, "That was my little joke, Inspector. Seriously, however, I suspected you up until a very short time ago. The biggest point in your favor was that the murder seemed to have been deliberately pinned onto you—and, of course, Hampton would have tried to divert suspicion from his own man. Even when you told Helène about the girl with the faked message, I thought that you might be inventing it to draw suspicion away from yourself. You will admit that your conduct was not reassuring. Gamboni was extremely disturbed to find you in here, for example. Disturbed and angry, poor man. He had been waiting months for Hampton's departure for Paris in order to get in here, only to have the room sealed by the police. It had taken him all day to obtain a duplicate key. Ah, well, as it happens, there was no harm done."

"You still haven't told me," Henry said, "what finally convinced you that I was innocent."

"Helène is efficient," said Zwemmer. "She telephoned me promptly when you mentioned the mysterious girl with the message. My agents in Italy were able to trace Signora Novari and confirm the story just before that unfortunate accident. Then I knew that you were innocent and that the murder was being pinned on you, for if you yourself had sent a girl with a message, you certainly would not have told anybody so, while at the same time denying any appointment with Trapp. Finally, I knew you could not be in league with Hampton when I saw that you had stationed the good Spezzi in the drive tonight. I much regret that I had to shoot at him, but he will be well soon. The police car was waiting outside the gates and rushed him to the hospital. Nevertheless, he should not have attacked me like that in the garden. I might easily have killed him in error."

"Tell me more about yourself." Henry was desperately tired, but Zwemmer fascinated him.

"I am afraid I had to deceive you to a certain extent," said Zwemmer. "My government had suspicions, and I was sent here in a double capacity, as delegate and secret agent. I have worked with Helène for many years."

"Where does Helène come into all this?"

"Helène was born German," said Zwemmer. "She and her parents were considered politically unreliable, and sent to a concentration camp when she was very young. I was working in the anti-Nazi underground, and we met when I helped to organize her escape with her mother. She was luckier than I; both my parents died. Helène went first to France and then, after the war, to England. I returned to Berlin. We kept in touch. It was no surprise to either of us to find the other enlisted for secret service duties. We had both hoped for political assignments, but the authorities—rightly, I think—decided that we were both too emotionally involved in such matters. So we found ourselves working together in the Narcotics Branch. We have been after Hampton for some years."

"And you finally got him."

"I would not say that." Zwemmer sounded grim. "He gave

himself up to us by this ridiculous and meaningless murder. I had not intended to bring matters to a head this evening, but I could not allow you and your wife . . ."

"I don't know how to thank you," said Henry.

"Don't thank me." Zwemmer was stating a fact, "I did not act to save your skin, although, of course, you would not have left the house alive if you had persisted in your refusal to go to South America. Hampton would have preferred you to go voluntarily, not from any humanitarian motives, but because bodies are inconvenient things to dispose of. No, when Gamboni telephoned me this evening, I was afraid that Hampton would spirit you away, which the police would have taken as irrefutable evidence of your guilt. The case would have been closed, and we might never have cornered Hampton. Even as it is, the affair is most unsatisfactory. I wished to take Hampton alive. It was Gamboni who killed him, as I was afraid he would if he got loose with that gun. So, we still do not know who was his agent in the conference. We still do not know who killed John Trapp, or why."

Henry looked out of the window. The sun was up now, and the lake was a beguiling blue, smooth as a mirror.

"I know the answer to all those questions," he said.

Zwemmer leaned forward. "You do? Then tell me."

"John Trapp was killed by mistake," said Henry.

"Ah. You mean that somebody else was the intended victim?"

"No. I mean that the whole thing was a misunderstanding, largely my fault."

Zwemmer looked at Henry with growing skepticism. "I don't pretend to understand you, Inspector," he said, "but please go on."

"We all thought that Trapp was killed because he knew too much. In fact, he was killed because Paul Hampton thought he knew too much, and all the time poor John knew nothing at all."

Zwemmer smiled grimly. "If you are right," he said, "there is a nice irony in the situation which appeals to me. But who killed him, and how?"

"Trapp was obviously not killed by Paul Hampton," said Henry. "He was in Paris at the time, and he could not have got in to the Palais des Nations. However, Hampton planned his murder, and forced an accomplice to carry it out—the accomplice who had been supplying him with secret information on the

172

conference."

"Who?" Zwemmer was insistent. "Who was responsible for that leakage? It is vitally important for me to know."

"I could tell you," said Henry. "But proving it would be a different matter. Please give me until ten o'clock this morning. I promise you that that will be the end."

The hired car was still in the drive, and Henry and Emmy drove back in it to Geneva. It was eight o'clock, and the town was stirring into its morning bustle. Already, sought-after parking spaces were filling up, and serious-faced businessmen with brief cases were hurrying to their offices. Bright, clear light whitened the gray stone houses, and the neat flowers in the public gardens glistened with color under the ministering sprays of an army of gardeners.

Back at the hotel, exhausted physically and mentally, Henry and Emmy clung to each other like lost children. The small squabbles of the day before had disappeared, burned up by the searing horror of the night. At last Emmy managed to smile and say, "Well, thank God that's over."

Henry did not smile back. "Dear Emmy," he said, "it's not over yet."

"What on earth do you mean?"

"Go and have a bath and get some sleep," said Henry. "I have to go out again."

"No. No, I won't let you."

"Please, Emmy." Gently, he disengaged her clinging hands. "I promise you, there's no danger. When I come back, please don't ask questions."

Emmy looked at him quickly. He seemed suddenly worn out, an old man. She squeezed his hand briefly and said, "All right, darling."

It was ten o'clock in the morning when Henry got back to the hotel. He came into the bedroom and went straight to the bathroom where, even though he was not dirty, he washed himself carefully from head to foot. Then he lay down on the bed beside Emmy. He did not move nor make any sound. After a moment or two, she put out her hand tentatively toward his, and grasped it. There was no answering pressure, but his fingers, encircled by hers, flexed slightly, in recognition and gratitude. Then, in spite of himself, he fell asleep.

At half past two in the afternoon, Henry woke with a dry mouth and the full, remembered horror to face. Emmy was dressed, sitting on the bed beside him.

"They've been telephoning since noon from the Palais," she said, "but I wouldn't let them wake you. It seems somebody has disappeared. They didn't tell me any details."

"Stay here, please," said Henry. "Wait for me. I'll be back."

He dressed quickly, and took a taxi to the Palais des Nations. The final expiation, the washing-out of all sins, was very close now. At the Palais, he joined forces with Colliet and Zwemmer, and drove off in a police car. Henry directed the driver where to go.

The beach was as empty and sunny as it had been the day before, except that there was a green cotton dress weighted down neatly by a big stone, and a letter in bold handwriting folded carefully into it. This was addressed to Henry, and he opened it quite calmly.

MY DEAREST HENRY,

Thank you for coming to see me. You see, I have kept my promise. Don't blame yourself, because I would have done this anyway, rather than be killed by Hampton, like the wretched Novaris—and make no mistake, I would have been killed, for I had become dangerous. My life is quite worthless, and it seemed to me a good idea to trade it for yours. I didn't realize that you were more than able to look after yourself.

I have left a full account of everything for Inspector Colliet, but this is just for you. Please don't judge me too harshly. I was brought up tough, and the actual, physical act of killing was not very difficult. Of course, I had no choice—it was kill or be killed. Nevertheless, the burden of it was too great to live with, especially after I came to know you. Please believe me that I was not spying on you yesterday.

I love you.
Mary.

P.S. You are very clever. I thought the tape recorder idea was foolproof. So much for vanity.

P.P.S. You will find the transcripts of yesterday's meeting in the green file in the office. They may need some correction.

It was not long before they found her, a slim, brown body in a black swimsuit, with a drift of auburn hair, floating quietly in toward the beach. Henry did not stay for the agonizing formalities. He asked the police driver to take him as far as the Pont du Mont Blanc, in the center of the city, and walked back to the hotel from there.

It was a blazingly sunny afternoon, and the streets were full of the slightly frenetic liveliness that is the essence of Geneva— the crossroads city, the city of brief encounters and unstable relationships, built on a foundation of placid prosperity; a foundation solid enough in itself, but slippery to the feet of the transient, the expatriate, the impermanent.

As he crossed the busy bridge and looked away down the lake toward Lausanne, Henry knew that his life could never be quite the same again. Old, unquestioned values had been turned upside down. The black-and-white view of morality which he had accepted as his middle-class heritage had gone forever. He forced his mind to consider the facts, clearly and brutally, so that they might have their full, salutary impact.

Mary had been a paid informer and a murderess. No amount of subsequent remorse or nobility on her part could alter that. And yet he had loved her, and his love, obstinately, refused to diminish in the face of what he now knew. He himself was a murderer, for he had caused Mary's death—Mary, whom he loved —as surely as if he had stabbed her as she stabbed John Trapp. Yet he felt neither guilt nor remorse, just an ineffable sadness which in its own way was right and true and the stuff of tragedy.

For Paul Hampton he could feel no pity, and yet his life and death had been curiously ennobled and etched with fire by Natasha, who loved him, and who was worthless. What would happen to her now? Henry had no illusions. As Paul's widow, she would be rich. She would indulge every frivolity, every passing fancy, every fly-by-night lover. She would grow old and painted and ridiculous, and a by-word for lechery, and she would never again love any man, or rediscover her one moment of nobility. Yet, having known it, she would never again be quite without honor.

And Zwemmer? He and Helène would pursue their dark star of vengeance, always on the side of the angels, always striving to deaden the pain, to cure the wound that went so deep in them that a thousand deaths, a thousand victims, could not begin to heal it. Henry remembered a moment, early that morning, when he had said to Zwemmer. "Why don't you marry Helène?" and had received the short answer, "Impossible. We have our work to do."

Thank God, Annette was not like that. Her wounds were superficial, of the flesh in every sense. Henry wondered if she would, in fact, marry Juan Moranta, and if Juan would have the magnaminity to accept John Trapp' s child as his own. Henry decided that he probably would. He had, after all, gone straight to Annette's side when he heard of her arrest, absenting himself from work on the excuse of illness; and he had stayed to comfort her even after he mus⸱ surely have heard of her pregnancy.

Henry smiled to himself as he recalled Annette speaking on the telephone in her apartment, the first evening that they had met her in Geneva. *"C'est un peu difficile ce soir, John,"* she had said, and because John Trapp turned up almost at once, he had jumped to the conclusion that it was to him that she had been speaking. But once he thought of it, he remembered that she referred to John always as "Jean," for their common language was French. What he and Emmy had taken for "John" was Annette's French-accented pronunciation of "Juan." Juan, mature, humorous and kind, the faithful admirer, ready to salvage the wreck of her grand, ill-fated passion for John Trapp. Henry hoped that Annette would appreciate what she was getting.

His mind ran on. Bill Parkington, stunned and inarticulate as a child in the face of Mary's confession, unable to reconcile in his honest mind her good and bad qualities; trying with desperate lack of success to reduce the matter to the simple terms of good and evil on which his life was built. Jacques Lenoir, volatile and irrepressible as yeast, already working on the story in his mind, blending and fashioning it into sufficient material for a lifetime of brilliant dining-out.

He thought of Alfredo, pale but quickly recovering in the Cantonal Hospital. Poor Alfredo, he was a little ashamed now of his ignominious part in the affair. . . ." But how was I to know, Enrico? He was creeping through the bushes like an assassin" . . . Zwemmer had sent him an enormous bunch of grapes, and Gerda was furious about the whole thing. Alfredo and Gerda had nothing to worry about. They had each other.

And he had Emmy. If it was true that their relationship would henceforward be different, it was true in the best possible sense. Their interdependence had never been more clearly demonstrated, and it had been spiced with the possibility, which would now always be with them, that each was capable of finding adventure elsewhere.

Henry walked slowly up the steps of the hotel in the sunshine. As he entered the foyer, the porter hurried over. "Mr. Tibbett," he said. "I have another message for you, that is, for Mr. Wilberforce Smith. His friend has had to leave the country unexpectedly, but he has left a forwarding address in Tangiers. I have it here, if you . . ."

"Put it in the ashcan," said Henry. "I'm going to bed."

/ Fifteen

It was a long time before Henry could be persuaded to talk about the Geneva case to anybody. Mary Benson's letter of confession to the police had been meticulous and fully explicit, and the dossier was closed. Emmy respected Henry's request, and asked no questions. It was some months later, when Alfredo and Gerda were visiting London, that Henry at last consented to explain exactly what had happened, and how he had arrived at the truth. In fact, he embarked almost eagerly on his exposition. The wound had healed, on the surface at least, and he was anxious to experiment, to make sure that the scar tissue was healthy and would stand up to harsh treatment.

"I hardly know where to begin," he said. They were sitting in the Tibbetts' London flat on a foggy November evening, drinking coffee round the fire. It seemed a world away from the opulence of the Villa Trounex, the polyglot splendor of the Palais des Nations, and the dancing blue of the lake. "The crux of the matter was that, as far as I or anyone else could see, only Annette or myself could have murdered Trapp, unless there was a conspiracy between two people to do it. For a time I considered the conspiracy idea, but at the time of the murder, the groupings were all wrong. I mean, I had established a connection between Helène Brochet and Zwemmer, but Helène was with Lenoir in the rest room and Zwemmer was with Alfredo in the conference room. Mary was with me. In any case, Annette, who was alone in the cloakroom, maintained that she could see the office door in the mirror all the time.

"Now, I knew very well that I hadn't murdered John, which

gave me an advantage over Colliet, who thought I had. So when evidence began to pile up against Annette, I was greatly tempted to believe her guilty. There remained, however, two facts which did not tally. One was her obvious, terrible grief when she found that John was dead. I didn't believe anyone could have faked that. The other was that she could not have taken the dagger. Both Paul and Natasha Hampton maintained that it was there long after she had left, and in fact the library was only empty for such a short time after our conducted tour that it would have been the greatest coincidence if nobody had seen her. I was prepared to believe that she might have been persuaded to take the note to John, but I was convinced she had not done the actual killing. I came back to my conspiracy idea. Was there, then, a connection between Annette and any of the men? I soon realized there was—Juan Moranta. He was in love with Annette."

"They're married now," Gerda put in.

"I know," said Henry. "Annette wrote and told us. Well, Juan loathed Trapp because of the way he had treated Annette, and if he had been concerned in the security leak as well, he might have been capable of murder. He could certainly have stolen the dagger during the party, but he did not arrive at the Palais next morning until John was already dead. He could, of course, have given the dagger to Annette sometime during the night. This meant, again, though, that she would have been the actual killer. I did toy with that idea, but it just didn't ring true, and I was more than ever convinced of her innocence when she failed to tell the police certain damning facts about me after her arrest.

"So I was faced with a nightmare situation, a murder apparently impossible on any hypothesis other than my own guilt. Once or twice I began to wonder if I had had a brainstorm and killed the man myself. It was only when I sat down and made out detailed timetables"—he grinned at Spezzi—"that a glaringly obvious fact leapt out at me. Trapp was a good typist. We all heard for ourselves that the typing was going on, steadily and without interruption, from at least a quarter past nine until nearly quarter to ten. Half an hour of solid typing at high speed—and what was there to show for it? A half-page letter unfinished in the machine. It was not a question of his having made several drafts, for the wastepaper baskets were empty. There was not another scrap of typing anywhere in the office. I don't know much about typing speeds myself, but I remembered that Marcelle had produced copies of the revised agenda, running to a whole foolscap page, in a matter of a few minutes. This opened up an entirely new line of thought."

Henry paused, and swallowed some coffee. The painful part of his monologue was getting close, and he dreaded it. He went on. "It was then that I remembered what it was that I had seen in the office with John's body, something that was missing when we moved up to the identical office on the floor above. It was Mary Benson's portable tape recorder. At once the idea began to take shape. A tape recording of the sound of typing, playing back through the closed door of an office where a dead man is sitting at the desk, thereby giving the impression that he is still alive.

"As soon as I accepted this theory, there could be no doubt as to who was guilty. Mary Benson arrived soon after John did, and followed him into the office. She, and only she, had ample opportunity to kill him before anyone else arrived. She had time to put a faked note into the typewriter and set the tape recorder going. It was she who kept everyone else out of the office, on the pretext that John did not want to be disturbed. For a while I was puzzled, because I had gathered from what Annette said that she had spoken to John personally in the office that morning; but then I remembered that, talking to Emmy about her quarrel with him the previous evening, she had said, 'I never thought I wouldn't see him alive again.' Clearly, when she told us that John said he didn't want to be disturbed, she was quoting Mary. A very natural thing to do.

"There were two other points to check. Could Mary have been the girl who took the message to John's apartment, and could she have slipped his answering note into my pocket? To answer the second point first: we all left her alone to cope with Annette after the murder. She was calm and efficient and organized us, and we all trooped off like well-trained sheep to the rest room. Mary actually said to me that she was going to give Annette a sedative,—and the First Aid Box, which contains aspirins, was in the men's cloakroom. As for the first point, she gave herself away, talking to me."

Henry looked down. He hated having to speak of the picnic by the lake. He said with a great effort, "She had overheard me telling Hélène Brochet about the girl with the message, but I didn't mention anything about the girl having insisted on a reply in writing. Yet she remarked on this to me. It was only afterward that I realized she could not possibly have known about it unless she had delivered the message herself." He paused, and sighed. "It was very ingenious," he said. "That is how John Trapp was killed."

"And what happened to the tape recorder?" Emmy asked.

"That must have taken some nerve," said Henry. "It was a perfectly ordinary piece of office equipment, and she simply left it there for the police to examine if they wanted to. Of course, they didn't bother. It was then taken up to our new suite with everything else, and she collected it, took it home as usual, and wiped the typewriter sounds off the tape. The recorder wasn't subject to the ordinary security regulations, because ostensibly it hadn't been used, since our committee had not started work. There was one thing I should have spotted. Mary told me she was never separated from her equipment, yet on the morning of the murder, the tape recorder was in the office, where she never worked."

"There are still a thousand things I do not understand," said Gerda. "How did she get the dagger, for instance?"

"The really vital part of this murder," said Henry, "was not who did it or how, but why. That was obscure for a long time.

"Bear in mind two facts. Trapp had no appointment with me; he only thought he had. Trapp did not write the note we found in the typewriter. The money which the police found in his flat belonged to Natasha Hampton. In fact, there is no reason to suppose that John Trapp knew anything at all about the security leak, *but his murderer did.* Now, Bill Parkington may talk too much, but he's blazingly sincere, and he'd never shoot his mouth off to anyone he didn't completely trust. However, after he got that cable about the security leak, and before the party, he went back to the Palais to do some checking up. Mary Benson was there, too, working late—she told me so. Bearing in mind that they were friendly—he'd had drinks with her outside office hours—it shouldn't have been too difficult for her to glean the truth from him, just as Alfredo did next morning.

"All well and good so far; but why, in heaven's name, should Mary then decide to kill the inoffensive John Trapp, of all people? And how did she get the dagger?

"Well, I started worrying that one out. The dagger connects her up immediately with the Villa Trounex, but she was not at the party nor, as far as I knew, had she ever been to the house. She did, however, admit to a slight acquaintance with Paul Hampton through her riding. Well, had somebody stolen the dagger and taken it to her? Somebody who knew about the security leak? At that time, that meant only Bill or myself, and Bill had already left the Villa Trounex when Natasha came down through the library and noticed that the dagger was still there. Right at the beginning, I made a joking remark to Emmy about one of the girls having burgled the Villa later that night. That was obviously a ridiculous idea, yet it had a grain of truth. I decided that either Mary had visited the house after everyone had left—an unlikely hypothesis, for the servants would surely have seen or heard her—or else somebody from the house went to visit her, taking the dagger along. Natasha is out of the picture, since she went home with John and stayed there. I was left with the choice of Paul Hampton or Gamboni. Now, the house is full of servants, and the chauffeur sleeps over the garage. Nobody could have taken a car out in the middle of the night without being heard. In fact, I rang the chauffeur and checked with him, and he was positive that no car had come or gone during the night. The next car that left the Villa was on perfectly legitimate business, taking Paul Hampton to the airport at six in the morning; and the chauffeur told me that they had, in fact, made a stop on the way through the town, not far from Mary's apartment. That clinched the matter. Paul Hampton and Mary Benson were in league. He had taken her the dagger and she had killed John Trapp. The whole thing was tied up with the security leakage. I felt I was really getting somewhere, but the question still wasn't answered—why kill poor, innocent Trapp?

"First I concentrated on trying to visualize the setup. I knew that Mary had had contact with Hampton through show jumping, and I guessed for myself what Mary told the police in her confession. Running his dope-smuggling business under the guise of respectable property deals here in Geneva, Hampton needed a contact in the Narcotics Section of the Palais. He met Mary, and started her off by exchanging the relatively harmless bits of information she gave him for a pony and equipment of her own. You must realize that horses were the passion of her life. Once started, he kept her at it with a nice mixture of blackmail and rewards, leading her deeper and deeper into the mire. Not," Henry added, with a burst of painful honesty, "that she probably needed much persuasion. She was as tough as they come, physically and mentally, and remained so almost to the end.

"Well, there's the situation on the night of the party. By then, Mary has heard or gathered from Bill Parkington that the leakage of information is known. As soon as she leaves the Palais, she must obviously contact Hampton and warn him, and how else should she do it except by telephoning him on his private line? As soon as I thought of that, everything else fell into place. The call that interrupted our tour of the house, which Paul pretended was from New York, must actually have been from Mary; and it was that call which signed John's death warrant. In fact, it was I, in all innocence, who caused his death."

"What on earth do you mean, Henry?" Emmy demanded. For Henry had never told her that particular part of the story. He did so now.

"When John came out of Natasha's room and ran into Paul and myself," he went on, "he was embarrassed—not to see Paul, who understood the situation perfectly, but to see me. For my benefit, he made up a ridiculously lame excuse; that he had been trying to telephone from Natasha's room, but that the line was engaged. Then, from pure impudence, he added, with a secret smile at Paul, that nevertheless his time had not been wasted. What he didn't know was that the private phones in Paul's and Natasha's rooms were on the same line, as I realized next day when I was there; and that Paul had, in fact, just been having a highly compromising conversation with Mary, which, had it been overheard, could have blown Hampton's racket sky high. Hampton knew that John envied and disliked him, and immediately read into his words a threat of exposure. Paul Hampton was a ruthless and very efficient person. He decided then and there to eliminate John Trapp.

"I must say, his mind worked fast and well. The killing must be carried out well away from the Villa Trounex. Mary must do it, but she must have a watertight alibi. He himself will be far from Geneva at the time. The question of a weapon presents a difficulty, for Mary has nothing suitable at hand; but by using the dagger which Juan and I have handled, Paul will also throw a scapegoat to the police. Meanwhile, Trapp must be prevented from talking to anyone else between then and the following morning. And what better method than to send Natasha home with him, thereby killing two birds with one stone, because it also gets her out of the house. You can see how beautifully it was all calculated.

"When all the guests had gone, Paul Hampton took the dagger up to his room and packed it in his suitcase. He then telephoned Mary on the private line, and told her that he would call on her early next morning. Soon after six, on his way to the airport, he visited her and gave her his orders. She was to make a tape recording of typing, and type the fake note, whose wording he dictated to her. She was to deliver the message, purporting to come from me, at John's apartment, and get a written reply which could be planted as evidence against me. This would ensure that John would arrive at the Palais well before anyone else. I was picked as the victim for no personal reason, but simply because I had handled the dagger, and because—as Mary must have pointed out to Paul—I had a date with her before the conference, so that I would be under her eye at the crucial time. I would like to think that Mary had qualms about killing John, but . . ." He paused. "In any case, she had no choice."

Emmy shivered. "I hadn't realized it was quite so cold-blooded," she said.

"That was typical of Paul Hampton."

"What do you mean by 'the crucial time'?" Alfredo asked.

"As soon as Mary had killed Trapp," said Henry, "she set the tape recorder going. She had recorded exactly a half hour of the sound of typing. So long as the tape was running, Trapp would be assumed to be alive, and it was vital that nobody should go into the office; it was equally vital that I should go in as soon as it stopped. No wonder the girl was nervous. She looked at her watch several times while I was with her, and she must have had a nasty moment when I looked like going into the office just before the typing stopped. She headed me off with a piece of uncalled-for flattery, and then practically pushed me in there the instant the tape ran out.

"Well, that's all there is to it. I was extraordinarily stupid in some ways. I suppose it came from being chief suspect myself, instead of playing the lordly police officer." Henry looked at Gerda and smiled. "I hope I'll be a rather more pleasant policeman from now on."

"The worst part of all," said Emmy, "was the Novaris. I suppose Hampton arranged that, too."

"Without a doubt, though it will never be proved. Hampton had thought of everything. He had arranged for the Novaris to be offered a considerable sum of money to trump up the story of an accident in the family and go back to Italy that day. All seemed well, and it must have been a shock to Mary when she overheard me telling Helène that I had seen Madame Novari before she left, and that she would recognize the girl with the message. Mary contacted Paul and warned him; she says so in her confession. Even she, however, was shocked by the prompt action he took. He had agents everywhere, of course, and could organize an accident like that quite easily."

"And Gamboni, who was he?" Alfredo asked.

"An adventurer," said Henry. "A sort of free-lance mercenary secret agent whom Zwemmer was employing to spy on Hampton. He knew very little about what was actually going on, but Zwemmer had offered him a considerable amount for certain documents out of the library. That was why he was so angry to find me in the library the evening after the murder. It was also why, happily, he informed Zwemmer of my arrival at the Villa at three in the morning."

"And this idea of trying to send us to South America?"

"That was a desperate move, when Hampton knew he was up against it. He was worried when he saw me going off in the car with Mary, and he lunched with you to get all the information he could from you."

Emmy blushed. "I'm afraid I told him quite a lot, now I look back on it," she said. "I was only thinking of Annette, and he was so kind and sympathetic. I told him you knew about the girl with the message, and that you'd seen Mahoumi."

"That didn't matter," said Henry. His heart was beating unpleasantly fast. "Paul didn't even know Mahoumi. He was just a crooked little man employed by Natasha for her intrigue. However, he knew Paul's reputation, and when Trapp was killed, jumped to the conclusion that Paul had arranged his murder out of jealousy; and he was in a panic that he might receive the same treatment for his part in the affair. When Natasha got in touch with him and demanded that he rifle John's flat for the money and the will, he saw his chance of decamping with the cash, out of harm's way."

"And what was Zwemmer doing there that evening?"

"He was after information," said Henry, "just as I was when I first saw Mahoumi. He still thought John might have been responsible for the leakage, and he was trying to find out all he could."

"You still haven't explained about South America."

"Well." Henry swallowed painfuly. "After our . . . that is, when Mary heard about the Novaris being killed, it was too much for her. She telephoned Hampton and threatened to confess and denounce him if there were any more killings, or if I came to any harm. Eventually he struck a bargain with her, as she thought. If I were to disappear, voluntarily, with my safety and a good living assured to me, I would be assumed guilty, and the case would be closed. She would then agree to say nothing, and she would not be required to give him any more information. Foolishly she accepted. Hampton certainly did want to get me out of the way, but I feel sure he would have done away with her, too. However, things didn't work out like that."

"Henry," Emmy spoke impulsively. "Henry, this wasn't in Mary Benson's confession. How do you know it all?"

"You promised me," said Henry, "that you wouldn't ask questions."

Later on in the evening, when the Spezzis had gone and Henry was already in bed, Emmy came into the bedroom in her dressing gown and sat on the foot of the bed with a final cup of coffee in her hands.

"I'm terribly sorry, darling," she said. "I'm afraid I put my foot in it. I've always wondered where you went after you dropped me at the hotel. Now I know."

Henry closed his eyes. "I had to, you see," he said. "They might never have caught her. I'm a damned policeman, and I couldn't let her get away with it, but neither could I go to Colliet and tell him the whole story and let the law take its course. I had to go and tell her myself." There was a long silence. "It was the worst thing I've ever had to do in my life. In a strange way, you see, I loved her. I don't suppose you'll ever be able to understand that."

Emmy nodded gravely. "I understand better than you think," she said.

She stood up and went over to the chest of drawers. She pulled open a drawer and took out something wrapped in crisp white tissue paper. Henry opened his eyes.

"What's that?" he asked.

"A handbag," said Emmy.

The paper fell away, and Henry recognized the shiny brown alligator skin which he had last seen at the Hotel Étoile.

"What are you doing with it?"

"I'm putting it in the dustbin."

Henry raised himself on one elbow. "But, Emmy . . ."

"Paul bought it for me that afternoon," said Emmy brusquely.

She went out, and Henry heard the lid of the dustbin rattle, and bang shut. When Emmy came back, she was smiling. "Oh, dear," she said, "we did both get out of our depths, didn't we?

I suppose we're just too dull and ordinary."

"And thank God for it," said Henry.

"Amen," said Emmy piously. She climbed into bed and took him gently in her arms.